a novel

"A delightful and engaging story with plenty of humor, tender moments, and the kind of character growth that will go straight to your heart."
—Rachael Anderson, USA today bestselling romance author

"I was drawn into this novel and didn't want to come out again! A captivating story with unexpected twists."
—Paula Kremser, author of *Sophia* and *To Suit a Suitor*

"*Lies and Letters* is absolutely delightful. This sweet and tender romance will capture the heart of all readers as headstrong Charlotte navigates the treacherous ground between duty and desire. I enjoyed every page of this charming book."
—Julie Daines, award-winning Regency romance author.

a novel

ASHTYN NEWBOLD

SWEETWATER
BOOKS

An imprint of Cedar Fort, Inc.
Springville, UT

ISBN 13: 978-1-4621-1984-4

Published by Sweetwater Books, an imprint of Cedar Fort, Inc.
2373 W. 700 S., Springville, UT 84663
Distributed by Cedar Fort, Inc., www.cedarfort.com

LIBRARY OF CONGRESS CATALOGING-IN- PUBLICATION DATA

Names: Newbold, Ashtyn, 1998– author
Title: Lies and Letters / Ashtyn Newbold
Description: Springville, Utah : Sweetwater Books, an imprint of Cedar Fort, Inc., [2017]
Identifiers: LCCN 2017006051 (print)
ISBN 9781462119844 (perfect binding : alk. paper)
Subjects: LCSH: Nineteenth century, setting; England, setting | LCGFT: Romance fiction
Classification: PS3614.E568 L54 2017 (print) | DDC 813/.6-- dc23
LC record available at https://lccn.loc.gov/2017006051

Cover design by Priscilla Chaves
Cover design © 2017 by Cedar Fort, Inc.
Edited and typeset by Hali Bird and Jessica Romrell

Printed in the United States of America

10 9 8 7 6 5 4 3 2 1

Printed on acid-free paper

*To the givers of kindness, the lights in darkness,
the friends in hard times. How you change the world.*

Other Books by Ashtyn Newbold

Mischief and Manors

Unexpected Love: A Marriage of Convenience Anthology

"Doubt thou the stars are fire; doubt the sun doth move;
Doubt truth to be a liar: but never doubt I love."

-William Shakespeare

Chapter 1

The scratching of a quill did little to settle my nerves. Neither did the pattering of rain, nor the abrupt plinking of the pianoforte from downstairs. In fact, all of these sounds produced quite the opposite effect.

Slamming my quill down on my writing desk, I jumped from my chair, striking my knee on the underside of the desk. The inkwell tipped, splattering my gown. I froze, staring at the teardrops of black. Propelled by a new bout of anger, I rushed at the door and threw it open.

I knew it was Clara at the pianoforte, rehearsing for a dinner party at which she was bound to humiliate us all. And as if the rain wasn't enough to upset me, my sister carried on with her horrifying display while I was trying to write a letter to my dearest friend, Alice. It had been two long months since I had visited her at Kellaway Manor, and I was itching to know if her eldest brother was still unattached.

I gripped my stained skirts as I stomped down the stairs. It was such a relief to stomp. In public, I was only permitted to *glide*.

"Clara! Quit that horrendous music and look what you have done to me!" My voice was a shriek, shrill from lack of use.

Clara's hands stopped for a moment, suspended above the keys. Her smile was tight as she took in my dirtied dress and ink-covered hands. Without comment, she resumed her playing with renewed vigor.

"Clara!" I rushed at her and threw the music off the stand, missing the burning fireplace by inches. The sheets fell to the ground like dead petals. "Content yourself with the fact that you will never be as talented as me." I placed my hand on her shoulder and leaned in close. "Nor will you ever be as pretty."

Her face darkened to a shade of cherry red and her brow creased. In anger or shame, I couldn't tell.

"A well-bred lady will always maintain an even disposition. I trust you haven't applied rouge to your entire face."

"Charlotte, stop!" She threw my hand off her shoulder. A dark smudge of ink stained her ivory sleeve.

I glanced at it with mock regret. "Oh, dear sister, forgive me."

With an animal-like grunt, she leapt from her seat and charged at me. Her palms slammed into my shoulders and I faltered, gasping. Clara was sixteen, two years younger than me, but we were similar in proportion. I regained my bearings and returned the action, throwing her back several steps. It was a fair fight, to be sure.

"I am going to sit beside Mr. Weatherby tomorrow, and you will be placed beside Mr. Connor's belching!" I screamed.

"Mr. Weatherby favors me!"

I scoffed. "What has possibly implanted such a fantasy in your simple head? He certainly wasn't charmed by your musical talent."

She cast me a look of contempt. "Do not ever speak to me again!" She gave me one last shove before crossing her arms. "I wish to play music, and I will play music, and you cannot stop me!"

I caught my breath, rolling my eyes. With the clean area of my hand, I brushed back my pale curls. "Very well, but you will never master the art as I have. You will *never* be like me."

She stepped closer, the light from the flames flickering over her face. I expected to see a look of hot anger, or inadequacy. But instead I saw pity. "I have never wanted to be like you, Charlotte."

"What is the commotion about?" Mama's feet clicked on the black and white tiles as she entered the room. The graceful air of Lady Pembury never changed. Attending a ball, a musical, or roaming the halls of our home, she walked the same. Her head remained at the same angle, and her striking green eyes always seemed to leak of disapproval. I stood tall at her arrival, knowing I was the daughter she had always favored.

"Clara," she gasped. Her eyes froze on my splattered gown, "what have you done to Charlotte?"

"I did nothing."

Mama's eyebrow lifted in doubt.

"She forced me to spill the ink," I stated. "I was writing a letter to Alice Kellaway when she ran into my room and tipped my desk."

Clara opened her mouth to belie the fib, but Mama stopped her. "That will be quite enough from you. Remove to your bedchamber at once."

"Charlotte is lying!"

Mama's expression hardened. "How dare you make such an accusation? You will not be dining with us at the Weatherby's tomorrow night. As far as they're concerned, you have caught a cold." Her eyes shifted to the leaves of music on the ground around the pianoforte. "And clean that up."

I stood back, fighting a victorious smirk. Mama left the room shortly after, and Clara bent over the sheets of music, blinking back tears. Rain continued its patter against the roof, bridging the gorge of silence between us. I moved across the room until I stood beside her. I picked up a page from the floor and handed it to Clara.

She lifted her gaze to mine, and what I saw there surprised me. Anger had faded into the depths of something heavier, a look I couldn't quite place. But it did little to dishevel me. Mama had taught me that eliminating the enemy can mean many things. It was a war of sorts, and securing a husband of rank and fortune required a famous arsenal. I figured that infliction upon family was merely part of the game.

I smiled at Clara in the dim light. "Forgive me if I steal away his heart." Then I turned away from her and smoothed back the golden curl that had fallen over my brow.

As I walked away, I yelled for Anna, my maid. It was late, and husband catching required a plentiful night's sleep. Only two months before, a plain girl had stolen the heir to Willowbourne from me. I was not going to allow my sister to steal Mr. Weatherby. He was one of Mama's top choices for her daughters, and I couldn't bear the thought of disappointing her again. Flirting came naturally to Lyons women, and if I was to win the heart of Harold Weatherby, then tomorrow night I would employ that great weapon to my advantage.

At breakfast, I pushed the food around my plate and stared out the tall windows. The rain had finally stopped, and tiny streaks of sunlight broke through the dark sky. I took a nibble of a biscuit, shifting my eyes between Mama and Clara.

"Where is Papa?" I asked, my voice nonchalant. "Was he not scheduled to return early this morning?"

Mama released a slow breath and straightened the pendant at her neck. It was a miniature of her own mother, who looked more like me than Mama did. My grandmother and I both had the same golden curls and pale blue eyes. I had determined that my skin was fairer, because an artist rarely depicts blemishes.

When Mama's breath was all the way out, she said, "Yes, he was due to arrive."

Clara looked up from her plate. Her eyes appeared puffy as they avoided contact with mine. "Don't you worry about him?"

Mama lifted her chin and dabbed her mouth with a napkin. "What you must learn is that in a marriage, settlements must be made. Your papa and I cannot bother ourselves with worry; therefore we have agreed to allow one another a sense of freedom. What your father does or does not do is none of my concern." She sipped from her cup. "He will arrive when he sees fit."

I made a note in my mind of her words.

Clara's scowl deepened. "He has been in London for a fortnight now. Don't you wonder—"

"Enough!" Mama barely concealed her glare behind the thick layers of rouge. "A woman is much better off keeping to her own affairs. The same is true for her silly daughters." After taking a huffed breath, Mama turned her attention to me. "Is your piece prepared for the dinner party this evening?"

I nodded. "I shall play more beautifully than any other lady there, I assure you."

Mama clucked her tongue and folded her napkin into a neat square. "You must do far more than that if you wish to win Mr. Weatherby, Charlotte. Many eyes are trained on him, but you must turn his to you."

"I will, Mama. Your daughter will be the mistress of Candleworth Manor." I chuckled deeply at the thought. "I will become Mrs. Charlotte Weatherby. Oh, it rolls off the tongue, does it not, Mama?"

She shrugged. "I would prefer that you obtain a title, but he is wealthy. I suppose it will do."

My face fell.

"Clara will be my last hope of possible ties to the aristocracy."

As soon as she said the words, I burst into giggles. Mama soon joined me, our laughter cutting the air like birdcalls. Clara shifted uncomfortably at her isolated corner of the table.

"Regardless of your success with Mr. Weatherby, I trust that you, Charlotte, will make an advantageous match. And what I ask of you, Clara, is that you . . . surprise me. Impress me if possible."

My sister's grip tightened on her fork before she scraped the final scraps of food from her plate and excused herself to the gardens.

Finishing my food, I watched Clara's retreating form out the window. She spent an unhealthy amount of time out of doors. I made it a firm endeavor never to spend more than one hour susceptible to the elements. It was preposterous the damage sunlight could do to a complexion.

There were still several hours before I needed to get ready for the dinner party, so I wandered through the house, trying to decide on an entertaining pastime. The music room was available. And so was the library, but nothing filled me with excitement. With thoughts of Mr. Weatherby and the dinner party that evening, I found it impossible to focus on anything else. After several minutes, I decided to stay in my bedchamber for a few hours.

When I reached the top of the staircase, I entered the first room on the right. Anna, my maid, kept it in acceptable condition. She had replaced my inkwell, I noticed, and the stains were scrubbed clean off my writing desk. I sat down in the chair and placed a sheet of parchment in front of me. Picking up the quill, I rubbed the plume over my lips, thinking.

At the Weatherby's tonight would be several guests, similar in rank to me, and close in accomplishment. Every lady would be vying for Mr. Weatherby's attention, and if I was to win it, I needed a plan.

I dipped the quill and positioned it at the top of the paper. I would start with what I'd been taught.

I titled it, *How to catch a husband: Charlotte's list of requirements.* Tapping my finger on the table, I began writing.

1. Always showcase on the pianoforte.
2. Always perform better than the previous lady.
3. Always let him choose the conversation, and always act interested.
4. Always dress in the latest fashion.
5. Always compliment him.
6. Always lean close when speaking and smile.
7. Always laugh at his humor.
8. Always steal his heart.

My mouth curled into a grin as my confidence returned. What had I been worried about? I had been taught what I needed to know, and my beauty was unrivaled in the entire county at least. My heart beat quickly, stimulated by my motivation. If Mr. Weatherby didn't send me flowers by tomorrow, then he was not worth my attention anyway.

With these firm thoughts in mind, I readied a new piece of parchment and finally finished that letter to Alice.

Chapter 2

*"Look like the innocent flower
But be the serpent under't."*

We left the house around six of the clock. Clara was in the drawing room when we departed, hanging her head and sniffling like a self-pitying dolt. Her hands were clasped behind her back, and thin strands of wet, dark hair clung to her cheeks where the tears fell freely. I flashed her a winning smile as I passed.

I walked to the carriage, shivering in the cold from the recent rain. It was mid-September, and the temperature was dropping more by the day, turning light summer breezes into chilly, still autumn air. I hadn't bothered to bring a miniature looking glass, for I had my appearance memorized from head to toe. I had insisted that Anna work nothing short of a miracle. Most of my hair was arranged on top of my head with pieces intertwining intricately like clockwork. Loose tendrils framed my face; my cheeks were rosy; my eyes were bright and perfectly matched to my dress—the color of which I called the sky. Any man would have to be blind not to notice me, or to want me as his wife.

When we arrived at Candleworth Manor, I stepped out of the carriage gracefully, lightly resting my hand in the footman's. The sky was speckled with stars, making me feel even more powerful and breathtakingly beautiful. Mama walked ahead of me, nodding at a couple arriving the same moment as us.

Once seated in the drawing room, I surveyed the guests with my gaze. Married women, four. Widowed, two. Young and unattached, nine. I felt the eyes of many men in the room wander to me, unfolding another bloom of pride in me. But where was my target? He wasn't yet in the room, so I would have to wait until dinner. The dining area was enormous, and the likelihood of receiving a seat near Mr. Weatherby was unlikely.

I watched the guests interact from my vantage point beside my mother. We were greeted occasionally by the brave men and women in the room, but most kept their distance. Mama had a tendency to intimidate.

A young woman caught my eye from the corner of the room, studying a sheet of music in her hands. I briefly recognized her from the previous London season. Her name was Miss Lydia Camden, and I knew that she was reputable on the pianoforte. Without a second thought, I stood from my chair and crossed the room to greet her.

"Miss Camden! Oh, it is a pleasure to see you again." I pulled my lips into a rehearsed smile.

Her eyes raised to mine in surprise. "Miss Lyons! The pleasure is mine."

"Why have you secluded yourself to this corner? I trust there are many fine gentlemen about to admire you." I eyed the music in her hands. It was Haydn's Sonata in C major, one I had previously played at a musical.

"Don't be absurd. It is you they are bound to admire."

I swatted the air and let a laugh ring through it. "Surely I will not turn a single head."

She smiled up at me from her seat. "Nonsense. You have much beauty to recommend you. I rely solely upon my performance."

"I am performing tonight as well."

Her face seemed to fall.

"When are you standing?" I leaned in as if sharing a secret.

"Second."

A burst of triumph spread through my body. I was to directly follow her performance. "And I am third! I look forward to your performance. Haydn is one of my favorite composers. Perhaps your talent will calm my anxious spirits. I do hate excessive attention . . ." I twirled a lock of my hair around my finger as I caught the eye of Sir

Edward Longleat. He was certainly my second choice among eligible husbands at the party.

"I wish you the best," Miss Camden said, recalling my attention.

"And I, you."

After an hour of tedious conversation, the group moved to the dining room. I was escorted by Mr. Hansen, a dreadful man that smiled far too often. I acted polite for the sake of the other members of the party, and noticed Mr. Weatherby's gaze travel my way on more than one occasion. Mama caught my eye with an eyebrow arched deviously.

When we arrived in the dining room, I was seated on the opposite length of the table as Mr. Weatherby, but nearly straight across. In no opinion would he be considered handsome, with his large nose and narrow eyes, but he was the wealthiest man in town, and his home was magnificent. I had taken note of it. The ceilings domed high, covered in paintings and decorated in crystal. The floors were made of fine marble, and the furnishings were in the latest French style.

So on the many occasions Mr. Weatherby's eyes were drawn to mine, I saw a husband I could be indifferent to. I could allow him freedom and he could allow the same for me. One day I could be hosting a party just like this one. Occasionally, I saw Mama's approving smile. And the thought of her approval eased something inside me.

"Mr. Weatherby, I understand you race horses at your leisure," I said in a coy voice, tipping my head at an angle I knew to be maddening.

He cleared his throat. "Indeed."

I waited, hoping for further explanation. Nothing.

"I cannot claim to know much of the sport. What of the activity attracts you?" My voice was sugary and my smile demure.

He was chewing, and I waited patiently for him to swallow the chunk of meat he had just lifted from his plate. "I see myself in the animals," he said. "A sense of adventure, a daring spirit. Very intuitive creatures, horses. They know where to turn when lost." He sipped from his cup and wiped his mouth with his napkin. His eyes roamed over me before he spoke again. "And in the wild, they know when they're being hunted."

I blinked twice. "How interesting!"

Before I could speak another word, he turned to the gentleman beside him and started a new conversation.

I slumped in my chair, unsure of my progress. I couldn't tell if Mama approved, because her eyes were trained on the elder Mr. Weatherby, and I recognized my own flirtatious expression on her face. I watched Miss Camden across the table, engaged in conversation with Sir Edward. Jealousy boiled in my stomach and I reestablished my next course of action. Surely I would outshine her at the pianoforte. I had no doubt.

After the ladies removed to the drawing room and the men had finished with their port, the first performer took her seat beside the harp. She was inept, to say the least, at the instrument. I breathed a sigh of relief.

When Miss Camden took her place at the pianoforte, I held my breath. Her hands plinked out the notes with accuracy, but she had simplified some of the complicated elements of the piece. It was novice, and my spirits rose more and more as I listened. When she finished, she stood shakily, beaming at the applause.

At last, it was my turn. I had brought no music, but had my piece memorized. It was a composition of Mozart, impressive, but too commonly performed to steal every attention. Haydn's work, the one Miss Camden had just performed, jumped to my mind. It was engraved in my brain, each note and dynamic. If I was to steal the show, I was to do it right.

Taking a seat on the bench I positioned my hands over the keys and played. I played with as much passion as I could manage. It was a lively and strong melody, and I lost myself within the powerful trills and flowing life of the sonata. Several gasps hit my ears from around the room, but slowly faded into silent awe. When I took my bow, I caught the eye of Miss Camden. In her face I saw the same expression I had seen in Clara the night before, but only now did I place it.

Hatred.

I smiled to myself. I could accept being hated if it meant being admired by Mr. Weatherby. I glanced toward where I knew he stood in the room. But what I saw on his face wasn't admiration—it was disgust. My smile faltered. That was not what I had expected. The ladies and gentlemen shifted all around the drawing room, leaning and whispering as I reclaimed my seat. I dared a look at Mama. She was sitting with unbendable posture, chin held high and eyes filled with pride.

Somewhat reassured, I kept my bearings and ignored the whispered remarks brushing the air like moth wings. Perhaps I had mistaken Mr. Weatherby's reaction to my performance. Or perhaps his expression was aimed at Miss Camden and her horrific interpretation of the song. Whatever it was, I found peace with the fact that I had accomplished what I came here to do. I came to be remembered, and remembered I would be. As I stole one more look at the guests, though, I wondered if being remembered for what I did tonight was for the better or the worse.

The shifting eyes continued for the rest of the evening. Yes, some people complimented my ability, but I also sensed some disdain. As someone who had always enjoyed attention, I found I did not appreciate this kind of attention. Not one bit.

As we were leaving, I gave one last attempt to obtain Mr. Weatherby's favor. But when I produced my signature coy smile, his eyes shifted away as quickly as they had come. He was rubbing his forehead and mumbling something to himself when the door closed him and the warm candlelight of the room from my view.

Mama looped her arm around mine in one stiff motion, and whispered, "Well done, Charlotte." Her voice was quick with excitement. "I am sorry to say I ever doubted you. Following Miss Camden playing the same piece . . . it was genius, to say the least. You exceed her talent for certain, especially with that particular song. I believe the audience was very moved."

I could picture the faces of reprimand and shock and disapproval, but Mama's words were falling over them like a shadow, bringing forward smiles and looks of envy.

"I worried it might have been too much . . ."

Mama scoffed loudly. "It would be a monstrous surprise if Mr. Weatherby doesn't call on you by morning. And Sir Edward could not take his eyes off you, especially after your performance. I daresay you have acquired new prospects."

My mind spun. Of course Mama was right. What had compelled me to doubt? As we entered the carriage, I brushed aside my worries and turned my thoughts to what dress I should wear tomorrow and which bonnet would most complement my eyes. If I was beautiful enough, then I could win any heart. I pictured my life as mistress of a grand house, hosting parties and presenting the home as mine. I pictured how my husband would dote on me, and he would grant me loads of pin money to spend in London. Then I could be off, and see him on rare occasions. When we grew older, he would retire to his library and I could spend hours perusing the shelves of the highest shops.

I placed my hand on my chest and sighed. If I played my cards right, that future could be mine. I would be happier than I had ever been in my life. Love was fickle and unlasting, nothing to aspire to.

I considered Mama and Papa. They had planned to marry from a young age, never compelled by anything but circumstance. Rarely did they speak, and both behaved as they liked. A match like theirs was drawn in fates and could never create such damage as a broken heart. A heart is fragile, and I considered it necessary to keep it from harm. Glassware was stored in sturdy cupboards, never atop a nursery table. It would be destroyed by the toddler's curious, destructive hands.

The sky was black when we pulled into the drive of our home. Crickets formed an orchestra through the still air as I walked toward the front doors. Our home, Eshersed Park, stood like a castle under the moonlight, the cream stone illuminated by fading candlelight shining through the windows.

Inside, I wasn't surprised that Clara didn't greet us. She was likely in her room with her face stuffed against her pillow, crying over her misfortune. The image brought a smile to my face. My curiosity couldn't be helped, so I climbed up the stairs to her bedchamber and threw open the doors. I was disappointed to see that her bed was free of a prostrate, weeping figure.

"Clara!" I called. "Mr. Weatherby has fallen madly in love with me!"

Nothing.

I walked to the window and stared down into the gardens. I was about to turn away when I noticed a single dot of light gleaming among the shrubs and squat trees. It had to be Clara.

Running to the back door, I stepped into the night air once again. After weaving my way through the intricate gardens, I came up behind my sister sitting on a large stone, her brown hair hanging in waves over her shoulders. Her head was bent over something she held in her hands. The candle was sitting beside her on the stone, bathing her face in an orange glow, and revealing the item in her hands. It was a book.

"What are you reading?" I asked, making Clara jump. "And what, pray tell, are you doing out *here* in the dark?"

She turned with the book pressed against her chest. Her eyes were wide, brimming with surprise. "What I am reading is none of your concern. I hear no news of an engagement, so I suppose your deception fooled no one."

I huffed a breath. "You are wrong. Mr. Weatherby was quite taken with my beauty and talent, and surely plans to court me."

She rolled her eyes and flipped the page of her book. Unsatisfied by her response, I lunged forward and ripped the book from her hands.

She gasped and whirled around on her stone chair. "Give that back!"

I examined the cover and turned my head to the side with disgust. "You are reading another of those silly romances, are you?" I snorted. "What do you suppose? The stoutly hero is going to ascend from the pages, desperately in love with you?"

She jumped for the book, but I pulled it away and out of her reach.

"Charlotte, give it back!"

"How do you believe in this nonsense? Such behavior is harmful to your health, dear sister." I leafed the pages open and tore out a handful of paper and inky, false words.

Clara stopped trying to reach the book, but melted into tears. "Stop! Stop!" She wrapped her arms around herself and leaned over, hiding her face from me.

I pulled out and crumpled another fistful of the pages. "You will thank me," I said. When I finished, I dropped the binding to the dirt and laughed.

"How can you be so awful?" She spit the words at me and tears fell slowly down her cheeks. "I hope you fall in love someday, Charlotte. And I hope he breaks your heart."

I shook my head with my hands on my hips. "Impossible."

She stooped over the bench, gathering up a few pages and organizing them in a neat stack. Amid her movements, she glanced up at me, eyes like stone. "You're right. I don't believe you even have a heart."

I kicked the remaining crumpled pages away from her reach before turning to leave. Before I moved, I said, in a voice just as hard, "That is because a woman is much better off without one."

The house was not silent as I had expected when I walked through the door. I could hear loud voices from near the front entry. Alarm bolted through me and I walked faster.

I heard Mama's words, shrill and unidentifiable, laden with sobs. As I came closer, I recognized the low rumble of Papa's voice. When had he returned? It must have been just moments before. Mama shouted something else, but I couldn't understand through the strong echo of the walls. Caution took over my steps and my heart raced as I made my way down the long hall and rounded the corner. I stopped with one hand on the wall, shocked by what I saw.

Mama was standing with her head in her hands, far from the composure I had come to know and expect. Papa was trying to console her. His hand was stiff and unfeeling on her shoulder. She jerked back and raised her face with a hard look. Papa's face was dark in a gaunt way, eyes falling back into hungry sockets, age displayed in every line.

"We will never recover from this!" Mama shouted. Her eyes moved to where I stood, now in plain view of both my parents. She ran to me, a wave of fresh sobs shaking her frame. "All I worked for! All I cared for!" The feathers of her headdress crumpled against my neck as she cried into my shoulder. She had never done such a thing in my entire life.

"We are ruined, Charlotte, utterly ruined! Because of *him*."

I pushed her away and took a step back, my wide eyes staring into her tear-filled ones. "What do you mean?" My gaze moved to Papa of its own accord. I realized it was the first time I had spoken to him in months. I had given up trying long ago.

He dropped his head and rubbed the back of his neck. He looked like a guilty child confessing to a nanny.

"Papa, what have you done?" The words scratched my throat.

He approached us, and his bloodshot eyes only blinked once. I expected a thorough explanation, maybe an excuse for Mama's reaction. But he spoke just two words. "I'm sorry." And then his slumping form retreated into the hallway and I heard a door shut. I couldn't breathe as the image of him faded. In all the years I had known him, he had never appeared so broken. I tried again to think of the last moment he had spoken to me, besides a brief word, but could think of nothing. My heart thudded with dread as I turned my attention to Mama. She had always been a woman of pristine composure. Something must have been terribly wrong.

With her face in her hands, Mama paced away from me and wailed into the open air, cursing Papa between gasps of breath.

Clara entered the house through the front door, freezing at the sight of Mama so uncollected.

"My lord has ruined us!" She whirled around and crossed the room to his portrait that hung on the wall. Her fingers slid over the copper frame, nails pressing into the canvas. I could see her ribs swell with a breath through the back of her gown. "He has gambled away the bulk of his fortune—our livelihood! And that is not the worst of it. He was caught cheating at cards in London among the *ton*. All the elite, the gentry in attendance, now know of our family's disgrace. He has no means to repay the debts! My husband is to be exiled to France and nothing will be left to us. Nothing!" She scratched her nails over the portrait of Papa in a quick slash, but it made no mark. With another cry of outrage, she pushed away from the wall and turned on us.

Despite our recent fight, Clara and I exchanged worried glances. Something within me was sinking at Mama's words. I struggled to draw a breath with this revelation tearing through me. Fear pooled in my chest so deeply I thought I might faint.

Everything I had planned—my living now, my living in the future—was being ripped from my grasp. Papa often found himself in gaming halls less than reputable. But relying on the game to preserve our fortune? And cheating? I had never thought him to be so low. My heart picked up speed and tears tightened a knot in my throat before splashing from my eyes.

"What are we to do?" I dared the question.

Mama wiped the tears from her face roughly and swallowed hard. "We can no longer afford this house. We will have to move to a despicable little home . . ." All of the sudden, her eyes lit up with urgency. "Charlotte. Yes, Charlotte, you are our only hope. We shall move to the North, where we are scarcely known. There you will meet all new gentlemen, none of whom will know of Papa's scandal. They shall not know of our fall in society. There you must win the heart of a wealthy suitor with your beauty. It is our only chance at redemption. I am much too old and Clara much too plain to succeed quickly enough."

My heart raced even faster. "But how—how?" I had never been unsure of my ability to catch a husband, but with the stakes so high, a new seed of fear bloomed inside me.

"No questions, Charlotte. You must do this." Her face had calmed a little, trained on me with determination. If only I felt it within myself. I was afraid, and for once I wondered if I could succeed. My confidence was wavering, and the feeling was completely new to me.

Mama paced the room with fresh speed. "Northumberland. That is where we must go. Perhaps Berwick? The place has been begging to be called Scotland for years."

Clara and I exchanged yet another glance. I saw tears falling speedily down her cheeks. "That is a long journey, Mama," she said.

"No, Craster! Yes, Craster will be perfect," Mama continued, ignoring Clara. "It is nearly as far as we can travel within the country where the people will have no idea who we are and from whence we have come." She put the back of her hand against her forehead and swayed on her feet. "I am feeling faint, now. The hour is late. Go to sleep. And Charlotte," she regarded me firmly as she stood near the door of her room, "I expect nothing short of a miracle from you. I have invested so very much in you. It is time you repay the favor."

Then she was gone, swallowed into the door of her bedchamber where her maid waited to assist her.

My shoulders quaked with a contained sob, and emotion tore through me so strong that I felt it tingle in the tips of my fingers. Was this really happening? I choked on a breath and my legs began to shake.

Unable to stay where I was any longer, I rushed away from the entry and up the stairs. My feet seemed to float, making me wonder once again if this was real, if any of it was real. I entered my bedchamber where Anna stood at attention.

"May I help you, miss?" she asked.

I turned my face to her and she seemed surprised at my tears. "Go! Get out!" I shooed her toward the door, my voice cracking.

She complied, her face draining of color as she went. I slammed the door behind her and pressed myself against the frame, my body shaking with fresh sobs. Were our circumstances really so fragile? I had heard whispers of debts before, but they were always accompanied by reassurances. That was no longer the case. Our living, home, and the Lyons name were now tarnished.

How could I find a husband now? How could I be desired? I had heard a tale of an earl's son once enticed to marry a tradesman's daughter. But how could I bridge such a gap as that? I turned to the mirror against my wall. My cheeks were streaked in tears and red splotches, but in my eyes I saw a flash of determination. Mama was right. I was our only hope. There was no other way to regain our wealth. Marrying well had never been as important as it was now. I was still a lady of high breeding, I reassured myself. I was still accomplished and beautiful.

After several minutes, I found myself unable to sit still. I took the candle sitting on my desk and opened my door. Flame in hand, I made my way up the stairs to the room that was calling me. I pushed open the heavy door and walked inside, touching the tip of my candle to the other unlit wicks.

The room blossomed in shadows and yellow light. I walked to the pianoforte that was positioned in the center of my music room. Clara's harp stood in the corner of the room, covered in a sheet. She had given up the pursuit years ago, and the instrument stood like an abandoned thing, deserted and alone.

I took a seat at the pianoforte and pulled music from the deepest parts of my mind. I played every song I had memorized. I was a slave to the music, driven by something other than the need to impress. The sounds drove through my skin and settled somewhere inside me, and then they pulled out the fear, the questions, and the unknown. I played and played until my hands ached and my soul begged for relief.

When I finally stopped, I felt the silence thrum around me, as if it had its own sound. I felt empty. Whatever was left inside of me had been poured out, deposited somewhere it could no longer affect me. There would be no more crying tonight.

I darkened the room again and returned to my bedchamber. I wasn't sure how much time had passed, but Anna was nowhere in sight. I didn't bother to ring the bell, and fell asleep in my dress. Exhaustion had trumped routine tonight. It seemed routine would be trumped by a great many things to come.

Chapter 3

"Hell is empty
And all the devil's are here."

Catching a Husband: Charlotte's list of requirements:

9. Always remember to smile, despite how you may feel.
10. Always display refinement, although you may not feel it.

These were the only two I could add to the list before my trunks were packed and my writing supplies were taken with them. Or rather, my *trunk*.

Mama had never been a woman to waste time. When there was a matter to be solved, she solved it. Mama had sought the confidential advice of her brother the day after we learned of our misfortune. Her brother dealt directly with the finances of the Duke of Rampton, and offered advice that she reluctantly took. All our possessions were to be sold—besides what we could fit in one traveling trunk. He had kindly offered to get them sold while we traveled, allowing sufficient funds for the trip and several months in our new home.

Now, two days later, we were preparing to journey to a mysterious coastal town. The thought made my stomach reel. I had never journeyed north past London. The South was where I had always lived. I didn't like the thought of living in a place where I didn't know what to expect. I hardly knew what I could expect from myself.

When I arrived on the main floor, I came face-to-face with Mama, Clara, and Papa. I wore my most comfortable dress while still remaining fashionable. The weeks to come would be dotted with atrocious inns and nonstop travel. I knew I would have to bid my farewell to Papa soon, but as I considered the thought, I realized how far we had grown apart.

I waited for feelings of sadness but they never came. Papa was going to be in greater poverty than we would be. Besides, falling from a position in the House of Lords was not easy to endure. But it was certainly deserved.

Clara embraced him quickly, her face firm, before moving outside to stand near the threshold. I approached him, and stopped a foot away.

"Good-bye, Papa."

His eyes flicked over mine and he rubbed his jaw. Then he grunted.

He *grunted*.

And turned away toward his study, choosing the books he would soon lose over the daughter he had given life to. But before he could enter the study, he turned to me one more time. "*Soyez bénis.*"

I thought I saw a twinge of regret in his eyes.

"*Soyez bénis,*" he repeated, "on your journey."

Be blessed.

As if the curse he had just given me could be reversed by two words.

I turned and joined Clara outside the door. I clenched my jaw against tears, suspecting that I was leaving this house forever. The thought suddenly filled me with panic. How would I manage sharing a maid with my mother and sister? How would I manage without so many rooms and sofas and instruments at my disposal? And no cook? We would surely starve. And what would happen when our money ran out? Only one distant connection had been found that might provide any support financially.

I was lost in my thoughts when Mama walked out to join us on the drive. There was something different about her face, she seemed . . . calm.

"Charlotte. Clara. There is another matter I have not yet discussed with you." She cleared her throat and smoothed the front of her gown. It was one of her finest, and immediately my mind was filled with suspicion. She continued in a clear, strong voice—the one I recognized the most. "My cousin has offered me, and myself alone, residence in his country house here in Canterbury. I truly despise the arrangement, but . . ." she wiped a tear I wasn't sure I saw, "it is for the best. The bulk of the disgrace will fall on me, so I cannot accompany you to Craster. The driver has my instructions. And Charlotte, you will keep me updated with your progress. I have intentionally chosen a dwelling near the home of the Earl of Trowbridge. Do not disappoint me."

A thousand words bubbled inside me, but I couldn't seem to push them past my teeth. All I could manage was, "You are staying?"

"It is the most advantageous arrangement for all of us." She didn't falter in her stance.

I felt betrayed, and my cheeks heated with the shame of it. "How will we manage? What if I don't succeed?"

Mama shook her head hard. "You will." She held out her arms to me but I stepped away, hot tears stinging my eyes. I had always found joy in flirting, showcasing my strengths, eliminating my shortcomings. But the idea of a comfortable living now felt so distant, I was strangled by it. I had no instructor by my side. Mama was staying here, coaxing her cousin into providing for her and sending her daughters to an unknown wasteland.

She moved her hands away nonchalantly, pushing back a stray curl. "The coach is waiting now, my dears. Remember me while you are away. Write often."

And with that she was inside the house again, a fading image of emerald green and betrayal. I made a sound, a deep burst of anger and disbelief. Clara looked shocked. I turned my back to Eshersed Park, the only home I'd ever known, and moved toward the carriage, something deep and wild and new burning in my limbs as I walked. How could Mama do this to us? I supposed she had no choice in sending us away, but she was staying in the comfort of her home county, and among friends and family. Clara was to be my only companion besides our maid. I considered neither my friend.

Clara stepped into the carriage behind me and we sat on opposite sides. The seats were cold and the interior of the carriage smelled of rusted metal. Her face was blank, something I couldn't read, and it bothered me.

"Do you realize we are likely to never return?" I said. "We could be away for years." When she didn't respond, my voice raised to a shout. "Our parents are to become strangers to us!"

She glanced at me wearily. "Have they ever been anything but?" Then her eyes filled with tears that she blinked away, and she turned back to the window.

I tried to ignore her comment, but it ate away at me from the inside. Mama had just as much affection for me as any loving mother would! She wanted the best for me, and nothing Clara said could change what I knew. So I closeted the unnecessary concern and focused on a new one.

"Where is our maid?" The carriage was rolling forward now, and Clara and I were the only occupants.

"She is not accompanying us."

I gasped, panic hitting me forcefully. "What? That cannot be true."

"I overheard Mama this morning. She is keeping Anna as her own lady's maid to bring to her new residence; she has released the others."

"But who will do my hair? Who will help us cook, clean, dress?" I stomped my foot against the floor of the coach. "How does Mama suppose I can catch a husband without a maid?"

Clara didn't say anything. I pressed my head against my seat, forgetting the restraints of a proper lady. How had so much misfortune hit me this quickly? It was hard to believe. So much weight was on my shoulders I could hardly bear it. Questions scraped at my skull like wood carvings. Despite how little I knew, I needed to formulate a plan. I had weeks of travel ahead of me, so I was bound to gain some advantage over my situation. As we drove closer to the unknown, I sunk deeper into my despair and stayed there. It was a place I had never been before, and I found I didn't like it. Not at all.

I never knew time could pass so slowly. A day felt like a week and a week felt like a month. We stopped at a different inn every night, and each was stuffy, disgusting, and full of weary, sweating travelers. After a few days, I accepted that I was one of them. Clara and I hardly spoke. We were both fully aware of our drop in station and lack of propriety. We were traveling unchaperoned, completely alone. It was entirely improper of Mama to put us in such a situation, and I struggled to keep my composure.

By the ninth night, the coachman informed us that we would arrive in Craster the next afternoon. Northern England was like a stranger to me, and what I would find there was a constant, maddening weight on my mind. What would our new home be like? How was I to find a husband who was able and willing to save us from ruin?

These questions plagued my mind the next day too. For several hours now I had noticed a drastic change of scenery. The air was thicker, as if it were wearing a cloak of mist. We traveled close to the coast, and I saw the ocean in the distance; the line between sky and water blurred in a line of gray. Prickly, dying plants patched the scenery like ugly sores. I almost cried. Although I had been asleep longer than I had been awake for so many days, I leaned back and fell asleep again, dreaming of the life I could no longer have.

"Charlotte!" I awoke to Clara's scratchy voice. "We've arrived."

I sat up, desperate to stretch my legs. Rain blew on the windows of the carriage as if it were eager to enter and wet my hair and make me feel even more ugly. So this was Northumberland. We had arrived in the little town called Craster. My first impression of the town was not what I had expected. It was worse.

Shaking my legs to stop their tingling, I stood, unlatching the door and climbing out of the carriage without waiting for assistance. My eyes widened at the wild scene before me. Cold, wet winds hit my face, stole my breath, and lifted my skirts. I tightened the carriage blanket around me and gaped at the house ahead. It was so *small*. A cottage would be an appropriate name for the structure. Wet, gnarled vines created a net over the gray-stoned facade. There were only four windows, two on the lower level and two on the upper. A scream formed in my throat but I didn't let it escape my mouth.

I could see the coast from here, where bright-roofed houses stood side by side, as if huddling together to stay warm in this wilderness. In a brief moment of optimism, I thanked fate for not finding me in a house like that. The ruins of a castle stood on a remote headland in the distance, blurred by the severe weather. I squinted through the rain at another lumbering building just up the road from our cottage. Its time-worn stone towered up and up, and was characterized by large cream pillars and many French windows. I assumed it was the home of Lord Trowbridge.

"On you go, miss. You'll catch a cold." It was the coachman, hefting my trunk over his shoulder.

I scowled at him. But I was freezing, so I trudged toward the house behind Clara with the coachman behind us. We threw the door open and walked inside. A musty smell filled my nose and I grimaced. Despite evening being hours away, everything was dim. Clara set herself to finding a source of light, and I walked around the corner, still feeling like a ghost, unable to absorb so much change.

The ceiling hung low and blank in the entryway, raised by pale green walls. The wooden floor creaked beneath my boots as I rounded the corner at the right. Here was a sitting room of sorts, with a settee, wooden chair, and stone fireplace. My heart sunk when I didn't see a pianoforte. I peeked my head through the door at the back of the room and found a tiny kitchen along with a wooden tub and washboard. I shuddered. We would be washing our own clothing. There must have been a way I could force Clara to do it. After all, I was on the inescapable quest for a husband. There was no time to focus on anything else.

Strangely, a narrow staircase created a parallel to the kitchen, giving way to a second floor where I assumed the bedrooms were located. I walked carefully up the stairs, running my hands along the walls to keep from tripping and cursed whoever constructed this home for its lack of windows. It was so dark, and with winter coming, it would only become darker. When I reached the top of the stairs, I found a short hallway and only two rooms. Both were furnished with a bed, desk, and to my relief, a mirror.

When I looked at my reflection, I cringed. My hair was still in the spinster knot Clara had styled it in. It was the only way she knew. My face was dull and my dress was dirty.

I don't know how long I stood there, studying my reflection and the room around me, but my daze was broken when I saw Clara walk into the room in the corner of the mirror. She was holding two lamps. I watched as she set them both on the writing desk, filling the room with a sense of warmth that didn't reach me. I turned around and walked toward the bed where I sat down, and she joined me.

"What are we to do?" I choked. "Look at me! How can I win Lord Trowbridge looking like *this*?"

She tucked her legs underneath her. "I will practice making your hair look better. And you will just have to wear the dresses you have." She paused, as if deciding whether she should say something else. "But Charlotte . . . you cannot try too hard. I don't care what Mama says. Any sensible man of wealth can sort out the fortune hunters."

I shrugged. "Then we shall hope he is a simpleton." I hated the fact that my pursuit of a husband was no longer directly related to me. Now Clara was involved and Mama cared more than ever. How could I please them all? And why should I?

Clara didn't smile at my comment. Instead she looked sad. "How do you do that?"

"Do what?"

"Consent to marry a simple man if he is wealthy or high class. Do you even care if he is agreeable? If he is kind?"

I rolled my eyes, annoyed. "Once we are married I will avoid his company as often as possible."

"But do you care if he is handsome?" she asked.

"How he looks is of little concern to me. People will not question my attachment to him. They will know that I was wise in my decision, no matter how unsightly he may be. Besides, I would prefer that he not outshine me in his appearance."

I thought she would be finished with the questions, but she pressed on. "Well then . . . what other attributes do you find attractive?"

Leaning back on my hands, I temporarily forgot our situation. My smile grew. "A large house, preferably with a memorable name. I do adore Grecian furnishings. Also his circle of acquaintances must be large, and—"

"No," she interrupted, "that is not what I meant."

"What *did* you mean?" I asked through gritted teeth.

She leaned toward me, a dreaming look in her blue eyes. "He must be kind, brave, and true. He must have a knowledge of literature and poetry and care for it. He'll have a tender heart, and care for others more than himself. But above all, he'll care for me." Her smile grew to a ridiculous size. "He'll love me."

I pushed myself off the bed and gave her a disparaging look. "Oh, my, you are such a romantic! Do you think men sit around their port speaking of such things? No. They don't love. They only desire. They care for nothing more than how we look, so we must care for nothing more than what they possess. Who they know. Where they live. It is the only fair way. The heart must remain an uninvited third party."

Her lips turned down in a pout and her brow furrowed. I had won the conversation it seemed. She stood and stretched her back. "We are each entitled to our opinion, I suppose. At least the task ahead of you will be easier because of your opinion. Love can make even the best laid plan go awry." She walked across the room to her traveling trunk and opened it, beginning to unpack her things. "I am finally seeing the benefits of being the plainer daughter," she mumbled.

I hurried over to where she was unpacking and planted my hands on my hips. "You plan to use this room? I was here first. I am older, so the larger room belongs to me."

She looked up at where I stood. Her eyes were weary, succumbing to my hard ones. "Why must you always have your way?" She shook her head. "Why must you only care for yourself?" I opened my mouth to speak, but Clara just hugged her trunk in front of her and walked to the room down the hall.

I was surprised by her reaction. Something inside of me wished for an argument. The past days had been so dull, I needed a reason to raise my voice and claim the upper hand.

I shut the door behind her and grimaced at the layer of dust on the wall behind it. My composure hung by a thread, but I clung to it still. Things could not possibly become worse than they already were. My fortune would turn. Despite what was written in my stars, I was going to force the hand of fate. I was going to find a husband in this misty town—one that could save the future I had planned long ago.

Too anxious to sleep, I picked away at my mess of hair. I needed to learn to style it on my own. It had always been a crowning feature of mine, and it was imperative that I showcased it in its best light.

After nearly an hour, I threw the brush at the wall in frustration. Several spiders emerged from a crack near where my brush hit, skittering across the floor toward me. Shrieking, I climbed on top of my bed. I brought my knees to my chest and buried my face into my skirts. Then I cried because there was nothing I could do to stop what was coming. And there was no way to stop the spiders. And there was no way I could achieve what Mama expected of me. Securing a fortuitous match had always been a dream of mine, but now it was an obligation.

And there was no such thing as an obligatory dream.

Chapter 4

"I would challenge you to a battle of wits,
But I see you are unarmed."

The morning light penetrated my eyelids despite its dimness. I groaned awake and sat up. I was still dressed from yesterday, wearing the most casual gown I owned. That needed to change.

I hurried over to my trunk with weak legs. Mama had only allowed us each to keep six dresses, and thankfully, I had kept my most flattering day dress—robin's egg blue with cream ribbon trim around the sleeves, neckline, and waist. Now came the difficult part.

"Clara!" I ran toward her bedchamber and pushed open the door. She was struggling to fasten the back of her dress, arms bent awkwardly over her shoulders. I stopped. "How did you do that on your own?" She was almost completely dressed. I couldn't even begin to undress without my maid to assist me.

She gave a huffed breath. Sweat shone on her forehead and she wiped her hair from her eyes. "It isn't so difficult. And I have long arms."

I raised an eyebrow at her. "When you are finished, come assist me with mine."

She crossed her arms. Only then did I notice the puffy, redness of her eyes. "Not everything is about you anymore, Charlotte. Mama is not here to favor you. She is not here to treat you like a princess and me like a burden. She abandoned us both! I won't accept orders from you ever again, and if you will continue to be selfish, then I will

28

only dress myself, and only cook for myself, and only kill spiders in my own room! I heard you shrieking last night."

I felt the weight of her words settle over me like an iron blanket. I needed her help, but I was not about to admit that. Being inferior was never an option. "Very well. I will dress myself. We leave for the village in one hour."

I stalked from the room, uneasy for a reason I couldn't name. Having an ally in this strange place was necessary, but how could I win Clara's respect without sacrificing my own? I was not a weak, silly girl who succumbed to her little sister. I was beautiful, capable, and governing. And I always achieved what I wanted.

Grumbling, I reached behind my back and looked into the mirror to begin unfastening the buttons of my dress. After nearly thirty minutes, I was wearing the robin's egg gown, wiping sweat from my own forehead. Now the hair.

I settled on a simple style I had practiced the night before. Luckily, I had brought an entire box of pins with me, so I could hide the many stray hairs and mistakes. I stared at my reflection and willed myself to be confident.

Before leaving, I dug through my things and withdrew a familiar sheet of parchment. Under the words, *Always display refinement, although you may not feel it*, I scribbled one sentence:

Always wear a bonnet out of doors. A mess of hair must always remain concealed.

The weather was surprisingly calm when Clara and I walked down the steps of our pitiful cottage. It would be a long walk to the village, and the air, although calm, was crisp and chilling through my cloak. I took it as a positive thing. Combined with the exercise, it would give more color to my cheeks. I was surprised Mama had found such a secluded cottage for us. As we came nearer to the village, I noticed that aside from our lonely home, all the other seahouses were grouped together as if they comprised a social circle I was uninvited to.

We passed the only grand home in the area, the one I thought to belong to Lord Trowbridge. The closer view was enough to take my breath away. It was old, and had a spooky feeling about it. The stone was dark and weather-worn, but the accents were fresh and belonged to the structure in an odd way. I could only imagine the home in winter, edged in frost and surrounded by leafless trees.

"How am I going to make his acquaintance?" I whispered. I didn't know why, but I felt like the house would hear me if I spoke too loudly.

Clara squinted back at the house as we passed it. "Gather more information. Surely some of the people we meet in the village will know of him."

I turned away, content for the moment. I was certain the house was haunted, and I wouldn't dare call it beautiful. That thing inside me continued to sink. As we walked, Clara began talking about the novel she was reading, and how everything she saw reminded her of it. It was exhausting.

"And that house is like the home of the poor Wilshire family. And the ruins of Dunstanburgh castle were once exactly like Helmsway castle, to be sure. Oh! And that woman reminds me precisely of the eldest Wilshire daughter."

The village was straight ahead, little more than a gathering of small street shops; the smell of fish pervaded in the air. I held my breath as we approached. The coast was so close now. I could almost feel the salty spray of seawater as I watched it crash against the rocks below the shallow cliffs. Fishing boats dotted the nearby water like splattered paint on a canvas of gray. I watched as a group of men hefted a net of silver fish into their boat, and I could hear their voices carrying over to my ears, much less refined and clear than the gentlemen of my acquaintance. My nose wrinkled in distaste.

"Oi, misses!" A thick-bearded man lumbered toward us.

Clara's eyes widened. "He is an exact picture of the villain of the novel."

I shushed her and quickly looped my arm through hers and tried to turn the other way, but the man was already beside us. "I 'aven't seen you about. Wha' brings ye 'ere?" He reeked of dead fish and ale.

"We are visiting a friend," Clara answered. "Good day, sir." Then we turned away and walked toward the market area, where less frightening people stood. I noticed another man watching us from down the path. His brow was furrowed as he watched the bearded man follow us.

"Ye smell like flowers. We don' grow many flowers 'round 'ere."

We walked faster, our footsteps exceeding even the rate of my heart. His hand clamped over my shoulder, stopping us. I shrieked, hitting him with my reticule. His eyes focused on it as it swung toward him. Then he snatched it from my hand and ran in the opposite direction, turning down a dark alley between houses.

I slapped my hands over my mouth, shock surrounding me on all sides. That reticule contained all our money for food and supplies for the next two months!

From the corner of my eye, I saw the other man—the one who had witnessed the scene—run past us and around the same corner. Were they accomplices in the crime? I supposed Clara would understand, as she had read so many novels. I looked at her in panic, but she seemed just as confused as I was.

I heard loud voices and violent crashes from behind the small house. My heart pounded. What was happening? Another sickening crash was followed by a low grunt. Eventually the noises went away until it was silent. Slow footsteps increased in volume toward us and I gripped Clara's arm harder, unable to move despite how much I wanted to.

The second man appeared, holding his hand to his nose. Blood flowed freely from it, soaking, I noticed, into the hem of his sleeve.

"Who is that?" I whispered frantically to Clara.

She tugged on my arm. "That's the dashing hero."

I didn't believe it for a moment. "Don't come any closer!" I shrieked at the man.

He scowled and rubbed his head with the other hand.

"We have nothing else for you to take!"

He stepped closer, eyebrows raised now. "You're jokin' me." Then he laughed. He *laughed*. "You suppose I went off and bloodied my own nose, do you? I was trying to get your things back, you ungrateful—" He stopped and took a breath.

Clara and I exchanged a glance. I cleared my voice. "You expect us to believe that you didn't intend to keep it for yourself?" I gave him an appraising glance. He wore clothing much more casual than I was accustomed to, with a worn leather coat rather than a styled one. He appeared to be slightly older than me, but by five years at most. His hair was black as charred wood, with eyes the color of calm seawater. For a moment they shone with disbelief.

"I'm going to pretend you didn't just accuse me of such a low crime." His eyes appraised me right back, then moved to Clara. "A simple expression of gratitude would suffice."

"I don't see our reticule in your possession."

He took a step back and grumbled something under his breath. Clara quickly thanked him for his trouble, but I kept my mouth shut.

The man gave his nose a final swipe, and I was relieved that the bleeding had stopped. I was weak-stomached when it came to such things. He narrowed his eyes at me for my silence but didn't press further on the matter. Instead, he half-grunted, half-spoke. "To make introduction, my name is James Wortham. You are new to Craster, I see. What brings you here?"

I raised an eyebrow as I spoke, ensuring that he knew he was below my notice. Trusting that word of Papa's disgrace hadn't reached this part of the country, I said, "My name is Miss Charlotte Lyons and this is my sister, Miss Clara. We are here visiting a friend."

"Who might that friend be?"

I threw a fleeting look at Clara. "Lord Trowbridge."

James chuckled. "Trowbridge doesn't have *friends*. Try again."

I scowled but quickly stopped myself. A lady must always maintain an even disposition. "Fine. But we are under no obligation to tell you why we are here. It is an errand of sorts."

He rubbed his jaw, a slow smile lighting his face. I chose to ignore the way it affected his appearance. He was very handsome in a rugged sort of way. I quickly banished the thought from my mind.

"Ah, a secret assignment." he said. "May I be of assistance? Adventure is scarce around here and I happen to know a great many things about this town."

I started shaking my head but stopped myself. "Very well. Tell us what you know of Lord Trowbridge."

"He's a dastardly fellow. Short, thick around the middle, not nearly as handsome as myself . . ." He grinned as if waiting for a response. When we said nothing, he cleared his throat. "Very well. He is entirely ordinary. Aside from his wealth and title, anyway."

I crossed my arms. "That is truly all you know?"

He straightened his collar and flashed another smile. "Well, of course not." He leaned closer. "But it seems to me you have a few secrets of your own. I'll keep some of mine in case you're ever interested in making a trade."

I almost screamed at him, but managed to maintain my countenance. Only just.

He looked down at the ground and chuckled. When he looked up, his face was serious again. "What was it that man took from you?" He was addressing me still, likely because I appeared to be the older sister. The reality hit me that all our money to sustain us for the next two months was gone. My throat tightened with the threat of tears.

"I'm afraid that reticule contained all our funds for the time being." I said it with my chin high.

"All of it?"

I nodded and a tear slipped from my eye. How had I come this low, crying to a man about my misfortune?

He rubbed the back of his neck. "Curse my angelic conscience." Then he mumbled some other things I didn't hear and nodded toward the village ahead. "Come with me."

Without a word, Clara and I followed. Mr. Wortham walked ahead quickly, and I nearly tripped over my skirts trying to keep up. He turned his head over his shoulder, addressing me with one eyebrow raised yet again. "Afraid to get your skirts soiled, are you?"

"Yes, in fact, I am."

He grinned and turned his head back around. "Then I'm afraid you've come to the wrong town, my dear."

Clara giggled in her throat and I shot her a scowl.

In the heart of the village, we walked past tall shops and short, crowded houses, much smaller than ours. People sat on the steps, talking, trading, and drinking. One man sat with a young girl on his lap, whispering in her ear as she cried, apparently trying to comfort her. His clothing appeared to have been worn for weeks without wash, and the little girl looked the same. Both their faces seemed to be sinking as if they were feathers tied to an anchor.

Mr. Wortham stopped and reached in a pouch around his waist. He withdrew a shilling and held it out in his palm to the man. Clara and I watched from behind as the men exchanged a few indistinguishable words. The coin ended up back in Mr. Wortham's pouch and he walked ahead.

Clara and I caught up to him. He gave me a sideways glance. "Poverty and pride have never belonged together."

"He didn't want it?" I turned around and stared at the little girl. She was sobbing again, rubbing her belly. I felt a twinge of grief as I looked at her. What would she give to have the upbringing I had?

"It seems my services are unwelcome to everyone today." I felt his gaze linger on me long enough to make me uncomfortable. "Yet still I try." He looked heavenward and back down again.

With Clara at my side, we followed Mr. Wortham off the path and toward the shore where dozens of men emptied their traps from the water. Lobsters, clams, and fish filled the boats where men loaded them in wooden boxes and carried them into the market.

"I'll supply you with enough for one week. But if you want more, you will have to work for it. Or you can ponder on the idea of payment by secrets. I would very much like to know what brought two all-the-crack ladies to Craster."

My usually smooth brow wrinkled in annoyance. "You would do very well to mind your own business, Mr. Wortham."

"Oh?" He lifted a bag of smelly dead fish. "Then I s'pose I'll keep these."

I didn't know why, but I pressed him further. "And always pronounce words clearly when speaking to 'all-the-crack ladies.'"

He dropped the bag to the ground and stepped toward me. His head tipped down and he gave me a stern look. "You would do well to stop pressing the temper of your means of survival. I'm doing you a service. Besides, I caught *'em* myself," he finished just to irk me.

"We graciously thank you, Mr. Wortham," Clara said, her voice quick.

He gave her a stiff nod and handed over the bag of fish. He tossed her a fast smile and said, "To you, Miss Clara, I say you are quite welcome." I thought I saw her blush. I rolled my eyes inwardly. No man could make me blush. Ever.

I wrinkled my nose at the smell of the fish. I was going to have to eat it. My stomach turned over and over at the thought. I had always delicately pushed my food around my plate when fish came in a course. Now I had to eat it for a week or go hungry. I didn't even want to think about after that week was over. Without money, we would have to find work. Mr. Wortham had mentioned working for our next supply of food, and I was afraid to know what that meant. But I wasn't going to tell him any secrets; *that* I knew.

"And when this is gone?" I asked. "How will we afford anything more?"

He raised both eyebrows this time. "Work," he affirmed.

"Work?" I refused to fall into the working class. If he could just provide for us until Mama could send a new allowance of money, I could continue through life in this wasteland without lifting a finger. I decided to employ my oldest and most talented tactic.

It began with a slight pout of my lips. Then I leaned in close. "Is there truly no other option? We are so very afraid and alone." I batted my eyelashes and smiled through them.

Instead of acting flustered, bending to my requests, Mr. Wortham surprised me. He stepped even closer to me. His closeness afforded me with a new view of his eyes. They were not only blue—they were streaked with green and edged in gray. "Aye, miss, but I would very much like to see you sporting a pair of fish-strewn breeches." A wink followed the words. Heavens, the man could flirt with the best of us.

I warned him with a look, accepting that my ploy was ineffective. I wanted to stomp my foot and demand my way, but I suspected this James Wortham would find amusement in such an act. "You will never have the privilege."

"A shame. But I happen to know of several more suitable employs for a lady. One of which may be of particular interest to you both."

I cast my eyes at Clara. "How so?" Clara asked.

"I am not at liberty to disclose the position at this time." He rubbed the stubble at his jaw. "Although, I am a tradesman of sorts, so something could be arranged . . ."

"We have no secrets to share!" I half-screeched.

His eyes widened. "It appears you do. Let us strike a bargain. I shall reveal to you what I know of Lord Trowbridge, and recommend you for any work you may seek, in exchange for a tale of your past and the meaning of your undisclosed errand."

I gritted my teeth.

"You have given me the impression that good deeds are unappreciated by you, Miss Charlotte. I should like to see you earn them." Then he smiled. Never had I wanted to slap a man in the face more than I did just now. "Good day, Clara," he nodded, ". . . and Charlotte."

The ribbon of my bonnet seemed to be growing increasingly tight. "You will address us properly." I managed to keep my voice even.

"I am under no position to take orders from you. And if you choose not to receive the information I have to offer, you could end up running my stand in the market, in which case, you'll be taking orders from me." His words hung in the air as he walked away with a nod and a victorious grin.

When he was out of earshot, I gave a frustrated sigh and stomped down the road in the opposite direction. The man was infuriating! His head was far above his station and he needed to learn to respect his superiors. I considered death in higher regard than taking orders from that rugged fisherman.

"He is quite handsome, is he not?" Clara said amid a giggle.

I snorted. "He is terrible. And stop grinning like a ninny."

She scowled at me. "He has been very kind. Perhaps if you hadn't been so flagrant he might have been even more charitable. Already he has helped us very much."

"Only with a smelly bag of fish," I mumbled.

"Would you prefer to be begging on the streets and selling even more of our things?"

That silenced me. The image of the little girl sobbing into her father's shoulder flashed in my mind. I imagined us in a parallel, me at her age, with my muslin gowns and ribbons with all the fine food and drink I desired, and her, wearing rags and going hungry under a dark gray sky. Something inside me ached at the thought.

"We need Mr. Wortham's help, Charlotte," she said, accepting my silence. "He seems trustworthy enough. And why should it matter if he knows a piece of our situation? You are not trying to secure a match with *him*."

I pulled my arm away from hers and tightened my cloak around me. "I don't trust him."

"Why? Is it because he is below our station? Not outrageously wealthy? Heavens, Charlotte, wealth of kindness may not be important among the *ton*, but I'm afraid we are far beneath their notice now. It is time you rely on something more than your beauty and talents to meet success."

I glared at her under my lashes. "You have been brimming with unwanted advice of late. I am the older sister. Therefore, I am the wisest. I say we do not trust Mr. Wortham. He is improper and ridiculous and disrespectful and—"

"Handsome," Clara suggested.

I rolled my eyes, refusing to agree verbally.

"I must own that it was refreshing to see a man maintain his head in the sight of you and your flirting." She laughed deeply.

It was humiliating, really. Nothing was right in the world here in the North. I was accustomed to lush woods, bell pulls, satin gowns, and a certain authority in the art of flirting. I had failed to make a match in the last season, despite being the prettiest debutante. I had been holding out for Dr. Owen Kellaway, whose heart had already been stolen. I had looked forward to another season in London—another chance, but now it would never come.

What if I failed to win Lord Trowbridge? Would Mama make other arrangements? Or would we be ruined forever? I shuddered at the thought of gutting fish in a pair of breeches while Mr. James Wortham relished in the sight. Sooner would I starve to death.

Chapter 5

"Friendship is constant in all other things."

I thought I felt it swimming in my stomach after I swallowed it. The fish had been painstakingly cooked after much argument over who should have to remove the heads. Luckily, the kitchen was already fully equipped, but unfortunately, Clara was just as unfamiliar with preparing food as I was.

I grimaced with distaste as I scraped the rest of the fish off my plate. If I hadn't been so hungry I never would have eaten it. With nothing to accompany the fish I was left with its lingering flavor. I stabbed my fork against the table and lifted my water with the other hand. I had noticed vegetables and fruits and even pies, puddings, breads, and tarts in the market. My mouth watered at the memory. Those foods I had taken for granted before now sounded like a delicacy.

My eyes drifted to Clara across our squat wooden table. With effort, she swallowed the last bite of her fish and scrunched her nose in disgust over the discarded skin on her plate. "I am telling Mr. Wortham what he wants to know," she said. "I refuse to eat this for any longer than a week. We need his help immediately. Even if we find work tomorrow, we won't receive our wages for a week at least."

I looked down at my plate. My stomach protested against my better judgment. "Very well, but we must be discreet. Or fabricate a story that he will believe. We cannot have him spreading gossip in the way we are here to avoid. And we must also demand the information he has of Lord Trowbridge."

"Of course." She stood and pushed her chair away from the table.

Something about the plan still didn't bode well in my mind. If Mr. Wortham was demanding so much of us in exchange for a favor, perhaps there was a way we could gain the upper hand. We only needed to find something we could hold over him. Anything.

Bright and early the next morning, I climbed out of bed, my back sore from the hard mattress. My stomach growled as I grudgingly wrestled with my buttons. I checked my reflection where a haggard, sullen face clouded the smooth confidence and easy beauty I had always known. It was purely manufactured by anxiety, an emotion I had only experienced over the prospect of another lady wearing my dress at the theater in London, or a pin coming loose in my hair. But now it was caused by problems of an entirely different sort.

I put a hand against my cheek and leaned closer to the mirror. I squinted. Soon my skin would resemble the color of that pitiful fish.

I stood in the midst of the seaside town an hour later, hands clasped firmly around a small basket covered with my shawl. I had stowed two of our brooches and a necklace inside, hoping to trade them for food. We could acquire plenty with such a trade. I was confident.

A sudden gust of wind stole my breath as I opened my mouth to speak to Clara. I readjusted my bonnet and tried again. "Where do you suppose Mr. Wortham has gone?" I wanted to try one last time to gain information about Lord Trowbridge from him, but I had no idea of where I might find him.

Her eyes shifted past crowds of people and small shops. Meat hung on racks above market stands and the smell of freshly baked bread wafted through the air near the bakery. My mouth watered.

"I would imagine we could find him running a stand or out by the fishing boats," Clara said.

As we walked, I observed the many eyes that shifted to us. Some bled envy while others merely appeared curious. A trio of women, one significantly older than the others, caught my attention. They were dressed at the height of fashion, and each sported neat hairstyles and an elegant air. They smiled at each other as they walked ahead of us. Giggles resounded from the two younger girls. They seemed to be close to my age. As they came closer, one girl with dark brown curls noticed us, whispering behind a gloved hand to her companions. They slowed and came to a stop ahead of us.

"Good day," the oldest lady said, her voice carrying a tone of surprise. "I had assumed we would be bereft of new faces in town today, but it appears I was mistaken." Her lips curved into a pleasant smile. "I am Mrs. Helen Abbot, and these are my daughters, Lucy and Rachel. We live just up the road at Clearfield house." She gestured in the opposite direction of our cottage where I could see a tall, neat home standing among a cluster of smaller houses.

"A pleasure to meet you," I said. "I am Miss Charlotte Lyons, and this is my sister, Miss Clara." I made a quick examination of the two girls. The one with the darker hair—Rachel, she had been called—was pretty enough, but nothing to worry myself over. The other girl, Lucy, I would need to watch a little more carefully. Her eyes were deep brown and framed in charcoal lashes. Her hair was also dark and curly, and her complexion was nearly perfect. She was a short, pretty, petite little thing, likely close to my own age. I masked a frown as I evaluated my competition.

"We would love to speak with you in greater length, as we are rather destitute of company here, but we are in a hurry for a fitting at the moment. Are you available for tea this afternoon?" Mrs. Abbot regarded us, her hazel eyes wide.

"Oh, yes, to be sure." I spoke in my most gracious voice.

"That is quite perfect then. We will receive you at two o'clock." Mrs. Abbot's smile was quite unlike any smile I had ever seen. It puzzled me. It was as if her eyes cared about her smile, and wanted to deliver it with sincerity.

"We thank you," I said, momentarily forgetting about all my other endeavors. And I found myself smiling back.

The butler welcomed us to Clearfield house at precisely two. With a pang of melancholy, it reminded me of our home in Canterbury. The home that was no longer mine. I lifted my chin, willing myself to forget my sorrows and melt into this refinement I was allowed to reclaim for an hour. Clara stood beside me, her blue eyes flickering between all the beautiful portraits, trimmings, and furnishings of the lovely house. Her mouth hung slightly open. She missed these things as much as I did. I was tempted to push her mouth closed with my hand and remind her that a proper lady never *gapes.*

Mrs. Abbot, Rachel, and Lucy were awaiting us in the sitting room. I entered first, bringing my eyes to a thoughtful gaze and my mouth to a slight curve. I had managed to tame my hair into something presentable, which I was quite proud of. The most important task I had in coming here to Clearfield was to develop a positive standing in town gossip. The look of screened envy Rachel threw in my direction was a promising start.

Mrs. Abbot welcomed us and beckoned us to our seats on the settee. Something lifted inside of me when I saw a pianoforte sitting in the corner of the room by the window. I sighed softly.

"What is it, dear?" Mrs. Abbot recalled my eyes.

I brought my expression back to neutral. "Oh, I was admiring your pianoforte."

She shook her head and swatted her hand through the air. "Oh, that old thing? It is an antique. But of course, that makes the sound all the richer. Would you like to favor us with a song? We would be so honored by your performance, wouldn't we, girls?" She raised her brows at Rachel and Lucy who nodded.

"Very well. But be aware that I am a bit out of practice." I thought I saw Clara roll her eyes.

I stepped up to the bench, fluently swept my skirts under me, and sat down. The keys were chipped and ugly in some places, but my hands found them and accepted their music anyway. I chose a piece I knew well, a sonata by Bach in A minor. Or rather, it chose me. I had copied the music into a journal from my instructor as a child, and had played it so often that I remembered every note. It was a stately, aching, and nostalgic song, a sharp contrast to the allegro pieces by Pleyel and the Scotch and Irish airs I had played most frequently as I'd grown. This moving piece by Bach came to me now for a reason I couldn't name.

Every bottled emotion streamed through my arms and through the keys and the air as I pressed the first key. It was the same experience that I'd had in the music room the night I had learned of Papa's disgrace. I forgot the time and place. As I swayed to the song, I forgot the eyes trained on me, expecting something of me that I could actually deliver. My fingers moved deftly over the keys, feeling every ridge in their imperfections, yet understanding the contradiction of their hauntingly beautiful sound. The sense of release was intoxicating, and when the song was over, my hands trembled, and it was all I could do not to cry.

The room was still. Before I could turn around, the silence was split by a most improper applause.

I turned my head in surprise. Clara's face was tight with emotion, but she smiled when she saw that mine was too. Rachel and Lucy's expressions were in combat between amazement and what I hoped was fresh envy. For the first time I wasn't pleased to see the envy. I had just shared a piece of something important to me, and it was new and rejuvenating. I had never delivered a song for the purpose of anything but accuracy and praise.

Mrs. Abbot rushed to my side with her hand pressed to her chest. "Miss Charlotte! You have broken my heart. You are a musician! That was truly exquisite."

I would have never thought it possible, but I felt bashful under her praise. It was different when my intention hadn't been to impress. My intention just then had been to release, and whatever I had released now belonged to every person in the room, and I felt raw and vulnerable from it. It was not a feeling I enjoyed.

When I reclaimed my seat, and all the ladies had recovered from my performance, we were presented with a tray of sandwiches and cakes, along with a kettle of tea and a cream pitcher. I wanted to eat it all. My stomach made a sound of ample agreement.

Mrs. Abbot sipped from her teacup slowly and then raised her gaze to Clara and me. "Do tell us . . . how long have you been here in Craster? It is a fairly small town and we have not met until today. It cannot have been long."

Truth and lies battled inside me. She was very kind, but without a doubt one of the most reliable sources of gossip in the area. If any eligible men heard of my situation, I could have no chance of making an acceptable match. Kindness could not come without a price. I had learned that lesson. Certainly Mrs. Abbot and her daughters were only trying to coax the truth out of me to feed their acquaintances enough of a scandal to keep them entertained.

I nibbled the corner of a cucumber sandwich before speaking. I wished I had pockets to stuff with the entire tray. "It has been less than a week, in fact. Our poor grandmother has been ill for several months, and thought the fresh sea air would serve her well. We accompanied her here to aid her as needs arise. Already the new scenery and air has livened her spirits."

Clara grumbled something behind her teacup.

"What was that, Miss Clara?" Lady Abbot asked.

Clara's eyes rounded. "Oh . . . may I—er . . . more cream, please?"

I stifled a laugh as Lady Abbot graciously added three more drops to her tea. Clara shot me a glare through the side of her eye.

"How very kind of you both," Rachel said. "We have always preferred life here in the North. We used to visit the southern countryside nearly every summer but I was always anxious to return here. Thankfully we haven't left the North for several years. It is necessary for my health and happiness." She half-smiled. "Have you come to appreciate these benefits yourself?"

I kept my face even. "I must admit I prefer life in the South. But more than anything, I enjoy visiting London during the season. Canterbury is relatively close to London, so I have had the opportunity to enjoy both." I pushed the empty feeling from my chest. I would never feel the same way about this desolate, sea-sprayed town.

Rachel swallowed a hefty chunk of cake. "I have never been to London. But I don't wish to. If I must marry, I will find a man in this very town so I am never forced to leave."

I studied her, wondering if she would continue speaking, but she was preoccupied by the tea tray. Lucy's expression tightened, then relaxed before I could wonder what it meant.

"Have you been acquainted with any others in the village?" she asked me.

When I didn't answer immediately, Clara spoke up. "Mr. James Wortham."

"Oh, but briefly," I added quickly. "We don't make it a habit to speak with such roguish, disagreeable society."

Mrs. Abbot's brow furrowed in a frown. "I must disagree. Mr. Wortham is quite respectable. He works for reasons of his own; he prefers to stay occupied. I find him to be a very amiable young man. I must come to his defense, of course, because he once carried Lucy all the way home when she injured her leg in town."

My breath came in sharply. "How improper," I half-mumbled.

Lucy reddened. "I was only eleven years old," she said quickly. "Never would I allow such a thing to happen now."

"What a lie!" Rachel said, her voice trailing with laughter. "You would, and you would thoroughly enjoy every moment."

Lucy opened her mouth to contradict her but seemed to change her mind. Clara giggled from beside me and I shushed her.

"Well, I would call the act kind." Mrs. Abbot smiled. "It is a rare soul that will engage in an act of kindness for nothing in return."

My mind wandered to the day before, when Mr. Wortham chased after the man stealing our reticule. I had assumed Mr. Wortham had intended to keep it himself, but he had only hoped to return it to us. I remembered the shilling piece he had offered the proud man and his hungry, dirty little girl. And then he offered us food for a week, without asking for payment. Something told me he wouldn't have accepted putting us in debt to him. Yet somehow I felt like he had.

It was a weakness he possessed then, too strong a conscious to refrain from assisting anyone in need, and too much pride to accept reimbursement. The man was obviously lacking great wealth, and for reasons besides lack of peerage or holdings. He gave it all away.

A thought stabbed me with anger. But he *did* expect something in return. He wanted my secrets, a payment I could never give. His

charity was not unending. It would expire after a week. Why did
we need his assistance? Mrs. Abbot and her daughters likely knew a
great deal about Lord Trowbridge. As for finding work—I shuddered
at the thought—Clara and I would need to do it alone. I was not
going to amuse Mr. Wortham by allowing him to pull us by a leash
into his charitable trap. He was cunning, but surely he didn't know
that I had been trained to be the same.

The conversation turned to our hostesses and how they came to
live in Clearfield house, Mrs. Abbot's husband, and their odd gar-
dening habits. As soon as I found the opportunity—a lull in conversation—I posed the question eating on my mind.

"What do you know of Lord Trowbridge? I have seen his lovely
estate and wondered what the owner of such a beautiful and haunting house could be like." I filled the proceeding silence with three
breaths. Finally, Mrs. Abbot found her voice between the shifting
eyes of her daughters.

"Regrettably, I must say I do not have much to tell. He typically
refrains from making appearances. He is an earl, a widower, and I
have only met him once, several years ago. His disposition was rather
reserved and a little pompous for my liking." Her voice faded at the
end.

To be a countess? It was more than Mama had ever hoped for. A
little grin lifted my lips. *Lady Trowbridge*. How lovely.

"Does he own a country or town house as well?" I pressed further.

"None that I know of. I have told you all I know. You have met
Mr. Wortham, and if I am not mistaken, he would be able to offer
you the most information about the earl. Not a soul knows Lord
Trowbridge like he does."

I tried very hard to conceal my clenched teeth. "Thank you. I
suppose I will take my questions to him." I glanced at the clock on
the back wall. We had already stayed for an hour, and I had eaten
my fill from the tea tray. I was going to avoid eating fish tonight if I
could manage.

My eyes flitted deliberately from the clock to Mrs. Abbot. "Oh,
the time. We really must be going. I thank you for your hospitality."

She stood, smiling with that same twinkle in her honey-colored eyes. "You are welcome to come calling any time you would like. It is not often we have such amiable and talented guests. And please do plan to honor us with your music again. It was absolutely stunning."

I thanked her and hooked my arm through Clara's. After Clara had offered her gratitude, we walked toward the door. Lucy and Rachel bid their farewells, and I thought I must have mistaken the disdainful look I had seen in Lucy's eyes before, for now they held nothing but kindness and smiles like her mother.

Mrs. Abbot grasped my hand as we were leaving. "Wish your dear grandmother well from me."

I thanked her with a false smile and stepped into the uncharacteristic calmness outside. Large black birds soared through the air, and I was tempted to cover my hair from their potential droppings. I shook my head in an effort to clear it, and took a deep breath. The air smelled of salt and rain.

"What an agreeable woman," Clara said, wrapping her arms around herself to keep warm.

I turned my gaze back to the house. There had been something different there; the house was loose and warm, not tight with indignation and insurmountable expectations, or cold with stares and harsh judgments. There was something genuine and comfortable about the afternoon that I couldn't claim to have felt before. Mrs. Abbot was friendly and spoke without clipped tones of disdain. Her smile was contagious, and I found myself wanting to confide in her.

But I wasn't ready to admit any of it to Clara.

"She was only trying to uncover a new topic of gossip," I said, even though I had given up on that theory by now.

Clara gave me a sharp look but didn't continue on the subject. She was silent for several moments as we walked. "You played the pianoforte beautifully," she said finally. "It was different. I had never heard you play like that before. What happened?"

I searched for a snappy retort, but something about the event felt too special to belittle. A piece of myself was still in that house, embedded in the walls and the keys and glass. Something inside of me lifted at the thought. It scared me, yet I wanted to go back and release even more.

I wanted to glare at Clara, or call her question absurd, but I couldn't. Instead I just shrugged one shoulder and squinted at the sun ahead, a dull, glowing circle behind thick, gray clouds. For once I didn't bother to stop myself, knowing full well the wrinkles squinting could create.

"I don't know." I crossed my arms tightly and tried not to think about everything I had lost, because the pain of it could come back, and I didn't have a pianoforte to unhinge it from my soul.

"It was truly lovely," Clara's voice pulled me away from my pensive thoughts.

My eyes shifted to her, but I said nothing.

"We should return tomorrow."

I shook my head fast. "We don't have time. I must meet Lord Trowbridge somehow, and that needs to be our only concern."

"And finding work."

Oh, yes. I grimaced. "We don't need Mr. Wortham's assistance any longer. In fact . . ." I lifted the basket containing the brooches and necklace I still held. "Let us go to the market and trade these for food and then find Mr. Wortham while carrying our purchases just to spite him."

Clara's brow furrowed. "How are we going to ever meet Lord Trowbridge without his help? And Mr. Wortham knows of a place we can work."

An idea came to my mind slowly, but rounded out into something that quickened my pulse. My mouth tightened into a smirk. "We will not be forced to pay him with secrets. We will discover a secret of his own and threaten to spread it through the entire town."

She raised a skeptical eyebrow. "How do you plan to do that?"

My mind raced. It would be near impossible to find something so ruining as quickly as we needed. What secrets could James Wortham be hiding? There was an idea close to the surface, I just couldn't quite grasp it. So Clara's question was unanswered. At least for now.

Chapter 6

*"With mirth and laughter
let old wrinkles come."*

I spotted Mr. Wortham by the docks. I stood with Clara above the short cliffs, watching his exchange with another man. There were dozens of men, really, all hauling crates of fish and dipping nets and traps into the shallow water. Other boats floated several feet out in the ocean while deep voices crowded the air with words unfit for a lady's ears. Roaring laughter met me as a group of men far to the left of Mr. Wortham drank out of amber-colored bottles and turned their dirty faces in our direction. I swallowed hard. I did not want to go down there, no matter my motives.

Clara gripped my arm and pulled. "Come then, Charlotte." My feet moved without consulting me as I tore my arm from Clara's grasp. We walked down the sandy pathway and I almost slipped on the steep decline. Twice. The rakish laughter grew in volume and Mr. Wortham cocked his head in their direction. Then his eyes met mine.

He looked mildly surprised that we would venture down here, but the expression settled into exasperation when he saw the basket of groceries I held proudly on my arm.

We came closer and he smirked. His black hair was mussed to put it kindly, but combined with a freshly shaved jaw and his eyes so closely matched to the sea, I had to take two breaths to assure myself that he was below my admiration. Handsomeness and all.

49

"Something tells me you didn't work for that load." He eyed our basket.

I lifted my chin higher. "Might I inform you that we are the daughters of a baron. Of course we didn't work for it."

"Ah." He rubbed his jaw. "The fish wasn't sufficient? Hmm." His face lit with mischief. "Employment doesn't come easily around here. Nearly everyone is searching for work. And I can't assume you found it without my help. So how, pray tell, did you come by such an abundance of food? Flirt outrageously with the costermonger, did you?" He narrowed his eyes at me, yet I still caught the trace of a knowing smile on his lips.

I gritted my teeth, understanding full well how unattractive such an expression was. "No. But how we came by this food is another secret I do not intend to share. I have come to tell you that I don't need your assistance. And I certainly will not buy it from you."

He shrugged his broad shoulders and crossed his arms over his chest. "Very well."

I waited for more, but he was silent. "Very well?"

He nodded. "Might I remind you I was willing to offer my assistance without charge before you showed such ingratitude." He turned toward the group of men still throwing whistles and jeering laughter in our direction. "Enough ogling and return to your business!"

The noises fell into slow grumblings. My mouth dropped open in shock and embarrassment.

"Now. I will be away for a fortnight, but if you change your mind by my return, you may find me around town." He tipped his head and turned on his heel. Then he sauntered away, leaving Clara and me standing in the misty, salt-ridden air among all the strange men.

I stomped up the trail, stifling a cry of outrage. I didn't care whether Clara followed me. I didn't care that I had all this fresh food and that I didn't have to eat fish tonight. I only cared that James Wortham had bested me once again. And I did not like that fact. Not in the slightest.

I was shivering in my bed when I awoke the next morning. My stomach wasn't growling like it had been the day before, so I considered that an improvement. Without a way to meet Lord Trowbridge for at least a fortnight while Mr. Wortham was away, I decided to direct my attention to improving my appearance. I was already improving on my ability to dress myself, but I still owned only a few gowns, and two of them were already dirty. I shuddered at the thought of washing them. I would just make Clara do it. Luckily, Clara had also learned how to keep our food fresh, so it would likely last another three weeks along with the fish Mr. Wortham had left us, although that would have to be eaten sooner.

I sat at my quaint writing desk and thought about what Mama might be doing right now. She was probably dining on a breakfast of biscuits, ham, eggs, and fruit, with all her lovely things intact besides her impeccable reputation. Papa had ruined that for all of us. I didn't pause to wonder about him. I hardly knew the man. I felt a renewed surge of betrayal directed at them both. Papa had sentenced us to this place, but Mama had sent us here alone. I couldn't decide which betrayal stung more.

During the week that followed, I fought Clara on the matter of washing dishes and our clothes, and on who would prepare our meals. I won most of the battles, but somehow the victory felt more bitter than sweet, and I couldn't understand why. There was one tub that we used for washing our dresses with washboards we found under the stairs. I also used it to bathe, but Clara was the only one who knew how to warm the water. After a few days, she refused to do it for me, but taught me the process. I felt like a maid, and it stung me to the core. I found solace in the fact that Mama should be receiving our letter soon—the one requesting more money. But it would still be at least a fortnight before we received anything. So I just sighed and rubbed my underthings against the washboards until my hands were pruned and cracked.

We called on the Abbots near the end of the week, and they were happy to receive us again. When they inquired after our fictitious grandmother's health, I felt a flutter of hesitation to continue my lie. I pushed the qualms aside and told them she was only slightly improved. When I sat down to the pianoforte again, my hands slid over the chipped, faded keys even easier than before, and I emptied more of my bottled emotions into a place I hoped could stop me from feeling them. But it wasn't so. I realized as I played that day, that in the midst of the song was when I felt most poignantly the abandonment and lost dreams and despair. But I also found a joy in it, born from the freedom the notes afforded me.

And I didn't care about the applause.

When Mrs. Abbot invited us the next day, I readily accepted, not only for the tea cakes and beautiful furnishings, but for the warm company and beautiful music I could create. We arrived at two o'clock as usual, and Mrs. Abbot greeted us as if we were old friends. Lucy and I had enjoyed a lengthy conversation about ribbons the day before, so she happily took a seat beside me. We all talked for hours, and I found myself smiling and even laughing in their company. When the topic turned to Rachel and her love for nearly every man in town, we teased her relentlessly, and I laughed until my stomach hurt at the look of lighthearted anger and embarrassment on her face.

In a jolt of sadness I realized I couldn't remember the last time I had really laughed. I had chuckled politely in social gatherings, but had it ever been genuine? Had I ever laughed purely out of enjoyment and fun rather than self-amusement or another's distress? The thought served as a sharp reminder that life here in the North was changing me into something I had never been before. I needed to be careful. Mama would not approve of any of it.

So I pressed down my laughter each time I felt it bubbling to the surface. I pulled my lips closed over my teeth in a prim smile rather than an obnoxious one. By the end of the day I felt better, as if I were once again in control of something. But that *something* didn't want to be controlled. Each day we ventured to the Abbots' house and stayed for hours. I practiced on the pianoforte until my fingers ached, even as something inside of me was relieved of a deeper kind of pain. Mrs. Abbot had assured us that we were welcome at her home at any moment, and she didn't press us to visit our cottage, which was a relief.

But I was feeling increasingly guilty about concealing the truth from her, and I didn't know how much longer I could do it.

I was scraping up the last of my dinner when Clara spoke aloud my thoughts.

"Mr. Wortham returned today. I saw him briefly when I went to the market today."

I pushed my plate away and sighed. "Did you speak to him?"

"No. I only saw him from a distance, coming off a boat. Have you decided how you plan to *threaten* the information out of him?" She smiled at her own words. I didn't find them amusing at all.

"No, I have not." I drummed my fingernails on the squat table. The man was manipulating us, and it was incredibly vexing.

"Have we received a letter from Mama?" Clara asked.

I had been watching the post for days and was disappointed every time, so I shook my head no.

We had been eating less than usual in an effort to make our food last until Mama sent the money, but despite our efforts we had just eaten the last of it. We would have to sell another one of our things, but eventually those would be gone too. It would still be another six weeks before our promised funds would arrive if Mama never received our letter. I prayed that she had. But still I knew that we couldn't rely on that. We needed a way to earn wages, and Mr. Wortham claimed to know where we could find suitable employment.

Regardless of the shame of it, Clara and I had spent a morning in the village asking nearly every person we passed if they knew of a place to work. Each had either mumbled a quick, "no, miss" and hurried by, or ignored us entirely. It seemed Mr. Wortham was still our only hope.

My head had begun to ache, so I retired to my room early. There was too much uncertainty ahead to be comfortable, and I was overwhelmed with unanswered questions. The dreams I had never thought I'd lose were quickly burning away to invisible ashes. My eyes closed against the searing pain in my skull and I endured night-mares of gaunt faces, dark skies, and worst of all—deceitful, green-eyed fishermen.

Chapter 7

*"A little more than kin
and less than kind."*

I was pulled from sleep by the sound of rain slapping my window. With little sunlight to tell me the time, I left my room and checked to see if Clara was still in bed. Her room was empty.

Hurrying down the narrow stairs, I was careful to duck my head below a loose rafter in the ceiling. When I peeked my head in the sitting room, I found her sitting on the low sofa, head bent over a letter. She looked up when I approached and waved the letter in a lackluster show of enthusiasm. She appeared to be disappointed, but I didn't dare ask. She extended the sheet to me. I took a deep breath and read.

My dear daughters,

I am indeed devastated that you must be among such uncivilized society. To rob you of your provisions was a most nefarious act and if I had been present, I should have stopped the man myself. My poor daughters! My heart aches for you, truly. Though I cannot condone that man's actions, I must advise you to be careful, for such things cannot be so easily reversed. Unfortunately, I am in no place to provide you with additional funds until the end of next month.

Life carries on here in the South. I am quite comfortable away from your disgraceful father and among my cousin and his agreeable family.

Clara, you must find employ in a discreet manner to provide for the following weeks. Charlotte, it is imperative that you make progress with Lord Trowbridge. I trust that you will win him over in a timely manner. Such a match would do much for our situation, and with him out-ranking your odious father, no one should mingle his disgrace with our family again. Do not disappoint me.

Sincerely yours,

Mama

I dropped the letter to my lap when I finished reading. Anger and fear coursed through my veins and filled my vision with hot tears. Mama was doing nothing to help us. I had been wrong to assume we were not entirely alone in this place. I hadn't even met Lord Trowbridge! How was I to secure a match with him as quickly as she hoped? I reread the last line: *Do not disappoint me.* The words inscribed themselves on my mind and throbbed against my skull. There was no time to waste. I needed to meet with Mr. Wortham and take what I wanted no matter the cost.

Clara's eyes were wide with anticipation as I looked up from the page and Mama's immaculate penmanship. She must have seen the determination in my eyes, because we both stood and hurried up the stairs to get ready.

The morning was new and, rain or shine, today I was going to find a way to meet Lord Trowbridge.

The plan was actually quite simple. Although I had tried my hardest to avoid falling into Mr. Wortham's trap, there was no way around it. I didn't have the time to find a ruining secret about the man, and even if I did, it would require getting to know him and spending time with him, which was not something I intended to do. Ever. Or rather, after today.

It seemed that Mr. Wortham's only problem was with me. He had shown no ill will toward Clara. I couldn't imagine why. According to our plan, I was to approach him in the village, thank him for all he helped us with, and secure his pity if nothing else. If he still refused, then I would tell him what he wanted to know—leaving out any specific details of Papa's situation.

I stood with my sister on the road before the fishing side of town. She helped me scan the coast for any sign of Mr. Wortham, but we couldn't see him. Surely he had a home. He couldn't live continuously out of doors. But the thought of him sitting in a chair by a warm fire just did not seem fitting at all. The Abbots had mentioned that he lived nearby Lord Trowbridge. That meant he also lived close to me.

After walking the streets for nearly half an hour, we decided he must not be out, and I stopped a woman as she passed us. "Do you happen to know where a Mr. Wortham lives?"

She scowled, then raised an eyebrow, as if it was an obvious question I should have known the answer to. "Up the road that way," she pointed in the direction of our house, "and take yer first right, he's the second house ye see." She gave me one last look of appraisal, then went on her way.

I handed my parasol to Clara and took a deep breath. "We will meet at our cottage again at noon. If I have secured a meeting with Lord Trowbridge, then you will accompany me. If my efforts meet with success, Mr. Wortham will be present to introduce us. But for now, I will go speak with Mr. Wortham alone. It is, in essence, a matter of business, so it can't be considered wildly improper. Not that anyone lives within the bounds of propriety in this town," I finished in a mumble.

"And I will be actively seeking work in town," Clara said, nodding her head.

I affirmed her words with a nod of my own. "Yes."

She gave me a little smile, the effort behind it evident. We were doing what needed to be done, but it felt strange and unusual, as if we were finally succumbing to the fact that we were not the same girls we once were. Those girls were evaporating into mist, breathed into the lungs of the unfamiliar people here, and transforming us into the same with each labored exhale.

Something else flashed in Clara's eyes as she turned to go, her shoulders less straight than usual. I watched her back as she walked, trying to puzzle out the meaning of that look in her eyes. But the wind was too cold, and the miniscule droplets of rain had grown in size. Clara had my parasol and I didn't want to ruin my hair, so I tightened my shawl around me and almost ran up the road toward Mr. Wortham's house. I recalled the directions the woman had given me and took the first right. His was the second house.

I stopped in front of it and pulled my shawl even tighter. There was a rough stone pathway winding around rich green plants, struggling to keep their color. Two peaks characterized the roof and met in the middle in a straight line with red tile slats between. The entire facade was mottled gray, like charcoal streaked on wood. It matched the sky. I squinted up at the stiff, intimidating home and found that it suited its inhabitant quite nicely.

Gathering my fortitude, I picked up my steps and took myself to the porch. Without hesitation, I rapped my knuckles against the door. I waited, hearing nothing inside. The house wasn't large. Surely he had heard me. I raised my fist to knock again, when the door was pulled open so abruptly I felt my heart skip. I quickly lowered my fist but not before it went unnoticed. A cocked eyebrow from Mr. Wortham was my chagrin.

"Miss Lyons." He looked surprised to see me. "What brings you here on this fine morning?" He grinned as rain continued to fall from the sky.

I didn't know if I was more surprised by his appearance or that he had addressed me properly. He was dressed . . . well. He wore a waistcoat, clean breeches, and a cravat—loosely tied, but cleaned and starched. The waistcoat was pale green, embossed with silver strands. My eyes flickered to the book he held in his hand.

"You—you can . . . read?" I asked. My voice was flat, not the smooth purr I usually employed around gentlemen. But Mr. Wortham wasn't a gentleman. He was a dirty, uneducated scoundrel. Yes. That was it.

"No. I merely use this book as a coaster for my jug of brandy."

I remained silent.

There was a sardonic smile on Mr. Wortham's lips that told me he had been jesting. "Of course I can read. I've known how to read since I was very young." He looked down at me with a stern brow, as if expecting me to challenge him.

"But you are a fisherman—er—tradesman, costermonger . . ." My words trailed off. What was his profession exactly? I remembered the shilling piece he had offered that poor man on the street. No fisherman would sacrifice that much of their wage so freely. And his speech. It was rough to the untrained ear, but significantly more refined than that of the other men I'd observed in town.

I was distracted by my thoughts—I didn't notice Mr. Wortham lean his head closer. "There's a great deal you don't know about me."

I studied his face for one second longer and tucked my questions away to analyze later. I realized with embarrassment that I hadn't told him why I was here. I hurried the words from my mouth, annoyed with myself for allowing this man to dishevel me.

"I have come to attempt to thank you for the assistance you have given my sister and me. It is much appreciated. I am very grateful, and would now venture to ask if you would be willing to share the information we so desperately need." I tried one more time at a coy smile and glanced up at him as my lashes fluttered downward.

He held the door open wider and ushered me inside, hardly glancing at me as he did. "I'll dismiss that obvious flirting as a desperate attempt to avoid your end of the bargain." He flashed me a smile. "Come in. We will discuss the matter inside before you drown."

I fought back a frustrated scowl as I stepped into the entryway and followed him to a room that looked like a small library. My nose was greeted with the smell of parchment, wood, and something masculine I couldn't name. Bookshelves bordered the room, stacked full and orderly with books. There was a round desk to one side near a low-burning fireplace. I sat on one side of the table and Mr. Wortham took his place across from me.

"Remind me of your inquiries," he said, leaning over to replace his book on a nearby shelf.

I narrowed my eyes. I had no doubt that he remembered perfectly. "Suitable employment and information pertaining to Lord Trowbridge. I have been told you know him well."

"Indeed, I do." He drummed his fingers on the table, staring at my face for several seconds. "For information on both subjects I require you to tell me where you came from, and also why. Craster is not London. Rarely do we have lovely young ladies storming our gates."

I searched frantically for a response. I could not tell him of our entire situation. My plan had been to inform him of the vague details, but I didn't trust him with any information that could spread to Lord Trowbridge and ruin my chance of winning him. It was already a remote chance, and I didn't want it to shrink.

I settled on telling half the truth. "We came from Canterbury to escape the disgrace of a relative." When he raised his brows for me to continue, I added, "A gentleman would not pry into the subject."

He dropped his head and chuckled.

"What do you find so amusing?" Anger clenched my fists.

He raised his eyes to mine. "You never considered me a gentleman before today. So why should I be one now? When I ran after your stolen reticule, or fed you for a week, I was not a gentleman because I wasn't dressed in the latest fashion, strutting about like a peacock in search of spectators. It is your prejudice I find so amusing, *Charlotte*."

The way he emphasized my Christian name hardened my resolve to give this man nothing that he wanted. He was hateful and disagreeable, and I could not stand him. "It is a precaution."

He shook his head. "It is blinding. Think of what you might miss if you overlook so many people. If you assume the worst, you will never see the best. Wealth and title are on the surface, easily seen and easily desired." Something in his face looked . . . sad. But it was quickly shaken away with a smile, and the subject change felt disjointed. "But I assure you, anything you tell me in confidence will remain discreet."

"Why do you wish to know so badly?"

"It is a precaution." He echoed my words with a smirk. "For an acquaintance of mine."

I was now even more confused. "Do explain."

His eyes bore into mine as he leaned across the table. "It would not be the first time this acquaintance has been pursued for his title and fortune—when beautiful ladies come to steal his heart with no interest in giving him one in return."

My stomach dropped. Did he suspect my true motive? I swallowed and smoothed my loose curls over my shoulders. I didn't know if it was a nervous habit or an attempt to look my best under his unwavering gaze. "You assume that is why I have come to this tragic place?" I kept my voice even. "How ridiculous."

He studied me carefully, and I managed to hold his eyes. After a moment, the firm line of his mouth lifted into a soft smile. "You came from a household of high regard, did you not?"

I nodded, so subtly I wasn't sure he noticed.

"You were sent alone. With just your sister? No parents?" His voice had lowered.

I was angry that he was prying into my life and asking so many questions. But the gentleness in his eyes undid the threads tying my delicate emotions together. A tear fell from my eye. Then two. Then three. I felt my lip quiver and imagined how pathetic I must have appeared. I thought my anger would counteract every emotion, but it seemed to only propel me into an even more uncollected state. I swatted at my wet cheeks.

With a sigh, he reached into his jacket and withdrew a hand-kerchief. As he extended it across the table to me, a small square of parchment fluttered out of its folds and landed directly in front of me.

Mr. Wortham noticed it quickly, a look of panic widening his eyes. Seizing the opportunity, and acting out of strange instinct, I snatched it off the table and stood, taking a step back. He stood too, making the table shake as he pushed away from it. I clutched the square in one hand. I stared at him. Silence lingered thick between us like a tangible thing.

"Give that to me, please." His eyes were fixed on the parchment, and I thought I detected a flush to his cheeks. Out of rage or embarrassment, I couldn't tell.

My heart beat quickly in my chest. I was hesitant to look away from Mr. Wortham, expecting him to rush at me at any moment. But too curious, I dared to flick my gaze at the parchment I held. It was distressed at the creases, as if it had been folded and unfolded many times. Small tears marred the edges like trim. I could see marks of ink showing through, writing evident within. Why was he so protective of this document? I smiled inwardly. This could be the thing I had been searching for—a way to gain the upper hand.

I took two more steps back and hastily unfolded the square.

He walked around the table, uncollected in a way I had never seen before. "That's personal," he grumbled.

But my eyes were already skimming the words on the paper. I didn't have time to read the whole thing, but I noticed the handwriting was decidedly masculine, and I caught several words that piqued my interest. *'Love,' 'dearly,' 'heart,' 'beauty.'* Mr. Wortham must have written it. Forgetting my tears, I grinned like a cat after catching a long awaited prey.

"A love note?" I laughed loudly in triumph. "To whom?" I scanned the top, but found that it was addressed vaguely as, *My love.* I snorted back another giggle.

He sighed and rubbed the back of his neck. "Something like that. Now give it back to me. Now." He took another step forward.

I held the letter behind my back. "Why was it never delivered?"

A muscle jumped in his jaw and I took it as a warning that I should have left the subject untouched. "Would you prefer that I wrestle it from you?" His voice was an eerie calm.

I gasped and raised an eyebrow in reprimand. "You wouldn't."

"Do you really believe that?" He moved even closer.

I skirted around him and stood in the doorway of the room, prepared to make an escape if needed. This letter was a lifeline, and I didn't plan to let it leave my grasp. "Just answer my question."

He remained silent, evidently grinding his teeth to keep from saying something awful.

"It is much easier to pry into the business of others, isn't it?"

His eyes flashed. "It was never delivered because she married someone else." He spit out the words as if they were poisoned. He crossed his arms tightly, as if to hold himself together. "She married a man of wealth and title. So forgive me, Charlotte, if I have suspected the worst of you. When your heart is broken by an act, it is never one you soon forget, and though I am not hunted for such a thing as fortune, I can imagine it is an equal folly to be loved for your holdings rather than your heart."

I pieced his words together in my mind, trying to make sense of them. "You cannot suspect I am here to secure Lord Trowbridge. He was a friend of my father's and I wish to meet him." I knew the lie was pathetic, but I no longer cared. I had an item of leverage in my hands now, and I knew precisely how I intended to use it.

He uncrossed his arms and fixed me with a look of reprimand. "I do hope that is true."

It took much effort, but I didn't look away from his intense gaze. That seemed to be answer enough, because his posture relaxed. His eyes returned to the letter, and I instinctively gripped it tighter. "Now, *James*," I appreciated the slight roll of his eyes, "I intend to keep this letter. And unless you provide me the information I seek, I will send it to Lucy Abbot *and* her father, binding you in honor to marry her." My heart pounded.

He watched me with scrutiny, his stare cold as ice. "You wouldn't do such a thing."

"I'm afraid there is a great deal you don't know about me." I repeated his words with a look of triumph.

I turned around and walked out the door, knowing he would follow me. I stepped into the crisp, wet air, and tucked the letter beneath my shawl to keep it from becoming soaked. Turning around, I watched James trudge toward me, an unforgiving look in his eyes.

I smiled. "I do not seek your good opinion. I am simply doing what needs to be done to receive what I want."

He approached tentatively. Every line of his face was drawn out in exasperation and irritation. When he stopped, he was only two feet away. "You would willingly ruin my life for a few pieces of trivial information?" His eyes seemed to touch my soul, and I knew he was expecting an answer. I found myself suddenly uncomfortable under his gaze.

Weeks before I wouldn't have hesitated to say yes. But something inside of me had begun to change, something I didn't dare examine for fear of what I might find. There was vulnerability in the answer "no," so without knowing for certain, I answered what Charlotte from Canterbury would say.

"Of course."

He ran a hand over his hair and muttered something I didn't quite catch. After standing for several moments in silence, he said, "Very well. Come with me." He didn't wait to see if I would follow, but walked up the path without turning his head. I took the opportunity to slip the letter in my boot unnoticed.

I caught up to him, struggling to keep up with his long strides. We walked in silence for several minutes, and soon I could see the rooftop of Lord Trowbridge's home, peeking out between flat dark clouds and emerald-green land.

"Where are we going?" I asked.

James gave me a look out of the corner of his eye that was more glare than glance. "As it turns out, both your demands come intertwined. You wish to know more about the mysterious Lord Trowbridge, and you are in desperate need of suitable employ. I hoped to know of your past before I recommended you for the job, but it seems I have no choice in the matter now." Another barbed look was cast my way. "Lord Trowbridge is seeking a governess for his young daughter, and I am taking you there to meet them."

I almost stopped walking. A governess? I didn't even know Lord Trowbridge had a daughter! Working in his household while trying to win his heart would be vastly improper. "Should—should you not call before barging on his door?"

He shook his head swiftly as the house came into clearer view. "I am always welcome."

I scrunched my forehead in confusion. "How did you come to know him so well?" We were in front of the enormous house now, and James moved forward, undaunted, up to the front steps. I followed, wondering if he had even heard my question.

I was about to ask again, when he rapped his knuckles against the door and answered, "I know him so well, Charlotte, because he is my brother."

Chapter 8

"To unpathed waters and undreamed shores."

There was little time to register his words. My mouth dropped open but I quickly forced it shut again. How could James be Lord Trowbridge's brother? The door swung open to reveal a butler, starched and neat, with a prim, ghostly face that sent chills up my arms.

"Mr. Wortham, I welcome you. Master Trowbridge will surely be glad for your visit." His eyes flicked to me.

James offered a smile only I could tell was still pinched. "Good day, Benson. This is Miss Charlotte Lyons. Please inform my brother that she is here in interest of taking on the responsibility of governess to Sophia."

The butler nodded and welcomed us into the drawing room. I immediately noticed a beautiful pianoforte in the corner of the room. It reminded me of the instruments I had played so often at lovely homes like this one. I knew it was not my place to play here, so to quiet my longing, I reminded myself I could play at the Abbots' the following day.

James had taken his seat on a sofa angled away from me. I cleared my throat loudly, calling his eyes. "How long did you plan to conceal this relation from me?"

He slid his arm over the top of the sofa and leaned back. One corner of his mouth lifted in a sardonic smile. "It is common knowledge around this town. You would have learned of it eventually without my help. You may blame your ignorance on a pompous inability to communicate with those below your station."

I glared at him. "Why did you pretend you were below your own station?"

"I didn't."

My forehead creased. "Then why do you work with the fishermen? Despite being a younger son, surely you have a better occupation than that."

"Fishing is a favorite pastime of mine, and it puts enough food on the table. I am not rich, you know." He straightened his cravat with a wide grin. "Besides, the men respect me."

I rolled my eyes. "How could you possibly enjoy fishing?"

"I invite you to try it sometime. Lowering a trap and later emptying it, pulling a net weighed down by fish, exercising patience. Wearing a lovely pair of breeches." He winked.

I shook my head. "Never."

"Would you attempt fishing? Purely for the joy in it?"

My nose wrinkled in distaste. "It is a man's sport."

He sat up straighter. "Oh? You find yourself incapable? I would have to agree."

"Surely it takes little expertise. Why should I try it just to prove you wrong?" The very idea was ridiculous.

"Because until then, I will presume you can only thread a needle through fabric and plink meaningless melodies on the pianoforte."

I looked away from him, crossing my arms. I was exasperated by his efforts to vex me. Without meeting his eyes, I said, "Might I remind you I have your love letter. If you wish to keep it from the hands of Lucy Abbot, then I suggest you stop teasing me." My face was shrouded in heat. He didn't know me. He didn't know how much the pianoforte meant to me. I had half a mind to just send the letter regardless of his fulfillment of the bargain.

The door to the room cracked open and a round, long-lashed eye came into view. Slowly the door eased open wider and a head of carrot-hued curls entered the room, followed by the rest of a tiny girl in a frilly purple dress. She could not have been older than six.

"Uncle Jamesy!" The girl ran forward and into James's arms.

He grinned, lifting her up with ease and setting her on his lap. "Oh, Sophia, you have become even bigger since I saw you last week."

She giggled, a high trill that made me smile. "So have you."

He frowned. "When you are all grown up, it is no longer a compliment to have become 'bigger.'"

She laughed as he poked his own stomach. James glanced at me, and I quickly tried to hide my smile, but he saw it.

"Who is that lady?" Sophia asked him, threading her little arms around his neck and frowning in my direction.

"That is Miss Charlotte. She is going to be your new friend. She will teach you how to be all grown up."

I opened my mouth to protest, still unsure if I should take on the job, but stopped myself. I would be living within the same household and under Lord Trowbridge's supervision, but also among other servants. To win his affection would be quite easy, actually. But would Mama condone the impropriety of the situation?

Sophia was still staring at me, a thoughtful look on her round face. I smiled at her without reservation, trying to somehow make up for the scowl on her brow. She was truly adorable. Perhaps being her governess wouldn't be so very bad.

"She is very pretty," Sophia observed, still watching me.

James shot me a sideways glance. My smile was still wide, and it seemed to catch him by surprise. His eyes lingered on me just a little longer. "She is."

That he should compliment me after my underhanded play this morning was unexpected. But more unexpected was the heat I felt rising to my cheeks. I hurriedly dropped my gaze from his. What was wrong with me? I did not blush! I had been called pretty too many times to count by various gentlemen. So why did his simple, uncalled for flattery affect me?

I stood and walked over to the little girl, forcing my eyes away from James. "Good day, Miss Sophia. If I could be half as pretty as you I should be lucky."

She gave me a shy grin, eyes dropping to her shoes, which she clicked together at the toes. The door creaked behind us and Sophia's eyes lifted, the hazel color shining with excitement. "Papa!"

I straightened my posture quickly, smoothed back my hair, and hoped with desperation that my cheeks were no longer flushed. I turned toward the door, eyes lowered beneath my lashes, displaying the look I had practiced while Mama held my looking glass.

Standing in the doorway was Lord Trowbridge. He wore a gold-trimmed waistcoat and a perfectly pressed coat. His shirt was ruffled and his cravat pristine. His face bore little resemblance to James. His hair was lighter and was tied back neatly. His mouth was a firm line and his eyes were like black tea. He was more handsome than I had expected, so I counted myself fortunate. Lord Trowbridge's eyes found Sophia and he smiled, reaching his arms out as she ran to him.

"There's my darling girl." His voice was low and scratched, like he had swallowed shards of glass. His eyes flicked to me, and he scowled, but stood up straighter.

James stepped forward. "This is Miss Charlotte Lyons. She is interested in becoming Sophia's governess. And I . . ." he cleared his throat, "highly recommend her."

I gave a coy smile and Lord Trowbridge looked away from me and at James, still scowling. "I expected an old, haggard sort of woman."

My eyes widened in dismay, but I quickly corrected them and continued standing with straight posture and a basic expression.

James laughed. "Not to worry. Miss Lyons is very well educated, and will suit greatly to little Sophia, I assure you." His words were edged in sarcasm only I could hear.

Lord Trowbridge didn't move a muscle. His stern brow made me uneasy as he looked between Sophia and me. I moved my expression to a more professional, stoic one, realizing that he seemed to despise the fact that I was young and pretty, and not wanting to emphasize those positive traits.

Lord Trowbridge looked at James, still frowning. "May I speak with you for a moment?" He cocked his head toward the door and James followed him out, shooting me a look. The door closed behind them and I could finally relax.

I dropped my hands to my sides and breathed out the breath I hadn't realized I'd been holding. I couldn't tell if he was impressed or hated me, but he seemed to think I was attractive at least. Lord Trowbridge was moderately handsome, with neat hair and fine clothing. His eyes were dark and stern, unlike James's open, clear, sea green ones.

I quickly stopped myself. Why was I comparing James with Lord Trowbridge? There was no comparison. Lord Trowbridge, I hated to admit, was far less inviting and handsome, but none of those things mattered. Lord Trowbridge was the prize to be won, and if Mama had chosen a man to deserve me, then he was the man I would pursue. I hoped he turned out to be a little more kind. Or maybe he could smile now and then. I shook my head swiftly. When did these things ever matter to me? He was wealthy and titled. Nothing else could contribute to my opinion of him. He was wealthy and titled, and I was to win his heart if I ever hoped to have a chance in the high circles of society again. Despite his reclusive nature—never leaving his home and making appearances in town—surely as his wife I could convince him to go out to London at least once a season.

I had nearly forgotten that Sophia was in the room. She was standing in the place her father had left her, looking up at me with a crease between her nearly invisible eyebrows. I could hear the low tones of voices outside the door, but couldn't decipher any words. Sophia had eyes and ears only for me.

"Your dress is very lovely," I said, breaking the silence. "You need only a tiara to be a princess." I related her to a princess because I knew how much I had wanted to be one when I was a little girl. There were few memories of my childhood I held so dear as the ones of when my nanny—though strict—softened enough to read to me from a storybook.

The crease between Sophia's eyebrows deepened. "Where could I find a tiara?" Her voice was so quiet I could hardly distinguish it between the voices outside the door and the swaying of the curtains by the open window.

There was something about her expression that was just so endearing to me. I couldn't help but smile. My eyes surveyed the room and settled on a piece of stiff twine that encircled and bound together three books. I walked over to the shelf and undid the twine, then tied it again in a small round. When I reached Sophia again, I placed it atop her curls. "That should do for now."

Slowly, like a twitch, her lips moved upward and into a smile. It felt as though a small force hit my chest. I had brought that smile to her face. How often had I seen that? I scraped my mind for a memory, a time I had withdrawn something other than outrage, envy, or sadness from someone's countenance, but could find only the smiles from Mama, the wicked ones paired with victory. But the pure joy I saw in Sophia's face now struck me somewhere deep inside.

She looked into my eyes and for a moment I saw my reflection in them. "Where is your tiara?" she asked.

I shook my head. "I don't have one." My mind wandered to the days when I lived at Eshersed Park in luxury, wearing pretty gowns everyday, eating four course meals, flitting around at parties, gaining the favor of every gentleman I saw but always moving to the next one, certain that none of them were deserving of me. I had felt like a princess then. Mama had been so proud. But now I felt very much like a commoner, and I had lost my crown.

Sophia squinted at me, confused, but didn't comment further. Her hands lifted to her head and her fingers traced the rough edges of the twine. She adored it. I imagined myself at her age, throwing it across the floor because it was too dull and brown.

The door opened and James walked in first. He looked satisfied, so I allowed myself a sigh of relief. Lord Trowbridge followed him in, darting a wary glance my way.

He cleared his throat. "Miss Lyons. It seems you are well suited to the position, so I will expect you here every morning at seven o'clock. You will instruct Sophia in her instruments in the morning hours, and her studies in the afternoon. We will discuss wages and other specifics when you arrive tomorrow." He gave me a stiff nod, then exited the room, his coat tails swishing against the frame.

I watched the footman close the door, and felt hopelessness wash over me. Lord Trowbridge obviously did not want me here. But what had I expected? That he would fall in love with me at first glance? Winning his heart would not be easy, but stealing a heart was something I had done before. Surely I could do it again.

James and I bid our farewells to Sophia and left the house. It was almost noon—the time I was expected to meet Clara at our home. I didn't want James to know where we lived, but he didn't seem inclined to leave my side. He was more of a gentleman than I thought. It irked me to no end.

"Do you have all you need, then?" he asked as we walked. I looked up at the side of his face. His jaw was clenched and he refused to look at me.

"I know you are angry, but it had to be done." I said, still looking up at him. "You would never have helped me otherwise. I intend to keep the letter in case you choose to bargain with me again."

His face snapped to the side, his eyes locked on mine. He looked as if he either wanted to call me a terrible name or pick me up and heft me into the ocean. Then his expression relaxed, and the fire in his eyes was gone. "You have outwitted me, Charlotte." He shook his head and with each turn his smile grew wider. "But you still have not proven me wrong."

"What?"

He grinned wider. "I have proven you wrong, surely. But you have not done the same."

I raised my eyebrows for him to explain. I stopped walking, knowing we were coming closer to my cottage, and I was ashamed to let him see it. His home was only slightly bigger, and he knew how desperate our situation had become. But if he saw our tiny home everything would be real, not just words painted on a canvas of mistrust.

"You thought me to be an impoverished fisherman, disagreeable, and nonrespectable. You wouldn't have imagined me to be second in line for a title, or that I was not so far below your own station."

I scoffed, rolling my eyes. "You did not prove me wrong, you are just a liar."

His eyes widened, but his smile showed that my diatribe had not pierced him. "You presumed I would not dare wrestle that letter from your grasp. Would you like me to prove you wrong again? I could reach in your boot and take it right now with no one around to stop me."

I gasped. "How did you—" I had been sure he hadn't seen where I slipped the note. He was cleverer than I gave him credit for.

He straightened his sleeves, nonchalant about the ordeal. I wanted to slap him.

"Based on your refusal to continue walking, I conclude that you would like to keep your residence confidential." He flashed a smile, highly amused by his own charade. "Unfortunately, if I wish to prove you wrong ever again, I must know where you live, so I may barge into your house and rummage through your things to reclaim the letter for myself."

I glared at him. "Are you *begging* me to send it to Miss Abbot?"

He laughed. "Ah, Miss Charlotte, but I do not beg." He drew a step closer. "I am *asking* that you do not send it. I am asking that you let me remain a gentleman. If you must keep it, don't send it. Please consider what ruining my life might do to your own." His eyes were sincere, and I looked away, knowing the last time he had looked at me like that I had dissolved.

What could be done to my life to make it worse? I had already fallen so low. It was as if I was at the bottom of a pit, and slick walls surrounded me, making it impossible to ever climb out. I imagined the wind whipping at my skirts, and undoing my hair, but the air around me was still. I felt like a porcelain doll, pretty and neat on the outside but empty and plain on the inside. Torn and vulnerable, hiding cracks beneath ruffled dresses and borrowed paint so no one would know.

I felt the pressure of James's gaze leave my face. I dared myself to glance up at him, but I felt a bite of shame that prevented it. I knew I could never send the letter. It was too cruel, even for me. But I couldn't hand it over to him without a fight. It would make me look weak.

"Well, I will leave you alone then," he said. He must have sensed how deep my thoughts were, because for once, he didn't try to breach them. "My brother expects you at seven o'clock."

I acknowledged his farewell with a brief nod; it was all I could do. He stayed for a moment longer, as if he wanted to say something more, but then I heard his footsteps fade out. He was gone.

I looked up and crossed my arms tightly. My feet felt rooted where I stood, and I couldn't even begin to riddle out the emotions I was feeling. I was aching to play the pianoforte, and I knew it was the only way to untie these feelings from me. So without waiting for Clara, I picked up my skirts and ran toward the Abbots' home, pushed from behind by the haunting hands of sunshine and stately houses.

Chapter 9

"The earth has music for those who listen."

Mrs. Abbot greeted me with her usual smile, and Lucy and Rachel were beaming as well. I immediately felt the warmth of their familiar faces and laughter wrap around me, calming some of my uncertainty. I hesitated, but decided to tell them about my job as Sophia's governess.

Mrs. Abbot's jaw dropped open. "Oh! I had nearly forgotten about his daughter. His wife died shortly after their daughter's birth." She looked concerned. "You assured me you and Clara were well enough off to care for your grandmother. Are you not well provided for?"

"We are just fine," I lied. "I work only to make her as comfortable as possible."

Mrs. Abbot put her hand against her heart. "How very generous of you."

I pushed a smile to my lips, and feeling a sudden and overwhelming sense of guilt, I moved away toward the pianoforte. "May I?"

All three women nodded emphatically. "Please do," Mrs. Abbot said.

Sitting down at the bench, I positioned my hands above the chipped, fading keys I knew so well. After taking a moment to wait for the perfect song to come to mind, I decided on a precise piece by Mozart. But I didn't play it precisely. I held some notes longer, some shorter, adding trills and melodies in the middle from other works.

I decomposed on the notes and let them carry me away with them. I loved the disorganization of the tune I was creating; I loved that nothing was required. The music embalmed my soul and removed the ache and fear. And so I played until my hands shook and tears streamed down my face. I didn't bother to hide them.

Mrs. Abbot came to stand behind me, a quiet rustle of skirts. Her genuine eyes met mine, and I noticed the wrinkles at the edges from countless years of smiling. I doubted I would ever have wrinkles like those. "What is wrong, dear?"

I wiped the moisture from my cheeks with quaking hands. "I don't know." That was all I said before I put my hands on the keys again and played. I played every song I knew. I was determined to force the sounds out of the instrument until the sounds of confusion and despair and shame stopped playing inside my head. I couldn't guess how much time had passed before I stopped playing, but when I did, my eyes were dry, and I felt lighter, and my mind was clearer. I was going to work in the home of Lord Trowbridge. I was going to marry him. Mama would be proud of me.

I stretched my back and shook my hands out at my sides. The room felt like a resonating echo of the music I had just filled it with. Mrs. Abbot, Rachel, and Lucy sat in stillness on the sofa.

I stood, feeling the sheet of paper slide against my ankle inside my boot. James's love note. I purposely shifted my leg again, making sure it was still there and not in the hands of Lucy. Despite his vexing qualities, I couldn't do such a thing to him. He hated me enough already.

"Thank you for allowing me to use your pianoforte, but I must go home." I pressed my lips together in a poor attempt at a smile. Giving up, I walked toward the door.

Mrs. Abbot followed me. I heard her steps louder than my own, and I silently begged her not to speak to me. I worried I might spill all my secrets along with my tears. When I stood in the doorway, I turned around to thank her again, but before I could speak, she reached forward and took my hand.

Her eyes held unspoken words of comfort, words that I didn't think even existed—maybe they could only be conveyed this way.

Right before I left, she gave my hand one more squeeze and those words threaded down her arm and into my hand, and ended up somewhere close to my heart.

If I even had one.

Luck had not met Clara in her search for work. When I returned to the cottage, she was there, complaining of how many mocking words and slammed doors she had encountered. Apparently no one wanted to employ a young woman wearing more than a ragged, out-dated dress. Perhaps James had been our only hope after all. I cursed him under my breath.

When I told Clara about the note, her eyes rounded in shock. I removed it from my boot and we had decided to keep it in my room in a small drawer on the backside of my writing desk.

"Have you read it?" she asked.

I shook my head. The note had been my ticket to meeting Lord Trowbridge and finding a job—it had turned out wonderfully. But I couldn't stop the pangs of guilt that struck me every time I thought of my manipulation. James had manipulated me too, hadn't he?

Regardless of where we stood on a ranking of cold-hearted influence, I would keep his words private. I would keep the note as a threat, but a meaningless one, and I would never send the letter. I knew it, but James didn't, so I had the upper hand. My brow furrowed as I considered this. If I had the upper hand, then why did I still feel as though I didn't?

Late that night, I lay in bed, but couldn't sleep. Nervousness fluttered in my stomach like a thousand hungry moths. I was due at Lord Trowbridge's home the next morning, and would officially be a working woman. I would earn wages and report to a master. Trying to win his heart in such a situation would be complicated. Searching every piece of advice I had ever learned from Mama, I modified them to fit my situation. Eager to remember my thoughts, I jumped from my bed, lit a candle, and retrieved the parchment I had entitled, *How to catch a husband: Charlotte's list of requirements.* Just below my last point, I penned my next line.

11. Always arrive for work in a punctual manner, allowing ample time to speak with the master about his interests.

I approached Lord Trowbridge's main entrance at precisely half past six. The gray, austere butler answered, a scowl written all over his forehead. "What do you suppose you are doing?"

I took a step back. I wasn't expecting that. "I am Sophia's governess."

"I believe the master informed you to arrive at seven o'clock, and you are to enter through the servant doors. Never here."

I bit back a retort and grumbled to myself as I turned and walked down the steps. The servant's entrance was around the back of the house. Trudging through the overgrown grass, I came to the door and pushed it open.

The smell of ham and eggs filled my nostrils the moment I entered. I passed the kitchen, ignoring the whispers and frowns from all the servants. Without asking for direction, I found a series of stairs that led to the main floor. After wandering for several minutes, I ended up in a remote hallway at the back of the house, and had to find my way to the main rooms of the floor. I walked past a small room with an open door.

Carefully, I leaned against the frame, out of sight, and peered around the edge. I jerked back immediately. Lord Trowbridge was sitting behind a desk, surrounded by papers and books. Calming myself, I arranged my curls and rapped my knuckles against the doorframe to get his attention. He glanced up, and I stood in plain sight.

"Good morning, sir," I said, maintaining a professional demeanor, as he seemed to prefer that. But I made sure my voice was still silky smooth.

He blinked twice. "You're early."

I remained in the doorway, unsure of the best way to respond. "Am I?" I sounded pathetically stupid.

He stared at me a moment longer, then tore his gaze away and straightened a stack of papers in front of him. "Come in."

I tentatively walked toward his desk. I tried to give a demure smile, but it felt . . . strange. It felt forced and unnatural. Deciding on another tactic, I tilted my head to the side and played with one of my curls as he spoke.

"I trust you know what will be required of you here. You will accompany Sophia everywhere she goes, you will instruct her in reading, writing, language, history, basic mathematics, and mythology. You will direct her on the pianoforte and in drawing and vocal talents." His eyes were in a constant flicker between his desk and my outstretched neck and twirling hair. I smiled and batted my lashes.

He cleared his throat and continued. "You will respect all other staff and teach Sophia proper manners. Specifically, you will teach her that outrageous flirting is never to be condoned. Especially toward an employer."

My smile fell and he looked down at his papers. I thought I saw a ghost of James's smirk on his face. "At seven o'clock," he emphasized the words, "my housekeeper, Mrs. Woodley, will direct you to your other tasks. You will be paid at the end of each week."

My face burned with embarrassment. I had never been accused of flirting before, at least by someone other than James. It seemed I was out of practice. When I remained standing there, he glanced up lazily. "You may wait in the sitting room where Mrs. Woodley will meet with you shortly."

Giving a polite nod, but grumbling inside, I whirled around and hurried out the door.

So it would not be as simple as I had hoped. If he could not be won by calculation and coy smiles, then how? I had never considered any other way. I needed Mama's help, but she happened to be hundreds of miles from here. I paused in the hall to take a shaky breath and calm my nerves. I remembered where the sitting room was from the day before, so I found it without much trouble.

When Mrs. Woodley finally arrived, I practically jumped from my chair, eager to escape the isolation of my own troubled thoughts. She was an extremely tall woman, very thin, with eyes so large they seemed to examine every detail of my appearance before I had the chance to blink.

She greeted me and introduced herself, then led me to the second floor. "This is Sophia's bedchamber," she said in a soft voice. "She will be ready soon, and you will wait here until she is presented by her maid. She has just outgrown the nursery, so you will take her to the library on the ground level where you will begin your studies. Breakfast is at ten, and you will meet in the servants' quarters to dine there, at which point, I will give you further instruction. Do you understand?" Her eyes grew impossibly wider.

"Yes." It was a concise, plain answer, but that seemed to be the rule in this household.

"Very well. I will return to my work." Mrs. Woodley disappeared in a hustle of apron and cap, and I was alone.

I leaned against the wall by Sophia's door, facing the opposite side of the wall. Portraits hung in an orderly line, and I noticed Lord Trowbridge in one, standing beside a woman. She had auburn hair and piercing eyes. There was something distant in her expression that did not match Lord Trowbridge. When they stood together, there seemed to be an insurmountable gap—a misunderstanding—that drew a look of sadness from Lord Trowbridge's eyes and a look of pride from the woman's. She was truly beautiful, and I could only assume she was his late wife.

The door beside me shifted, and I darted my eyes toward it. Sophia stepped out, led by the hand of a severe-looking maid. "She insisted on wearing a piece of dirty twine on her head," the maid huffed. "I simply could not talk her out of it."

Sophia gave me a little grin that I returned. A bloom of endearment opened inside me at the sight of the mangled, ugly twine pinned atop her head. "Certainly not," I said. "A princess mustn't go without her tiara! It is bad form." I winked at Sophia and she giggled. It was a rewarding sound. Perhaps the best way to win over Lord Trowbridge would be to win over his daughter first.

"Come with me, Sophia, and we will begin your morning studies." I held my hand out for her to take and she held it with a firm grip. I smiled down at her as we walked toward the staircase. She held her head upright, with her shoulders back and chin high. I wouldn't need to teach her how to walk with elegance—she seemed to have mastered it already. Or maybe it was the twine wrapped in her curls that gave her confidence. I grinned at the thought.

As I began teaching her, I found that she was already very intelligent, and seemed excited about the prospect of learning. At her age, I dreaded my lessons, wishing to be taking tea with Mama and her friends instead. I found myself smiling at nearly every word Sophia said, and wishing I didn't have to try to correct the adorable pronunciation errors in her delivery.

Eating breakfast and later, lunch, with the servants was a new experience, and not one I particularly enjoyed. By the time I returned home that afternoon, I was exhausted.

"Is Lord Trowbridge already smitten?" Clara asked me at dinner. I thought I caught a tone of sarcasm in her voice.

"No."

She chewed and swallowed. Her eyebrows lifted. "Surely he is already planning the wedding." She chuckled and I glared at her.

"He seemed to hate me, actually."

"Oh, dear. Was a curl out of place?"

I still felt like I was being mocked. "It will take time, but he will realize I am a perfect fit for him and his daughter. She adores me, you know."

Her eyes turned downward and then flashed with pity. "Is he the sort of man you could ever love?"

My mouth dropped open in disbelief. "You are still obsessing over the idea of love, are you? Have you seen it? I declare I never have. Love in a marriage is a far off exception, never the rule. I suggest you stop dreaming of it, and stop advising me to care. I never have loved, and I never will."

She paused in thought for a long moment. "Mr. Wortham's note. He must have been in love before."

"More likely it was a foolish adoration of some woman he hardly knew."

She sighed and stood from her chair, lifting her plate and carrying it to a small basin to clean. "I admire your strength of mind sometimes, Charlotte. I could never do what you are trying to accomplish."

I rolled my eyes, annoyed by her attempts to advise me discreetly against fulfilling Mama's request. "You could never do it because he wouldn't look twice at you."

She scowled and scrubbed her plate, splashing water over the edges of the basin.

I drove my fork into my fish. I thought I would be through with eating fish by now, but it was the most affordable option, and without my wages coming for a week, my plate would be covered in soggy scales for a few more days at least. The fish reminded me of James and his words today about how I hadn't proven him wrong. It seemed I had claimed the final word with Clara, but not with James.

I explored my mind for an idea—anything to put that infuriating man below me once again. I looked out the window at the waning light above the distant coast. The fishermen were tiny dots as they lowered their traps into the water to remain overnight. An idea struck me, and a slow smile curled my lips.

Energized by new excitement, I stood from the table and walked over to Clara. "Wash this." I handed her my plate.

She impaled me with a look. "No."

I had forgotten that Clara no longer bent to my requests. Kneeling down beside her at the basin, I painstakingly scrubbed my dishes, disgusted by the wrinkles the water put in my fingers. I debated whether or not to tell Clara of my plan, and decided against it. I was to do it alone.

So when everything was clean, I went to my bedchamber and closed the door. The sooner I slept, the sooner I could prove James wrong. The fishermen, usually including James, always met at the docks early in the morning to empty their traps. If I made it sooner, I could empty them all without assistance, and leave the bags of fish on the shore, with a note from me. I giggled against my pillow. James was in for a surprise, to be sure.

Chapter 10

"We know what we are,
but we know not
what we may be."

I didn't sleep. I had been exhausted from my first day of
work, but every time my eyes closed, they opened again
with undying excitement. I knew it was absurd to be so anxious,
but it was as if there were a wild thing inside of me, thirsting for an
adventure full of daring and victory. Stealing the love letter from
James had not been enough. He needed to see that I was capable of
more than just quiet deceit in a moment luck brought to me. I could
formulate my own plans and carry them out without any qualms.

At four, I rolled out of bed, careful not to rustle the blankets or
creak the floorboards. Clara would surely object to my outing, and
I didn't want to awaken her. The house was black, and I didn't dare
light a candle, so I reached out my hands to feel for my writing desk.
I found a sheet of parchment and my quill and wrote a quick note to
James. I was sure my penmanship was appalling, but I doubted he
would notice. He would be focused on the words, not their appearance. I giggled again, but slapped my hand over my mouth to mask
the sound. When I finished, I stood and held the note up to my
small window, letting the pearly moonlight bounce off the small,
misshapen words.

To Mr. James Wortham,

I grew tired of 'pulling a needle through fabric' and decided to assist you. Have I proven you incorrect? If not, please let me know what I must do, because surely I am capable.
Always at your service,

C.L.

I folded the paper and set it on my desk while I dressed. I wore my darkest dress, an emerald green that would hopefully help me blend in with the darkness outside. I didn't worry much over my hair, letting it fall over my shoulders with just two pins to keep it from falling in my eyes. I retrieved my note and tucked it in the top of my sleeve. I didn't trust my boot to keep it dry once I was near the water.

With all the arrangements in place, I grabbed my cloak and sneaked down the stairs and out the front door. I was pierced by the coldness of the morning; chill, damp air threaded around my arms and legs as I walked. Tendrils of light threaded through the sky in the distance, indicating that the sun was trying to rise. I had roughly one hour to empty the traps, leave my note, and return home unnoticed.

On mornings when I couldn't sleep, I often watched out my window as the men arrived by the coast. It was always half past five, and they always pulled the traps out one at a time, lifted them to the sand, opened the latches, and dumped the contents into crates. It seemed simple enough.

But now that I was fully awake and shivering in the cold, I was beginning to doubt the wisdom of my plan. I banished the worry from my mind. If I arrived at the docks and realized it was too difficult, I could return home and James would never know that I had failed. But the prospect of success bore me forward with a devious smile pulling on my lips.

I could see the outline of the coast in the distance, a jagged line between water and land, garnished with rocky cliffs and deep green plants, dulled by the lack of light. My heart pounded hard in my chest, and I walked faster. Fear was catching up to me now, stepping on my heels as I hurried down the incline of stone and dirt to reach the boats. It was vastly improper to be out—especially at this hour— alone. I was beginning to wish I had invited Clara to accompany me. The task would be easier with an extra set of hands.

I surveyed the area with a fast sweep of my gaze, half-expecting to see a pair of menacing eyes glowing in the dark. Relieved, I deter- mined that I was alone. Calling on the excitement I felt before, I rushed forward and stepped onto the thin wooden docks.

There was enough light now to see six heavy ropes bobbing in the water with gentle waves. I reached forward and tested one of the ropes with my strength, and it moved slightly. I pulled harder. The worn rope scratched against my hands, and I felt it lift only to drop again with the weight of dozens of threatened fish. After taking a step back, I took a breath, rubbing my palms against my skirts. It would be difficult, but not impossible.

Stepping off of the docks, I moved quickly toward the boats. They were anchored to shore, where several empty wooden crates were stacked. I lifted them out and positioned them along the edge of the water where I could easily reach them once I pulled the traps out of the water.

Satisfied with the arrangement, I stepped back to the docks and onto the slimy, moss-riddled boards. The water level seemed to become drastically deeper just a few feet away from where the traps were placed, so I pulled on the ropes to drag the cages farther into the sea, where I could rely on the water to make the load lighter for as long as possible, before they showed their true weight once in air. After rolling up my sleeves, I grasped the first rope and tugged. I had to lean back for added weight.

The trap rose higher in the water, and I moved my hands down the rope for a better grip and pulled again. The top of the trap had come into my view now, angry, rusted metal. Inside, the brown shiny shells of some sea creature came into view. I couldn't tell what it was in the light, but I wasn't sure I wanted to know. Grunting, I heaved the trap onto the docks, but only halfway. I stopped to catch my breath and gasped when I noticed the rope sliding out of its knot around the handle of the trap.

I dropped the rope and lunged forward. The trap was slipping, rattling over the edge, inches from dropping back into the water, with nothing tethering it to my reach. Without thinking, I fell forward and thrust my fingers between the bars to stop it from falling. The weight of the cage was too much, and it pulled me forward by my hands, wedged inside the trap. I cried out in pain. Jerking one hand from between the bars, I used it to grasp desperately at the edge of the docks.

My other hand was holding all the weight now, and the trap crashed against the underside of the docks. I screamed, trying to twist my hand free, but the trap only clamped harder on my fingers. Pain shot through my hand like millions of jagged knives and the edges of my vision sparked in black and white. I pulled against the trap, hard, but that brought on a series of popping noises that only intensified the pain and flashed stars in front of my eyes. The sound of sobbing reached my ears, but I was unsure if it was coming from my own voice. My arm was on fire, and my head was clouded by tears and heat. I didn't know if I could still feel my fingers.

Crying out, I shook my hand roughly, with all my strength, and felt the trap sliding away. The change was abrupt, and the new onslaught of pain intense. I was held only by the fingers now, and I bit my lip to focus on something other than the pain. With one last hoarse scream, I shook my arm at the elbow and released my hand from the trap's unrelenting teeth.

The water seemed to shift as the trap sunk, glowing with the dull morning sun. My head pounded, flashing between dark and light. Sharp, searing pain was my only anchor to consciousness and I gripped it tightly as I struggled to lift my hand from the water. Afraid of what I would see, I moved backward on the docks, still lying on my belly, dragging my arm in the lapping waves. I blinked hard against the urge to faint. Something wasn't right.

I looked down at the water. Streamers of red followed my arm as it moved, and clouds of pink rose to the surface where I was before. Terror flooded in my chest and I staggered to my knees, raising my hand out of the water in one swift motion. My vision blurred one last time, and I saw a faint outline of my hand, dripping with water at first, then blood, and more blood. Something was missing. *Something isn't right.*

Then I tipped into the water, joining the waves of pink and landing hard on my back where the water was only a few inches deep. A sheet of parchment floated behind me, reminding me of a dead leaf falling, falling, falling.

Loud voices echoed in my head like a gong—deep tones I recognized but couldn't quite place. Strong arms pulled me from the water. And a haunting lullaby put me to sleep.

"That should do for now." A grainy voice swam in my head, scraping the surface but never quite reaching. "When she awakens I will administer more laudanum. I had hoped an amputation wouldn't be necessary, but she slept through it, thank the heavens. The pain will be intense, but she should sleep again under the medication."

"Will she be all right?" The new voice belonged to Clara.

"It appears so. It will be a long healing process, and she will need plenty of rest to recover from the blood loss. It is most fortunate that you were there at such an opportune time, Mr. Wortham. Otherwise she might have bled to death or drowned."

A whimper from Clara followed the words.

"That will be enough for now, Mr. Watkins." James's rich, low voice caught my attention.

My eyelids fluttered, and I was aware of the tiny movement as if I hadn't moved at all for a long period of time.

"Oh, dear . . ." It was Mrs. Abbot's voice. "She is awakening now."

"Ah." A shuffling sound and the clinking of glass bottles. "Mr. Wortham, yes, please come assist me."

A strong hand slid gently under my neck, and I was awake.

My eyes opened and every sense came alive, and I was aware of my surroundings—the Abbots' sitting room. I was aware of the bulk of bandages covering my hand, and the excruciating pain beneath them. My chin was quivering, I could feel it, and two hot tears slipped over my temples.

A bottle met my lips and I swallowed the acrid liquid that flowed into my mouth. I coughed, and the soft hand lowered my head to a pillow.

"Go back to sleep, Charlotte," James said from somewhere above me. I was aware—fully aware—of his eyes looking down at me with concern, and his fingers brushing over my forehead. "Everything is going to be just fine."

My eyelids were drooping; my head was filling with fluff once again. No. Nothing was fine. James was helping me. He had rescued me. That was certainly not right. I couldn't make sense of anything else. Consciousness was fleeting, and my last thought entered once, and was gone. *If I had been James, I might have left me there in the water after how I had treated him. So why didn't he?*

The second time I opened my eyes, I was alone. I found the clock on the wall, and read three. I tried to lift my head, but it protested with the full throb of a headache. Everything around me was dull, the colors, the sounds, even the pain was less acute. I dared to lift my arm, using my other hand for support.

I squinted, trying to cut through the lens of dizziness I was staring through. My right hand was wrapped from halfway up my forearm to the tips of my fingers. But the shape was wrong. My fingers were wrapped at different levels, some so low I wondered if they were even there at all. I tried to move my hand, but it brought renewed pain to the area, and the bandages were too tight anyway.

"Charlotte's awake!" I hadn't even noticed the door open. Clara stood there, hand pressed against her chest. Tears fell from my eyes all over again.

She walked over slowly and knelt on the ground beside where I lay on the sofa. The door widened and Mrs. Abbot entered. Lucy, Rachel, an old, unfamiliar man, and finally James followed behind her. My gaze settled on him. His jaw was firm but his eyes were weary and troubled.

The old man—I guessed he was the surgeon—shooed Clara away from my side and knelt in her place. He peered at me from behind thick spectacles. "My name is Mr. Watkins. How are you feeling, miss?"

I shook my head, the embarrassment and terror of the entire situation catching up to me. He was going to tell me about my injuries, and I was afraid—very afraid of what he would say.

He stared at me a moment longer, his gaze so heavy with pity I felt close to suffocating in it. "Unfortunately, a large portion of the skin of your hand was torn away, but I tried my very best to replace it. As for the fingers, the damages were most severe. I'm afraid the fifth finger was beyond repair, and also the upper half of the forefinger. And most of the middle. I will be available to aid you through the recovery. But I will not put it lightly—it will be long and intensive."

I stared at the bulk of cloth wrapped around my hand. It couldn't be true. "May I see it?" I croaked.

He shook his head. "I'm afraid not. We will change the bandages regularly, but I must advise you against looking until the stitches have been removed in a few weeks."

It was likely sound advice, for I was squeamish when it came to blood. I was breathing heavily. I didn't know when that started. Tears continued to fall freely from my eyes, but I tried to slow my breath to keep from sobbing. I was embarrassed enough already.

"May I ask what compelled you to the docks so early in the morning?" The surgeon was looking at me, his thick, gray eyebrows drawn together.

James released a slow sigh that drew my eyes to him. He ran a hand through his hair and stepped forward. "It was me." He turned his eyes to mine.

Mr. Watkins frowned, looking between James and me. "You were meeting him there alone? In the dark?" He scowled in confusion and disapproval. Awkwardness hung in the air.

"No," James spoke up, "I challenged her to it. I told her she couldn't do it. I had no idea she would really try." He shook his head and looked at the floor. A muscle jumped in his clenched jaw. "It is my fault."

Mr. Watkins looked even more confused, but instead of inquiring further, he just shook his head in almost a twitch, and returned his attention to my hand. "It would be best if you rested a bit longer, miss. The laudanum is still fading and you have lost a considerable amount of blood. We will attempt to change the bandages this evening when I return." He turned to Mrs. Abbot. "Please do not hesitate to call for me if there are any problems."

She nodded grimly. He doffed his hat before leaving the room.

I pressed my head into my pillow, hoping it would somehow drown out the sounds around me. I wanted to sleep again, to excuse this all for a dream, but the pain in my hand was a sharp reminder that I was *not* dreaming. I couldn't speak. The threat of tears tightened my throat again.

Mrs. Abbot came over to my side and placed her hand on my shoulder, so gently I hardly felt it. "Try to rest, my dear. You have been through quite the ordeal." I looked up at her eyes full of sympathy and regret. She wasn't looking at me with disgust like I had expected.

But I was disfigured! I was ruined, buried even deeper in shame than I had been before. I imagined that Mrs. Abbot was Mama looking down at me from above. With all my concentration I tried to imagine the accepting, caring look Mrs. Abbot was displaying also showing in Mama's eyes. I focused, drawing every memory together, and realized I had never seen that look in Mama's eyes before. She would never accept me this way. She would never love me. Lord Trowbridge would never have me. I was completely and utterly ruined. Nothing could save me now. No one could ever love me now.

But had I ever been loved before?

As I tried to fade back into sleep, I turned my head to the side, where I wouldn't have to see all my spectators and their expressions. I couldn't bear the disgrace.

So my eyes drifted across the room, at the tall, rustic pianoforte. The chipped keys seemed to mock me, and they drove into my chest and struck me with a new onslaught of pain, a pain I had never felt so keenly in my life. My hand was ruined. I had lost the pianoforte today too. That same ache I had been feeling for weeks now blossomed inside of me, bruised, bleeding, and broken. Only now did I realize it was my heart.

At dinner, I was brought a tray of all my favorite foods. Clara must have told them. It wasn't the usual meal food, but lemon tea cakes, grape juice, and treacle pudding. I had loved all of these things before moving to Craster, and Clara must have spent a great deal of time having them prepared. I drew a deep breath of unexpected gratitude and looked upward at the face that brought them to me. It was Rachel.

She smiled down at me. "Hopefully this will help you recover some of your strength." She placed the tray on my lap, and her eyes flickered to my wrapped hand. She swallowed.

"Did you see it?" I asked, my voice trembling.

Rachel averted her eyes and stepped around the sofa to sit beside me. Her large eyes shone bright and beautiful in the candlelight. I could only imagine how unbecoming I must have looked. The fingers of my perfect, undamaged hand touched the stringy ends of my hair. It was dirty and crusted in sea salt.

"Yes," Rachel answered. Her voice had softened, as if sharing a deep secret. "When Mr. Wortham carried you in here, I thought you had died. You were so very pale, and there was so much blood . . ." My stomach sickened and Rachel's eyes focused on something in the distance. "I didn't know what had happened until I saw that Mr. Wortham was holding his jacket tightly around your hand. When he placed you here, the surgeon arrived shortly after, and so did Clara. I was sent to retrieve water, and when I returned, your hand was exposed."

My heart pounded quick and weak. "How terrible is it, truly?"

"Mr. Watkins was able to stitch most of the skin back in place, but there will be scars. And the fingers . . ."

I already knew. My lips pressed together and I choked on a sob. I was pathetic, sitting here sobbing about something that couldn't be reversed. At first, being sent here, I thought my dreams were gone, every hope of happiness was erased. But I had still had a chance. There had still been a future with Lord Trowbridge I could have chased. I could have made Mama proud and lived in comfort all of my life.

But now there was nothing left for me. No man could ever see past the crippled, disfigured hand I now bore. I had lost my beauty and I had even lost my music. My heart filled with so much aching despair that I felt it would burst. How was I to release it now? It would be impossible to play the pianoforte, to send everything that made me hurt away and into the sky where it could no longer touch me. Instead, it was resigned to fester in my heart until it destroyed me.

"Where is Clara?" I asked.

"She is meeting with Lord Trowbridge and his daughter. She insisted that she cover the position of governess so the two of you should not lose your income."

I released a shaky breath, drying my tears. Of course Clara was there. She had risen to a duty without questioning it. She never hesitated to step up and help me, even when I was so terrible to her. I sat back in the revelation, feeling increasingly horrid. James had rescued me, even when I had threatened to ruin his life and mocked him for being in love. I had manipulated him, and yet he still continued to show me kindness. How could he blame himself for what happened? The fault was mine entirely. The thought chilled me to the bone.

"Thank you, Rachel." It was all I could say. She nodded tentatively, as if she didn't know what else she could do. After a moment, she stood and left the room.

I looked down at my tray. Everything looked delicious, and I hadn't eaten anything today, but I couldn't bring myself to take a single bite. The pain in my hand was returning to its fullest degree, and my arm shook as I lifted it close to my face. I was unbearably curious. Part of me couldn't believe what had happened until I saw it with my own eyes. I breathed quickly, trying to move the parts of my hand inside the wrappings. I stifled a cry as it rubbed against the bandages and a circle of blood appeared, soaking through the thinnest layer. My stomach lurched in disgust.

Unable to sit here any longer, I summoned all my strength and lifted the tray off my lap, biting my lower lip against the pain, and set the tray on the table in front of me. The dishes rattled against each other as the tray landed harder than I had anticipated. My head was feeling clearer by the minute, so I sat up straighter and eased my way to the edge of the cushion.

Pushing up with my good hand, I planted my feet on the ground and stood. The room spun for a few seconds, and I stabilized my balance on the arm of a chair nearby. When I felt in control, I walked over to the bench of the pianoforte. I didn't know why, but I sat down. Tears clouded my vision, blurring the black and white of the keys to a murky gray. And then I placed my left hand on the keys and plinked out a plain melody.

I closed my eyes and tried to feel the music, to let it heal me, but nothing happened. Without the synchronization brought by both hands playing in unison, the song was bleak.

Pressing harder on the keys, pounding, anger coursed through my veins. My hand tensed into a fist, and I hit the keys three more times, until my knuckles were red. Then I dropped my face down to my arm and sobbed.

The door to the room opened, and I heard someone enter the room. There was no rustled skirts or dainty footfalls. I lifted my eyes, squinting through angry, hot tears.

My eyes immediately widened when I saw James standing beside me at the pianoforte. His brows were drawn together with concern. I straightened my posture and breathed deeply. The pain in my hand was slicing through the ache in my heart, and I was relieved that I could stop feeling it for a moment.

James was silent, standing above me. He looked like he was about to say something, but I spoke first.

"Why did you do it?" My voice was a hoarse croak, almost a whisper.

He looked confused. "What?"

I leaned against my arm resting on the keys, creating an ugly sound of mismatched notes. "Why did you rescue me from the water? Why would you help me after everything I have done to you?"

He rubbed the back of his neck and gestured at the bench. I scowled in confusion, but realized he was asking to sit. Pushing my dress out of the way, I moved over, and he sat beside me, just touching. Glancing at the door, I breathed a sigh of relief. It was wide open. At least something was bordering on proper.

James turned his eyes on me, and I looked back for one quick moment, then looked away. Why did he have to sit so close? For a reason I couldn't name, my broken heart beat a little faster.

"I would never, *never* leave a person in your situation, Charlotte. Not even my greatest enemy. I am not that man."

I sneaked a look at his face. He was sincere.

"Am I your greatest enemy?"

A smile touched his lips. "Only if you wish to be."

I moved my gaze to the lump of ivory bandages around my hand. Everything about this day was so very confusing, and all of it terrifying. So I couldn't blame myself for thinking, in that moment, that no, I didn't wish to be his worst enemy. But I would never admit to it, of course.

When I didn't reply, James stood and offered his arm. "You really should be resting. Watkins will be by soon to assist with your bandages."

I looked up at him and back at the keys of the pianoforte. Every inch of me ached, knowing I could never play the same again. The accident this morning had stolen my beauty of appearance and my beauty of accomplishment. I was nothing now. I had nothing left.

I stood slowly, and wrapped my good hand around James's arm. He was strong, and I couldn't help but notice the muscle underneath his coat. We stepped up to the sofa and I sat down, keeping my posture until he moved to leave the room.

"James—" I stopped, realizing I had called him by his Christian name. "I—er . . ." I tried to collect my thoughts, unsure of what I meant to say. I felt as though I had never stumbled over my words before now. James's eyes were locked on mine, awaiting the words I didn't know I meant to say. "I wish to thank you . . . for what you did today. It was the way of a gentleman, and I am . . . sorry if I ever thought you otherwise. And please—please do not blame yourself for what I did." My voice came out soft and weak. It was humiliating and pathetic that I had even tried to carry out his challenge. Surely he never expected that I would.

He stood there, a shadow of surprise crossing his expression. "Then I must ask for a secret in exchange for my services today." He smiled and his eyes shone with amusement.

"Very well." I searched my mind for a secret to share, but found only one that I was willing to. I breathed deeply. ". . . I do not hate you."

He raised an eyebrow. He was hiding another smile. "That is to be the secret, then?"

I nodded.

"I shall not reveal it to a soul. You may carry on with the glaring and menacing words, and only I will know you don't mean any of it."

It seemed impossible, but I was fighting a smile. "Some of it will remain sincere, I assure you."

He dropped his head and chuckled. It was deep and rich, and somewhat endearing. Surely I had injured my head today along with my hand. Otherwise I wouldn't have been thinking such nonsense.

"How could I have suspected otherwise?" He looked up, smiling.

For a moment I forgot. I forgot about the searing pain in my hand and the humiliation of my new deformity, and the reality that I would now never have the life and marriage I always wanted. I forgot that no one could love me, or that I had lost my music. I just remembered James's smile, and I tucked it inside of my soul like a gift.

The door swung open and Mr. Watkins marched in the room, a small case hanging at his side. "Oh, dear." He stopped. "Have I interrupted something?"

James took a step back and shook his head, ushering the small man forward. When the surgeon was standing beside me, Mrs. Abbot and her daughters entered the room followed by Clara.

"I would suggest you avert your eyes, miss. I don't carry smelling salts. I would appreciate if you did not faint," Mr. Watkins said, peeling back the first layer of bandages.

I was overwhelmingly curious, but I did as he said, keeping my eyes trained on the ceiling. I was grateful he had asked me to look away. As much as I wanted to see my hand, I was even more afraid of *what* I would see. Perhaps if I didn't see it, then I could forget the injury even existed.

Clara moved to sit beside me on the sofa and I moved my eyes to her. We had hardly spoken since the day before, and I had been anything but kind to her. Yet she had still been kind to me. Why did these things keep happening?

I could tell the surgeon was on the final layer because I had to bite my lip against the pain. The bandage was sticking, and he had to pull it away from the raw skin. I felt the touch of air against my hand.

"You have fetched the water?" Watkins looked at a maid who I hadn't noticed enter the room. She handed him a bowl. Her eyes flashed to where my hand was, and she took a step back, paling slightly. That was not a good sign.

"This may sting a little."

He lifted my arm and I felt in a sudden rush, water pouring over my hand. It was soothing and painful all at once, the touch of cold water cascading over my hand that I couldn't see. He moved it away from the water and wrapped it in a towel to dry. I grimaced. The rough fibers of the towel scratched against the skin.

"Now this may sting a lot."

I watched as he doused a towel in a clear liquid and moved it toward my hand. I stifled a scream as every part of my hand roared. Instinctively, my arm contracted, trying to pull away. Clara reached forward and gripped my arm to stop it. Soon Watkins had everything bandaged again, and I could stop looking away. I wiped a stray tear off my cheek and took a deep, slow breath.

Mr. Watkins packed everything up in his case and flashed me a rueful smile. "The pain should subside very soon. Not to worry." His thick spectacles were sliding down his nose. "I will return tomorrow night."

I gave a stiff nod and watched him go through the door. James was standing in the corner of the room, arms crossed. His forehead was creased as he watched me. It struck me that it was evening, and he was still here. Had he been here the entire day? Each time I had awakened he had been present. It puzzled me.

"I will be going now," he said to Mrs. Abbot, as if reading my thoughts.

She smiled at him. "You have been of wonderful assistance to our Charlotte. We cannot offer our thanks enough."

Her phrase, *our Charlotte*, stuck out in my mind. So she had not forsaken me yet.

James glanced at me one more time, and I gave him a weak smile, hoping he knew I was grateful. Then he turned and left the room with long strides.

I sat up straighter and turned to Clara, desperate to turn the attention to someone else. I was drowning in four gazes, and I needed to escape them. "How did you enjoy Sophia's company?" I didn't want to mention or think about Lord Trowbridge right now.

"She is a wonderful little girl." Clara's eyes lit brightly. "She wondered where you had gone."

I gave a soft smile. "She will adore you."

"Did *you* give her the crown made of twine?"

I nodded and my grin widened.

"She will not take it off." Clara shook her head and laughed.

Releasing a deep sigh, I sat up straighter, preparing to stand. Mrs. Abbot rushed forward, stopping me. "Where do you think you are going?"

"I would like to return home." I looked up at her, eyes wide. I was feeling much less faint and had already trespassed on her hospitality the entire day. And I needed to distance myself from the looming pianoforte that I knew I could never play again. Our cottage didn't have one, so I could coach myself to forget.

"Nonsense. The walk will likely exhaust you. Spend the night here, and Clara will go to tend to your grandmother. Won't you, dear?"

Clara's eyes met mine first before she nodded. Guilt stabbed at my conscience with unfamiliar strength. Mrs. Abbot still didn't know the truth about why we had come here. She deserved to know every word. She had proven to me that she could be trusted, so why had I still kept the truth from her? I released my breath slowly, realizing it was because I was ashamed. I didn't want her to think any less of me than she already did. I couldn't afford it.

Clara was about to leave, and my eyelids were growing heavier by the minute. Mrs. Abbot was right. I needed to stay.

Mrs. Abbot moved around the sofa to stand beside Clara. "Lucy and Rachel will accompany you on your walk. It is darkening outside and I should hate for you to be afraid or lost." Clara smiled as Lucy and Rachel willingly linked their arms through both of my sister's.

"I will see you tomorrow evening, then," Clara said to me as she moved toward the door.

I mustered up a small smile and said, "Thank you." I was sure I had uttered those words more today than I had in my entire life. It was not as difficult as I had always imagined. I had always been strong, and I had always thought that thanking others would made me weaker somehow, submissive. But now, I *was* weak, and speaking those two words, *thank you*, was strengthening in a profound and strange way that I didn't understand.

Clara looked surprised, her gaze lingering on me just a little longer before she turned around and walked out the door.

"I have a room prepared for you upstairs." Mrs. Abbot gripped my elbow and helped me stand. "I believe you will be comfortable there. I have assigned a maid to help you get cleaned and dressed for bed."

We reached the top of the stairs and Mrs. Abbot retreated to the main floor. A young lady's maid, likely the one Lucy and Rachel shared, helped me wash and dress and darken the candles in my room. I had assumed my rest during the day would have been sufficient to keep me awake later, but my eyelids drooped as I climbed into bed. My hand throbbed with every beat of my heart, because today, both had been broken together.

The maid turned to leave and I uttered one last thank you before fading into sleep.

Chapter 11

*"Love me or hate me, both are in my favor.
If you love me, I'll always be in you heart . . .
If you hate me, I'll always be in your mind."*

Mr. Watkins changed my bandages in the morning and I still didn't look. When he left, Mrs. Abbot joined me in the sitting room. I was on the sofa, facing the pianoforte. I traced my gaze over the wooden, cracked edges and the sheets of music perched on top. Nothing moved but my eyes as I evaluated every inch of the instrument. Despite my inability to empty my emotions through my music, I felt an unmistakable void within me. I was an empty, battered shell, swept up from a sea of unknown emotions and heartache. I could feel Mrs. Abbot's gaze on me but I didn't look away from the pianoforte until she spoke.

"I am so sorry, Charlotte. I know how much the instrument meant to you." She draped her arm over my shoulder and squeezed my arm. "But all will be well. You will find happiness."

I glanced warily at her honey eyes and warm smile. Her face was wrinkled in different places than Mama's, though they seemed to be the same age. Mama had deep wrinkles between her eyes from frowning. Mrs. Abbot had tiny wrinkles at the corners of her eyes and curved ones by her mouth from smiling and laughing. The difference was striking.

"How will I?" It seemed impossible now.

"Make the choice. Choose to be happy through every circumstance, fortunate or not."

I sighed. "How can it be that simple?"

Her head tipped to the side and she sighed too. "It isn't simple. But what you must do is find all the good, all the kindness within yourself and use it. Helping others find their happiness is the best path to finding your own."

I squeezed my eyes shut with shame as I remembered that I had not been good to Mrs. Abbot. She did not deserve to be deceived. Unable to keep up my pretenses any longer, I said, "I must confess something."

She sat back, her hazel eyes wide in anticipation. "What is it, dear?"

I took a deep breath. "I did not come here with my grandmother. In fact, I never had the opportunity to meet either of my grandmothers. It was all a lie." I bit my lip, waiting for her reply.

She gave a small smile and paused for several seconds. "Clara has already informed me of that."

My eyes widened. "When?"

"Just yesterday. She begged me not to tell you until you confessed it yourself. She knew you would. But please, provide me an answer to this: What are you trying to hide from me?"

I swallowed. "We had agreed not to tell anyone the true reason we were sent here, Clara and I. So I came up with a story that seemed plausible, but I cannot continue to lie to you. You have been much too kind." I paused. "But I must ask that you keep what I am about to tell you a secret between us. I trust you are not keen on town gossip."

She watched my face closely and didn't hesitate. "Of course. What you tell me in confidence will be safe, I assure you."

"Thank you." I breathed deeply, trying to decide if this was a wise idea. It was too late now. I had to tell her. Speaking far too quickly, I relayed to her every detail. Papa's gambling, how Mama sent us here alone, and how she expected one of us to make a beneficial match to save the family from ruin. Mrs. Abbot listened in silence and her focus didn't stray for a moment.

When I finished talking, she gave me a soft smile—nothing disapproving and unkind. No disdain or anger. It surprised me.

"You should have told me before. I would have kept your secret safe."

I breathed out slowly and looked away from her face. "But you do not understand, do you?"

She patted my arm. "I would never ask so much of my daughters. And since your mother is not here, though I suspect she would advise you differently, I will say this: Do not do something you will regret. Don't sacrifice happiness for the sake of something like a tarnished name. Don't enter into a marriage where you will be alone and unhappy for the rest of your life. Wealth and prestige are not everything."

"But my mother demands it of me." I looked down at my hand. "Although I cannot see how a man could overlook a flaw such as this."

She smiled. "The right man will. He will see all the other things that outshine it."

I wanted to roll my eyes, but her words were so genuine I couldn't do it. Even if I didn't believe her. "I hope you are right." I said.

Feeling weary, I leaned my head on her shoulder. She was such a kind woman, caring and selfless. How did she accept me after all I had done and said? It was something I didn't know how to understand.

I didn't know when or how, but I fell asleep there, feeling comfort and safety like I never remembered feeling. Mama would have complained of my face wrinkling her sleeve. But Mrs. Abbot never did.

Winter was coming, and the temperature was dropping consistently. I had been home for several hours before Clara came through the door with a basket of groceries. Her dark hair was swept over her eyes from the wind and the door slammed loudly behind her, pulled by tendrils of chilled air.

She set the basket down near the door and smiled, her cheeks flushed from cold. "Charlotte! How are you feeling?" She hung her cloak up in the small entryway and joined me on the ragged sofa.

"Better. I'm not so tired as before, but the pain is still intense." I sighed, seeing the joy in her eyes. I wondered if I would ever see it in my own again. "You look happy."

Her smile dropped in tiny increments. "I am sorry, I really shouldn't be, what with your condition, but I just cannot help it. Today was wonderful. Sophia has such a natural talent for reading! We have only been helping her for three days and already she is much improved. And Lord Trowbridge joined us for my lesson on a proper tea." Her grin returned to its full size.

"And that makes you smile?" I asked. "Did you not find him very . . . severe?"

She stopped. "You had nothing but good things to say of him before. I find him very agreeable. And I base none of my opinion on his wealth or title." The words were hard, but she quickly put on an apologetic expression. "I'm sorry, Charlotte. You may like to know that Sophia would like to visit you soon. I gave her a poem to memorize and told her once she could recite it, then she would be allowed to come see you. It is serving as effective motivation." She offered a small smile.

My lips turned up at the corners. At least now I had something to look forward to. "She is such an adorable little girl."

Clara nodded. "She is."

Then silence hung in the air between us. After several seconds, Clara grinned again. "Mr. Wortham was there today. He plans to stop by tonight to see how you are feeling. Very thoughtful of him, don't you think?"

I jerked upright. "He cannot come here."

She shrugged. "I have already invited him. And why not?"

"He is going to rummage through our things until he finds his love letter. He warned me of it before. He might have been teasing, but I find it hard to tell." I frowned, worry pulsing within me.

"Based on all you have learned of his character, you still assume he would do such a thing?" Clara raised a speculative eyebrow.

I considered her words. It was true. He *had* proven himself worthy of trust. He was safe. And why did I need the letter anyway? It was pointless to keep it now. My conscience would not allow me to use it against him, not after all he had done for me. But he did not know that. He could still view me as a threat, as a terrible, selfish person. The thought made my stomach turn. I did not want him to think badly of me. I halted my thoughts as quickly as they came. Why did I care so much?

"I suppose you're right." I sighed, straightening my skirts over my lap. I thought of the note hiding in my room on the second floor. I could easily return it to him tonight, but curiosity was climbing steadily over me. What did the letter say? Who was the woman he had loved before? He must have loved her very much—enough to have his heart broken when she chose a man of wealth rather than him. But how could he blame her for making a decision like that? It was the only sensible option. Any woman of sense would have chosen the same path.

I moved my gaze to the stairs, itching to climb them and read the words he wrote to her. But I couldn't do it. I would keep the letter, yes, but I wouldn't send it or read it. I wouldn't send it because it would ruin him. I wouldn't read it because surely James wouldn't have me trespassing on such a personal thing. But I would keep it because . . . I didn't know why.

Clara recalled my attention by moving toward the kitchen. "After dinner, Mr. Wortham and the surgeon will be coming by. I would have invited Mr. Wortham to dine with us, but for now we can only afford food for the two of us. But we will be paid soon by Lord Trowbridge." She smiled again and stepped into the kitchen.

I couldn't see her anymore but I could hear her humming as she worked. I sat on the sofa, confused by her jovial mood. Although my head ached, I welcomed it as a distraction from the pain in my hand. Listening hard to the tune Clara was humming, I leaned my head back and strained my ears to hear every familiar note.

I recognized the tune as one our cook used to sing at home. The words played over and over in my head, coming back to my memory one at a time, until I remembered the entire song. Cook only sang it when we were young, and never when anyone else was around. I never knew if she intended for us to hear, but she sang it while she worked and while we waited in the back corners of the kitchen for the opportune moment to steal leftover cakes or dough.

As Clara repeated humming the verse, I sang the words softly, barely a whisper so she wouldn't hear.

The sun arising after me
Flowers growing in the land
While dirt and flour stain my hand
'Tis the place I am to be.

Care and thought in preparing tea
As life demands work for wage
Inside a cruel and bitter cage
There is a place I'd rather be.

On the edge of a peaceful sea
Where feast comes a daily sport
Every gentleman I may court
'Tis a place where I am free.

But through the ashes I soon see
Happiness indeed is found
Within a soft and humble sound
There is no place I'd rather be.

The words ended, but Clara had stopped humming before the final verse. I hadn't thought of that song for so many years. I bathed in the silence that followed, contemplating the meaning of the words I had never considered before. Cook must have written the song herself, singing it in secret, perhaps singing it to cheer herself up. She had hated working in our home but something changed her mind. Something had given her the ability to be happy there. But how? I thought of the line, *Inside a cruel and bitter cage.* How can one be happy in confinement? How could I ever come to be happy here in

Northumberland? It was not my choice to be here and it was not my choice to be happy.

After dinner, I returned to my place in the tiny sitting room, closing my eyes against the humiliation of presenting the dirty, unfashionable house to guests. Surely Mr. Wortham would be disgusted. Even his quaint home was much more presentable than ours.

It wasn't long before a firm knock sounded at the door and I rose to answer it. I didn't want to appear incapable of performing such a simple task.

Mr. Watkins stood on the other side of the door, eyes round and scolding. "You must be resting!" He scurried through the doorway. I poked my head outside, scanning the area for James. He wasn't here yet.

"Miss Lyons. What is the degree of pain . . . ?" he began with all his questions, but I only half-listened, answering only when required. I kept my eyes firmly on the door as the surgeon changed the wrappings on my hand, still not daring to look at the injury. I was watching for James's arrival.

When the new bandages were in place, a second knock came from outside the door. I tensed, nearly jumping from my chair to block the door, but thought better of it. Clara stood and swung the door open, bringing a burst of icy air into the house. I shivered.

James tipped his head, ducking below the squat frame. His eyes fell on mine and he smiled, just a slight lift of his lips and the corners of his eyes. I shivered again.

"I see I have missed the excitement." He walked farther into the room and stood behind Mr. Watkins. "How's the patient faring?"

"Quite well, quite well." Mr. Watkins stood and began gathering his things, seemingly in a hurry. "My work is complete." The small man was gone before any other words had been spoken.

James came to stand beside where I was sitting. He tipped his head down to look at me, a shade of guilt hovering over his eyes. "Are you truly well?" His voice was soft, and it brought a telltale quiver to my lip. I locked my jaw firmly, refusing to cry in front of him *again*. I focused instead on the question that had been bothering me. "Why are you here?"

I looked away from him as Clara melted into the dining area, leaving us alone. A mischievous smile twitched on the corners of her lips.

James sat down beside me and I scooted to a distance that allowed me to breathe normally. I did not like the way he affected me. Not at all. He leaned his elbows onto his knees and turned his head so he faced me.

I maintained his gaze with effort, willing myself not to notice the shade of blue his eyes looked tonight, and how the edge of gray was overriding the usual green. I noticed anyway.

"You may end the charade, Charlotte. We are alone." He winked, smiling more with the left of his mouth.

I raised my brows. "What charade?"

He chuckled softly. "Don't think I didn't notice that cold stare. I haven't yet forgotten your secret."

I realized how tense I was, shoulders straight and features firm. I relaxed all at once, slumping my shoulders and smiling. "I didn't mean it . . . I'm sorry."

"You didn't mean the glare, or you didn't mean the secret?" He leaned an inch closer. "Do you hate me after all?"

I shook my head, feeling like a ninny for my grin, but unable to control it. "I meant what I said. I don't hate you."

He sat back, seemingly pleased with my words. "So you love me then."

I jerked my gaze to him. To my relief, he appeared to be teasing. "I do not!" I leaned forward to emphasize my words.

He smiled wider, putting on an expression of presumptuous arrogance that made me laugh. "Surely you must love me. I have never encountered a woman who does not."

I considered swatting him with my bandaged hand, as it appeared very much like a club, but didn't only because it would hurt me more than him. I was laughing, still shaking my head. "I do not love you."

His smile softened and one eyebrow arched. "So if you don't love me, and you don't hate me, then what?"

I took a breath, enjoying this strange conversation. "Something in between." He seemed far too satisfied by my answer, so I added, "But much closer to hate."

He shook into laughter, and I joined, feeling free and light. I had never laughed with a man before. All my conversations with men had been calculated and boring, never entertaining and genuine. I tried to stop laughing, embarrassed by the sound. At parties, Mama had instructed me to keep my laughter at an appropriate volume and tone, as a gentleman didn't want a silly wife.

I eyed James carefully, expecting him to be appalled by the display I had just created. But he didn't seem to mind at all. And I was not trying to win his favor, so his opinion should not have mattered anyway.

He shrugged, his laughter subsiding. "I suppose that is fair." His eyes met mine again and I looked down, feeling uncharacteristically shy. I was fairly certain I had never been *shy* in my entire life.

"You never answered my question," I said, my voice returning to normal. "Why are you here?" I forced myself to look at him again.

His face became serious, and he was silent for several seconds. I waited, heart beating faster from the weight of his gaze. And then he shook his head and stood, taking a step back. "I don't know. I— needed to see if you were well, and you are, so I must be going now." His voice was quick.

"James—wait . . ."

He turned around, halfway to the door. What was his sudden hurry? I searched my mind for something else to say. "That was very kind of you. I would not hate it if you visited again." I didn't know where the words were coming from, and I didn't know why I wanted him to stay.

He gave a brief nod of his head. "Thank you." And in a matter of seconds he was gone.

I realized I had been leaning forward, nearly falling off the sofa. I fell back against the cushions, and felt my brow furrow in confusion. What had compelled him to leave so suddenly? I bit my lip in worry. Had I done something to offend him? I stopped my thoughts as quickly as they came. Why did it matter? Only days before I had planned all my words, hoping to offend him. But now, as much as I hated to admit it, I didn't mind his company.

Chapter 12

*"God has given you one face
and you make yourself another."*

$\mathcal{I}$ counted the flakes of snow on my windowsill every morning until there were finally too many to count. So instead of counting the ones already there, I counted them as they fell. *Twenty-five. Twenty-six. Twenty-seven. Twenty-eight—*

"Charlotte!" Clara's voice cut through my meditation and I jumped. I could hear her bounding up the stairs. I had taken to rising early in the morning, so Clara hadn't left to work yet. She appeared in my doorway, breathing heavily, and held up a paper with a wax seal. "A letter from Mama."

I scooted over on my bed and she sat down beside me, tearing the seal. In her previous letter, Mama had promised us money at the end of the next month, which was only three weeks away now. But with Clara's employment as Sophia's governess, the money was not the most pressing issue anymore. I tipped my head over the paper, reading quickly.

My dear daughters,

I hope you have been well these weeks. I imagine the weather has been colder than you are accustomed to, and it is my dearest wish that you are warm and comfortable. Unfortunately, I come with dreadful news. The freezing weather has not been well for my cousin's wife, and she has fallen ill. We fear she may die soon. But among happier things, the home is quite grand and beautiful, and my cousin, Mr. Bentford, is even more amiable than I remember. He does not treat me with the same disdain the rest of the county has adopted.

Charlotte—why have I not heard from you? I must insist that you write me the details of your courtship with Lord Trowbridge. I am eager to know how you are succeeding. I hope you are not boring him with conversation. Has Clara learned a proper way to arrange your hair? With the lack of sunlight, I presume your complexion has not been damaged. Clara has assured me that she was hired as a governess. Not a respectable position, but suitable enough to keep you well fed and to maintain your figure. Please write me soon, if only to put my nerves at ease. You owe your success to me and our family name. I expect your response sent in the post no later than today.

Yours etc.,
Mama

I was shaking my head as I finished the letter. I had nothing to say to her! I looked down at the bandages covering my hand. It had been a week since the injury, and I still hadn't looked at the damage. Mama could not know about it. Perhaps I still had a chance at a suitable match. If Mama didn't know about my hand, she could rest assured that I was still making progress. I needed only to lie a little bit.

Standing, I hurried over to my writing desk. I needed to tell her that all was well. She couldn't worry about my success. I still had time; perhaps Lord Trowbridge would still have me. Perhaps—

I looked down at the desk and the sheet of parchment I had placed in front of me. The ink and pen were on my right. My right hand was certainly incapable of writing. I stared at the pen as tears burned behind my eyes. My penmanship had been so admired. I had spent years perfecting it, penning letters to friends almost daily. Here was yet another thing I had lost.

Tightening my good hand into a fist on the desk, I built a dam inside me against the torrent of emotions threatening my composure. How was I ever to reclaim my place in society if I couldn't even

111

write a simple letter? Never mind the ugliness or the shame of how it looked. Little by little my hand was robbing me of everything I ever held dear.

I took a deep, shaking breath. "Clara?" I didn't turn around. I swallowed. "I need—will you write a letter to Mama for me? Please."

Her skirts rustled behind me and then she appeared beside my chair, kneeling at the side of the desk. "Of course." She hesitated. "What do you wish to say?"

Turning my gaze to her, I gave her a look of gratitude. She was looking up at me, concerned, careful. Her eyes were wide and clear, nothing like the hard, defensive look I usually saw when telling her how to help me. The difference was astounding, and I saw in her face a willingness to assist me, despite all my unkindness toward her. I had not demanded that she write for me, but I had asked. She was submitting to her own will for once instead of mine.

I stood and gestured at the chair for her to sit. "My note will be brief."

Clara smoothed out the parchment and dipped the quill in ink, holding it poised above the sheet. "How shall I begin it? 'Dearest Mama'?"

I thought about the endearment and hesitated. I stopped myself. Of course. Yes. *Dearest Mama.* I nodded. "But we shall not mention the hand."

Clara shot me a glance. "Why ever not? She may be concerned."

"I fear she would disapprove," I said in a quiet voice. My eyes flickered back to Clara and I cleared my throat, changing the subject. "Dearest Mama. You endeavor to know how I am succeeding with Lord Trowbridge. I have captured his attention, to be sure."

Clara's eyebrow rose but she started writing.

"I have spent a great deal of time with him and think his attachment to me is growing deeper by the day. I believe I shall marry him yet." Clara's shoulders stiffened and the pen stopped. I ignored it. "I am doing all I can to secure his affections, but he seems to be tentative and rather slow. Have patience and I will win his heart." My words sounded plain and dull to my own ears. I finished with, "Your beloved daughter, Charlotte."

I smiled as Clara finished writing. "There. That should afford us a little time." I tried to sound happy, but found the effort exhausting. Lord Trowbridge's affections were miles away from me, and I doubted it would even be possible to win him now. We would live in the North forever, and Mama would remain in Canterbury, visiting London every year and enjoying the society but eating the chagrin of her name. Perhaps she would return for us after all, or take us to live in a new place where I could find another man to pursue.

My shoulders slumped and I moved to sit on the ground, leaning my head against the wall. I had never sat on the floor before, but found it to be strangely comfortable. I tucked Mama's disapproving gaze out of my mind and brought my knees to my chest. I sighed.

"What are we to do, Clara?" My voice had changed to a desperate tone. I looked up at her. "Lord Trowbridge will never love me now!" I held up my hand and dropped it to my lap, cringing. "Mama will write again, and I cannot continue to lie to her. She will discover his indifference to me and she will despise me for it."

Clara crossed her arms and leaned over. "You are *still* beautiful. And if you are correct, that beauty is all a man cares for, then that should be enough." Her voice was soft. I thought I heard sadness in it. I looked up but she smiled in an effort to contradict her voice. "Do not give up."

I puzzled over the look on her face. The smile was forced. She played with a piece of hair, obviously uncomfortable with my study.

"Perhaps you could marry him," I said.

Her eyes flew open wide. "What? No." Her cheeks were flushed pink.

"You have a much better chance than me. You see him every day, and you find him agreeable." I smiled as her cheeks turned even darker. "You have grown attached to him, haven't you?" I exclaimed.

She crossed her arms in defense. "I have not!"

Laughing, I sat forward and crossed my legs in a most improper, girlish manner. "It is quite obvious."

I studied her face as it melted into a confession. She moved over to my bed and sat down, slumping her shoulders in defeat, but with a faint smile curving her lips. My smile was wide as I walked over and sat on the bed beside her.

She sighed and fell back on the blankets, eyes fixed on the ceiling. "I don't know what to do, Charlotte. He is much too old for me, surely. Why would an established, widowed earl such as he consider marrying a silly girl ten years his junior? It simply isn't logical."

I scowled at that, feeling a strange reversal of roles. "I thought you believed in love? If there is anything in the world that isn't logical it's love." I rolled my eyes and looked at her again.

Her eyes were cast down now, and she lay there, twisting a loose thread on the waistband of her dress. She looked so distressed and afraid, and I felt a sudden surge of protectiveness toward her. I had always tried to make her feel inferior to me, remind her of her lack of talents and beauty, but seeing her now, I was overcome with hatred— for myself. I had been so unkind. So selfish. So belittling. The realization stabbed at me with pain stronger than the ache throbbing in my mangled fingers.

Clara bit her lip and I saw a tear streak down her temple. Had I done this to her? Had I changed the way she viewed love? What had once been a giggling, romantic girl was now cold and sad and afraid. My heart quaked within me. What had I done?

She took a deep breath, breaking me from my thoughts. "I still believe in love. But I—I am not worthy of him. Lord Trowbridge is too wealthy and he bears a title, and—"

I cut her off, shaking my head. "Why are you speaking like this? It's as if you were me."

"But I am not you, Charlotte! That is precisely right. I am not pretty, and I am not flirtatious, and I am simply not talented. He will never have me." She sat up, blinking back tears.

I stared at her, surprised. I never knew how much it affected her, being compared to me all the time. Her hair was crinkled from laying down, and her round cheeks were splotched with tears, and her clear blue eyes were wet. Looking at her now, I noticed what I hadn't before—she *was* beautiful. She was adorable, really. Besides that, she was kind and forgiving and humble. She was *not* like me.

My heart beat fast, and I found myself wishing *I* could be like her. How had I been so unkind to her all these years? What benefit did it bring me to treat her so poorly? Guilt crept into my soul with an inky blackness I couldn't ignore.

I was appalled by the way she was speaking. It had annoyed me so much before to hear of her romance novels and ridiculous dreams, but seeing them dashed was so much worse.

"I should be very surprised if he does not fall madly in love with you." I smiled and clasped her hand with my whole one, feeling the threat of tears in my own throat. "I have treated you as less than you are all these years, and for that I apologize. I think I was just . . . incapable of treating you with the kindness you deserved." A tear slipped out of my eye despite my effort to hold it. "I'm sorry."

She looked surprised at first, then blinked back her own tears and smiled. Without any words she leaned forward and hugged me. I squeezed her back, a sudden surge of gratitude filling me, head to toe, for this sister I had taken for granted.

I sat back. "What is it about Lord Trowbridge that you adore?" I grinned as her cheeks reddened once again. "Is he kind? Is he brave and true?" I racked my brain to remember the words she had used to describe the man she hoped to marry. "Literature," I remembered. "Does he care for it? And care for others above himself?"

A small sigh escaped her lips and she grinned, nodding.

"Now all that is left is for him to love you." I was hardly aware of my own words. I sounded like a romantic dolt, and far from logical. Since I had a heart now I needed to keep it in check. "That should not take long at all."

She laughed softly, wiping a stream of liquid from under her nose. I laughed, snorting by accident. Her eyes widened and she burst into giggles, and I followed. Certainly I had never truly *giggled* before today. It was actually quite enjoyable. She released a slow breath and choked on a laugh.

"Now how are we going to make him love you?" I asked.

She shook her head. "That is not how it works. I can't make him love me. He can't make himself love me either. It's all up to his heart."

I stopped myself from rolling my eyes again. "Very well. If his heart possesses any level of intellect, then it will choose to love you. If not, his heart is irrevocably stupid, and you are better without him."

She grinned and put a hand over her mouth to cover it.

"Mama never specified that it had to be me that married him," I said. "It could very well be you." A shard of grief hit me as I looked down again at my bandaged hand. I would grow up to be an old spinster maid. Mama would come to prefer Clara over me. A deep determination grew suddenly inside me. No. I would find a way to make Mama happy. I would still make a good match, just not with Lord Trowbridge. And if no suitable man could overlook my hand, then I would not marry at all. Surely Mama would understand.

I shook my head in an effort to clear it and smiled again. "You must wear your lavender dress today. With the matching ribbons!"

Clara jumped from the bed and hurried toward the door. "May I borrow your ivory shawl?"

I grinned. "Yes!"

She ran from the room, reminding me of the time we had filled our skirts with pastries from the kitchen, holding the hem up to create a basket. Cook had chased us over three floors before we surrendered. I smiled at the fond memory.

A few minutes later, Clara was standing by the front door in her lavender gown, shining with excitement.

"You are beautiful." I smiled.

Her brow furrowed for a quick second then smoothed again. "Thank you." She twirled once and took my shawl, walking down the steps. I waved and closed the door behind her.

The house was quiet now, and I stood at the door, remembering the letter Clara had just written for me to Mama. I chewed my lip, considering disposing of it, writing instead the truth about my injury and the hopelessness of me winning Lord Trowbridge. After much thought, I decided to send it anyway. It would keep me in Mama's good favor, and it would do no harm. Mama would simply be surprised if Clara won him instead of me. The only one that wouldn't benefit from the arrangement was me. But that did seem to be the trend lately, so I contented myself with it.

When Mama returned for us, I would convince her to allow me another season in London—another chance. My hand could be concealed somehow. All would be well. I could still have what I had always dreamed of. In fact, with the responsibility of winning Lord Trowbridge now primarily Clara's, I felt a strange sense of freedom. She could save us from ruin; my life and dreams were mine again.

I sat down on the sofa in the sitting room where James had sat beside me the night before. We had laughed and talked, and nothing had been premeditated and forced. I tried very hard not to, but I smiled at the thought. I had never heard him laugh like that before, and I found myself craving the sound. I wanted him to come visit again so I could pretend at how much I hated him and keep it a secret that I was beginning to think of him as a friend.

I shook my head of my thoughts, calling them ridiculous, and leaned my head back on the arm of the sofa. Why was I thinking about James? Against my will, my heart beat faster at the thought of his smile and sometimes blue, sometimes green-gray eyes. I thought of Clara's list: He must be kind, brave, and true. James was certainly kind. Too kind. And he was brave. He had fought a man for our reticule, after all. True, love of literature, selflessness . . . I marked them on the checklist in my mind. And handsome. Much too handsome. A new realization struck me harder, and something began to sink inside me. How could I deserve someone like that? I didn't. I did not deserve James.

Sitting up, I stopped myself. Why did that matter? I did not want him anyway. He was too far below my station, too poor. I was being absurd. Quickly covering the new tracks in my head, I moved back to what I was comfortable with.

Leaning my head back again, I took a deep breath and thought of my grand house and pretty dresses and perfect match. No James, no North, no gray skies or rocky coast.

No struggles, no disappointments, and no heart.

Chapter 13

"Love looks not with the eyes."

Mrs. Abbot ordered a tray of my favorite lemon tea cakes when I came to visit. It had been a week now since I had seen her, and she welcomed me with my favorite sweets.

"Thank you!" I put a hand against my belly, feeling a faint rumble. "I fear I might eat them all."

She laughed. "Please do! I know they are your favorite. Although I suggest you save one for Sophia. If not, she may duel you for it."

My smile widened. Sophia and Lord Trowbridge were coming with Clara this afternoon. I pushed the tea tray to the opposite side of the table, hoping the distance could offer me a little control. I flexed my injured hand slowly, careful of the stitches beneath the now thin layer of bandage. The stitches would be removed soon, and I was not looking forward to it. I let my gaze wander to the pianoforte, allowing a wave of grief to settle over me once again. Being so close to the instrument was a sharp reminder of what I had lost. I closed my eyes and imagined the music floating through the air, sifting out the heavy, painful things from my heart.

"Oh! I think they are here!" Mrs. Abbot exclaimed. She called her daughters to the room and we all sat facing the door, waiting for the butler to let them inside. I straightened my posture and listened to the sound of feet in the entryway. Then a clear, soft voice echoed, "Where are the cakes?"

I grinned, recognizing Sophia's voice. The butler grumbled a reply and Sophia came skipping around the corner. She stopped when she saw me, her face molding into a shy smile.

"Good afternoon, Sophia! I have missed you." I smiled when I saw the twine coiled on her head.

She stepped forward and stopped just in front of me. Without another word, she unwrapped a similar piece of twine from around her wrist and presented it to me, grinning without reservation now. "I brought a crown for you too."

I laughed, taking the tan piece of string from her. "Why a crown for me?"

"Because you said you didn't have one." She shrugged, tipping her head to the side. My heart warmed inside me and I placed the twine in a ring on top of my curls.

Sophia's smooth forehead scowled. "What is wrong with your hand?" Her voice was careful.

"It was . . . broken." I held it out to her and she leaned closer, studying it.

"Where are these fingers?" She pointed at the place where my fifth finger should be, and at the shortness of my index and middle fingers.

I moved my hand away. "Gone."

She looked up, her round eyes concerned. "Do you miss them?"

I couldn't help but smile at the sincerity of her question. "Indeed." I took a breath. "There is very much I miss about them. I require assistance writing, dressing, and arranging my hair. And I miss playing music." My voice was hushed as I spoke to her, as if sharing a secret. I looked up at the doorway of the room, where Clara, Lord Trowbridge, and James were being greeted by Mrs. Abbot. I looked again. I hadn't known James was accompanying them.

He caught me looking at him and smiled. My breath lodged in my throat and I cleared it, returning my attention to Sophia.

She clasped her hands together in front of her and rocked back and forth. "You should do what Papa says to do."

My brow furrowed. "And what is that?"

"When you miss something very much, just think of every good thing you have. Think of all the good things you have been allowed to keep, and hold onto them tight. Then you don't miss the other things quite so much." She gave a small smile. "That is what I do when I miss my mama."

I marveled at the wisdom of such a young girl. "I will try it," I assured her.

Her smile grew and she turned around. "Uncle Jamesy!" She ran across the room and landed in James's outstretched arms. "I didn't know you were coming."

He chuckled. "I hoped to surprise you." His eyes flickered to me and I wondered if he knew how much his appearance here had surprised me. I thought of the last time I had seen him. He had left so abruptly and I hadn't seen him for a week since. I puzzled at the time that had passed. Had it been only a week? It had seemed much longer than that.

Clara walked in the room and sat in the chair beside me. Her cheeks were flushed yet again, and her smile was wide. I followed her eyes—they were on Lord Trowbridge.

"He asked me my opinion on his waistcoat color today," she whispered to me. "I told him to choose the green. He looks well, does he not?"

It was true. It seemed that Wortham men and the color green were designed for one another. James had worn a green waistcoat once. Today he wore blue.

Lord Trowbridge looked across the room at Clara. I sat up straighter in my seat, looking for any connection between them. The faintest hint of a smile crossed his lips and Clara's eyes fell down, focused intensely on her hands in her lap. I found myself close to laughter. "You must hold his gaze," I whispered. "Smile in return. Don't let him see how he affects you."

She scowled. "It may be easy for you, but I am a novice. Besides, you have never been affected by a man."

Out of the corner of my eye, I saw James walking toward the settee where I was sitting. My heart quickened. "That is not entirely true," I mumbled to myself. I quickly straightened my hair and tried to appear unconcerned when he sat down beside me.

"What a lovely accessory." He grinned, his gaze on the twine atop my head.

I reached up and touched it, laughing. "Sophia insisted that I wear one too."

He shrugged. "I find it quite becomes you." It was less his words but more the smile that followed that forced my eyes away from his face.

Why did he look at me like that? It was horribly unnerving. I felt something at my neck, burning up into my ears and cheeks. No. No no no. I was *not* blushing.

My gaze darted to Clara and she raised an eyebrow. Her lips quirked into a smile.

I ignored it and recovered my senses. I looked James in the eye. "Don't make the mistake of assuming that flattery will improve my opinion of you. You are still far below 'love,'" I said in a quiet voice. I allowed myself a small smile.

He laughed, leaning toward me and whispering, "Don't make the mistake of assuming that I care." The lighthearted look in his eyes shifted, and he shook his head subtly. "I mean to say that you look lovely. Whether it improves your opinion of me or not." He quickly flashed a smile, as if trying to convince me he was merely jesting. For a moment I thought he would stand up again and storm out of the house like he had the week before. I wanted to ask why he had done that, but I didn't know how.

My heart fluttered in my chest and I dared another look at his face. He was sincere. I searched my memory for the last time I had looked in a mirror. It had been two days at least. I shuddered. He must have been wrong. I did not look lovely, but the compliment still fluttered my heart, and the look in his eyes made me strangely breathless.

I scooted two inches away before offering a simple, "Thank you."

He nodded, his eyes never leaving my face, and leaned toward the tea table. I watched as his hands deftly poured the tea pot and cream. I looked down at my hands, embarrassed. It would be strange to sit here and not drink any tea, but I feared I couldn't pour it without spilling.

I looked around the room where everyone else was now sitting around the table. Mrs. Abbot was engaged in conversation with Lord Trowbridge, and the room was growing quieter.

Taking a deep breath, I reached my good hand toward the teapot, hoping my injured hand could be sufficient to steady my cup. But as my hand moved close to the handle, James stopped it with his own.

My eyes flew up to his and he handed me the cup he had just filled. "I was filling it for you." He gave a half smile—just a little quirk of his lips and warming of his eyes.

A slow melting started at my head and made me weak all over. I scolded myself for feeling that way, for admiring James's kindness. It simply wasn't acceptable. I thought it would be strange to thank him again, so I smiled instead and darted my gaze away, trying to focus on Clara and Lord Trowbridge.

"Are you very fond of music?" I heard Mrs. Abbot ask Lord Trowbridge.

"Indeed, I am." His eyes flickered to James. "He may murder me for saying so, but my brother is an impeccable musician. He is far too humble to boast of it."

James straightened and smiled, releasing a fast breath at the same time. He lowered his eyes. I had never seen his confidence waver like this. "My brother exaggerates."

Lord Trowbridge shook his head. "I don't. He has a great talent for it."

Mrs. Abbot turned toward James. "You must play a song for us!"

He looked at his brother, eyes hard, but smiled. "Since I have been betrayed, I suppose I must."

Lord Trowbridge laughed. I was surprised by what seemed like a drastic change in his personality. I wondered what had changed him. He never smiled before. His eyes flickered to Clara and she grinned at him, making him smile even wider. *Ah.*

My gaze drifted to James as he stood and walked to the pianoforte. I felt a pang of jealousy as he sat down and positioned his hands over the keys. He sat in silence, and I listened, waiting for the first note to ring through the air, wondering which note it could be, and which note would follow. I tried to match a melody with the way he sat, the way he talked and laughed, and the way he lived. But it was impossible. There was too much depth in his eyes and in his heart. A thousand melodies flitted through my mind but none of them fit, and when the first note rang through the air, my breath caught in my chest.

I watched in awe as James played a song I had never heard before. His hands pounded the keys strongly, then melted into soft trills that wrenched at my heart and left me captivated. The song was haunting, happy, and full of aching despair, all at once. It was not intended to be special, but the way he played it made it so. The notes that he chose to play suited him to perfection, and I hoped the song would never end. I loved it.

When the notes softened again, I knew the performance was coming to an end. I realized I had been holding my teacup so tightly it could have broken in my grasp. My throat tightened as a tear slipped from my eye. I swiped it away unnoticed.

The last note hung in the air, and the room burst into applause. I set my teacup down and almost clapped my hands too, but stopped myself. *There was yet another thing I could no longer do.* I held my hands in my lap quietly, feeling a fresh wave of emotion overcome me.

James stood from the bench, accepting the compliments from around the room. Lucy grinned up at him and he smiled back. She said something, but I didn't hear. He laughed.

My heart sunk a little further. Lucy was much kinder than me, surely she deserved him. Perhaps I should have sent his love letter to her after all. She seemed to like him well enough, and he didn't seem to be very opposed to her anymore either. The thought made me sad for a reason I couldn't explain. Then his eyes met mine from across the room and I caught my breath again. I hoped my tears had dried away.

"I didn't know you could play so beautifully," I said as he reclaimed his seat beside me. "Whose piece did you play? I have never heard it."

"It is mine," he said, meeting my eyes.

"You cannot be serious!" I struggled to find the words for how I felt. "You are—you are a magnificent composer."

"Flattery will not win my good opinion either, you must know." He grinned, and I found myself thoroughly enjoying this little joke we now shared.

My eyes wandered longingly to the pianoforte. James noticed. "Do you play as well?"

I dropped my gaze and shook my head no. "Not anymore." I remembered, embarrassed, how I had been the day of my injury, sitting on the bench, pounding on the keys and crying. James had sat beside me. Surely he knew how dearly I loved the instrument. Or perhaps he had excused the whole thing as a tantrum. As I imagined how I must have appeared, I felt a fresh wave of humiliation. A tantrum was much more like it.

"Music will not part from you unless *you* abandon it." His eyes were serious, and I had no choice but to listen. "How do you suppose music will find you if you keep it trapped inside an instrument?"

I held up my injured hand. "But I *cannot* play the pianoforte without fingers. It simply isn't possible. I will never play the same way again, no matter how intently I try."

He studied my face for a long moment. He was thinking, jaw clenching and unclenching, eyes moving fast. A slow smile lifted his lips. "Yes. You will."

I scowled. "How?"

"Are you otherwise engaged tomorrow afternoon?"

"Not at all." I was still confused.

"Do you think Mrs. Abbot would object to us using her pianoforte?" he asked in a quiet voice.

"She assured me I was always welcome. But why—"

He stopped me. "I am going to teach you."

"Teach me what?"

He leaned forward, smiling widely. "How to play music the way you did before."

He was being ridiculous. I stared at him with disbelief, tempted to roll my eyes at him like I used to. "Very well. But I still don't believe it is possible."

"I have proven you wrong before, have I not?"

I pressed back my smile behind compressed lips. "I daresay . . . I hope you can do it again."

James chuckled. "I intend to."

I looked into his smiling eyes, and dared myself to hope, to trust. If nothing else, it would be an enjoyable afternoon with a friend. A dangerously handsome, endearing friend. Another cursed blush tingled on my cheeks. Drat. I would need to enforce some very effective protection around my newfound heart if I wanted any hope of keeping it.

"Until tomorrow then," he said.

Chapter 14

*"If music be the food of love,
play on."*

We had agreed to meet at two. I wore a shawl wrapped tightly beneath my cloak to keep warm. Large flakes of snow landed on my shoulders and head, and I looked up, watching them spiral from the sky in pretty flurries of white.

My stomach fluttered with nervousness. I didn't know exactly what James had planned, but I was excited, moving with quick steps across the snow. There was no way I could really play the same, but he seemed to believe I could, and so I leaned against that belief.

When I arrived in front of the Abbots' home, I walked up the steps, careful not to slip. The butler let me in and Mrs. Abbot was there to meet me. I tried to smooth the wet, melting snow out of my hair but gave up when I realized it was bound to look horrendous no matter how I fixed it.

"You walked here? Good heavens, Charlotte! You shall catch a cold!" She took the wet cloak off my shoulders as if it were a dangerous thing, shaking it and handing it to the butler. "I could have sent a carriage, you know. Poor Rachel and Lucy have caught the same cold and are confined to their rooms, sleeping at this late hour."

"Oh, dear." I looked toward the west hallway. "I hope they recover soon." I was surprised by the genuine concern I felt for them.

"I am sure they will, not to worry." She gestured to the drawing room door at the right and I followed her in and we sat down. "How is your injury healing?"

I hesitated. The pain and swelling had decreased significantly, but I knew that soon the stitches would be removed and soon after the bandages would be minimized and I would have to see the damages. I could no longer avoid it. The bandages had become a blessing to keep me blind to what had really happened three weeks ago. I took a deep breath and smiled. "It is healing very well."

She smiled, but there was a hint of disbelief in her expression. "Everything will be all right, Charlotte. You will find a way to be happy." A tear glistened in her eye as she squeezed my arm in an effort to comfort me. I found it strange that she cared so much about me—my concerns and fears and hardships. Mama had never cared about those things.

I didn't notice the front door open again until the cold air floated through the house and touched my skin and gave rise to chill bumps. I turned to see James walk through the entryway and into the drawing room to join us.

He gave a charming smile. "Thank you for your hospitality, Mrs. Abbot. There simply isn't a pianoforte that compares to yours," he said. He could sound very refined when he cared enough to do so.

"I am glad to hear it. Please do not hesitate to grace this home with your musical talents. I don't understand how I have been so fortunate to have two of the most talented musicians of my acquaintance play on my old, antique instrument." She pressed a hand to her chest. "You have both touched my heart."

I smiled through my nervousness. At least Mrs. Abbot would be here with James and me, keeping things on a comfortable level of propriety.

Mrs. Abbot's smile widened. "Well then. I will leave you now to tend to my daughters."

No. "What?" I kept my voice from sounding panicked.

"Rachel and Lucy need my company. Surely you understand." I thought I saw a spark of mischief in her eyes. "You will be required to share the drawing room with no one but Mr. Wortham. In peace and quiet."

I almost protested again but thought better of it. She gave one last smile and flitted out of the room. The room suddenly settled in silence and I was still facing the door. I counted to ten in my mind, wondering which second would be the most natural to turn around on. Eleven. Twelve. Thirteen? I could hear myself breathing.

"Are you ready to be proven wrong?" I heard the smile in James's voice as it cut through the air.

Turning to face him, I was relieved that he was indeed smiling. The tension in the air slackened. "You have surprised me before. Are you going to present me with a new hand? Conjure up a set of whole fingers?" I raised an eyebrow at him.

He stepped closer. "No," he looked down at me, tipping his head, "but I am going to offer you a share of my hand, if you don't mind."

I scowled in confusion.

Without warning, he reached forward and took my uninjured hand in his. I thought I would be startled, but he held it with a gentleness that warmed me from the inside out. My heart skipped. His hand was soft and rough at the same time, gentle and strong. I tried to pull it away, to censure him for being so bold, but I was weak from the unexpected gesture of his touch.

"I'll show you," he said in a quiet voice.

I swallowed, nodding my agreement. He guided me by the hand across the room and we stopped by the pianoforte. He motioned for me to sit on the left side of the bench, and to my dismay, he sat beside me again. I stared at the keys, unable to look up at his face, knowing full well how close it would be to mine. "I don't understand . . ."

He pointed at the music on the stand. It was a piece I recognized. "Do you know this?"

I nodded, my eyes filling unexpectedly with tears. It was one of my favorites. "Quasi una Fantasia," I said in a hushed voice. "Beethoven."

His smile was gentle as he swept his gaze over my face. "You are quite fond of the composition, I see."

I sighed. "Very much."

He lifted a finger and traced a line down the middle of the keyboard. "You are responsible for every note to the left of C. And I will cover what remains."

Scanning the music, I focused on all the notes my left hand would need to play. It was mostly chords, all of which I remembered perfectly. Hope slipped out of its hiding place and grew inside me. "But how will we keep the rhythm?"

"You play how you wish, and I will keep with you. Today, I am simply your other hand." He was smiling again, I could feel it. I kept my eyes glued on the music, and pretended I couldn't feel the way his breath tickled my hair against my cheek. Why must he sit so close? I supposed it was because we were sharing the pianoforte, and the bench was only designed for one. I breathed deeply and moved as far to the left of my seat as possible. There.

"This is absurd." I laughed, but positioned my hand over the keys anyway. James followed, and his other arm pressed against mine as he played the first note with his right hand. I added my chords to the song, clunky and slow at the beginning, an uneven mess. I focused on the sheet of music, willing myself to forget the notes that belonged to James, and remember only the notes that my left hand could play. The melody was soft, slow, hauntingly minor. I let it permeate my skin, where it lived inside my bones. This sonata already held so much of my heart.

After several minutes of the simple, slow chords, the music shifted, growing more complicated and lively, and my focus intensified. James left spaces that I filled, adding my own notes along with the others, and soon the music was one piece, a flowing melody that an outside ear could never guess belonged to more than one person's hands or heart. I found home in the song, and the familiar buzz of bottled emotion came pouring into the air through our array of notes. Anger, despair, disappointment, fear. But something was different. I did not find contentment in emptiness. Instead, I drank from the song—joy, relief, belonging, until I was utterly and irrevocably filled.

My hand moved to the rhythm of my heartbeat, and my heart pounded in time with the song. I had nearly forgotten James, sitting beside me, playing the same way, keeping nothing in reserve. My heart ached with the silence of fading echoes, shattered in the beauty of the trills, and came back together through the length of each fermata. The execution was flawed yet it was somehow perfect.

When my focus broke and the last measure faded, I sat there, melting into the proceeding quiet. I realized I had leaned even closer to James as we had played, and I subtly pulled away. I could breath a little easier now, but I was disappointed at the same time.

Thick silence thrummed in the air between us, and I wished I knew how to break it. My eyes shifted to the side and I turned my head up to look at him—the movement slow and careful. My heart skipped when I saw his face—the way he was looking at me. There was a sort of quiet awe in his eyes, a sort of admiration I couldn't describe. His hand was still on the keys of the pianoforte, but slowly he lifted it, brushing his fingertips across my face, moving my hair from my eyes. A hot, tingling blush erupted where he touched my cheek. I wanted desperately to pull away, but found I lacked the strength. His gaze grew more intense when it met mine, seemingly searching every inch of my face. He breathed in, moving closer as he did. I didn't move, heart pounding, waiting.

All at once, something shifted in the air, in his eyes, and he pulled back, putting several inches where there had just been only one breath. The warmth I had felt moments before vanished, and I stood, unable to sit so close to him for another second. He stood too.

I turned, facing the window, trying to focus my attention on counting snowflakes. What had just happened? I wrapped my arms around myself to distract from the awkwardness and keep myself warm. Was he about to kiss me? I shook my head, excusing the thought. But then another, more disturbing thought followed—did I want him to?

I decided to face him again, to say something to lighten the tension. "The song was . . . perfect. How did you know it would work?"

He was looking at me in that same strange way but for just a moment longer. Then he smiled. "I told you music would not abandon you."

I swallowed hard, fighting back a sudden surge of emotion. *Music would not abandon me.* A realization struck and fear caught up to me. But what if it did? How could I play music without James?

Surely he would not stay with me forever. I had already been abandoned before. By Papa. Mama.

"But will you?" I asked in a quick voice. I was immediately embarrassed by the question, but something deep inside me needed an answer.

He stared at me in silence for a long moment before saying, "No. I will be here, should you need . . . anything. Anyone."

I smiled in gratitude, wondering why I had been sent to cross paths with such a kind person. He had given back what I thought I lost forever. Together we could play music, and I didn't want him to ever leave. For more reasons than one. "Thank you for being such an exemplary friend these last few weeks, James."

He drew closer, smiling down at me. More than anything, that smile was the perfect gift.

"Since you have proven me wrong twice now," I said. "I suppose it is my turn. I failed once," I paused, holding up my hand, giving a sideways smile, "but my next attempt will be easy."

He scowled in a gentle rebuke. "Don't do anything dangerous."

I shook my head. "It is safe. I mean to promise you that I will not send your love letter to anyone. In fact . . . I will return it to you if you wish."

I waited for his reaction, studying his features. His mouth was a firm line, and his eyes were deep, thinking. "Keep it."

I threw him an inquisitive look.

"I have no use for it now." He smiled, but it seemed forced. "But thank you." He leaned closer. "And I never thought you would send it."

"Yes, you did." I crossed my arms.

He grinned. "You just wanted it for yourself."

I shook my head fast, laughing. "No!"

"Surely you have inserted your own name in the address and read it to yourself each night, begging fate to make me love you."

I gasped. "You are being ridiculous. No. I thought we had agreed that it was I who didn't love you. You, on the other hand, could be very much in love with me." I was surprised at my own words.

"Then your dearest wish will have come true." He chuckled at my expression that followed. There was no possible way to turn the joke on him. He was too quick.

I sighed in frustration. "Well, if you don't believe I intended to send the letter to Lucy, then I will just return home right now and dispose of it. Will that be sufficient to prove you wrong?"

He feigned a thoughtful expression. "No."

"How so?"

He smiled in a teasing way, tipping his head closer still. I was leaning against the windowpane now, and found that there was nowhere else to go. James put his hand against the window, just above my shoulder. "The pain of unrequited love was simply too much to bear, so you destroyed the letter in a fit of heartache and misery."

I found breathing incredibly difficult, and my heart raced.

After a moment, he dropped his hand and took a step back. I could speak again. Rolling my eyes, I said, "Very well. I shall find another way to prove you wrong."

"Nothing dangerous."

I nodded. But I found myself captivated yet again by the color of his eyes, the width of his smile, the memory of his most recent laugh. The line of his jaw and the sound of his voice. James had once written his heart into that love letter. Little did he know the most dangerous thing of all would be for me to keep it.

I had no experience with love, but what I was feeling now, looking into his eyes, was certainly new. I didn't know if I believed in it, but if anyone was capable of proving me wrong, it was James. I was in danger. Falling in love with him would be much too easy. And love was a hinderance, a weakness, and I couldn't afford it.

But there was one more thing that was bothering me. I hesitated. "Who is she?"

He frowned in confusion.

I took a breath. "Who is the woman you loved before? Who was the letter intended for?" I hadn't known I had these questions, but now that I was speaking them, they all came spilling out. I tried not to look at his face, for fear I was offending him. I remembered what he had said before, that she had married a man with a large fortune. Had she truly loved him at all? Or had she just chosen to be smart?

James rubbed his forehead and looked at me from under his eyelashes. "I'm afraid I must postpone that story for another day." He pulled out his pocket watch and his smile turned rueful. "I must be getting to the docks." He snapped the watch shut and nodded, suddenly reserved and proper. Why did he always do that?

"You are leaving?" I asked. Without thinking, I reached out and stopped him, gripping his arm. He froze and his gaze traveled to my hand. His jaw was firm as he looked back at my face. I dropped my grasp and he shook his arm, as if my touch had disgusted him. I stepped back, embarrassed.

"Yes. I must be going." He gave another obviously forced smile. "Good day, Charlotte."

I frowned. "Good day, then."

James nodded and turned around for the last time before leaving the room. I listened closely until the butler shut the main doors behind him. My cheeks burned yet again, but this time in shame. What had I done wrong? Had I spoken too freely? I stared at the door, wondering why his rejection stung so badly.

I crossed my arms and sat down on the settee and decided it was best that he leave. It would be best if I didn't see James Wortham for a very long time, in fact. I did not appreciate what he was doing to my heart. It needed to stop. Mama expected an advantageous match from me, and I expected that of myself. I had grown too weak and careless. Even if I was not going to catch a husband here in Craster, I was most certainly not going to fall in love.

My new endeavor was clear, and after bidding Mrs. Abbot farewell, I hurried home with determination in my step. When I arrived home and walked into my room, I closed the door behind me and sat at my writing desk. My right hand would not suffice, so I wrote with my left. The words were sloppy, but it didn't matter. I blew the ink dry and looked at the title of my newest list:

How not to fall in love with James Wortham: Charlotte's list of requirements.

1. Never spend time alone with him.
2. Never laugh with him.
3. Never admire the color of his eyes.
4. Never think about kissing him.
5. Never let him make me blush.
6. Never look at his face for more than three seconds.

I finished the list with that for the moment and sat back in my chair, feeling stronger and more in control. I studied the words, silently praying that I would be able to read them tomorrow. My left-handed penmanship was atrocious. I took a deep breath, focusing on my list and my determination. For good measure, I inscribed the words on my heart, the only place I would never forget them.

Chapter 15

*"So shines a good deed
in a weary world."*

ord Trowbridge walked Clara home the next afternoon, and I watched from the window as they approached the cottage. Half my face was concealed behind the moth-eaten curtains, and I strained my vision to see their expressions. I could see the pink of Clara's cheeks even from my vantage point. I also couldn't miss Lord Trowbridge's adoring grin. He reached for her hand and kissed the top of it in farewell.

I slapped a hand over my mouth, trying to hide the sudden and unwelcome giggle that bubbled from my chest. It came out anyway, loud and girlish. *Well, that was certainly uncalled for.*

Lord Trowbridge walked away and I threw the curtains back over the window and bounded down the creaking, narrow staircase. I met Clara at the front door just as she pulled it open. She shrieked in surprise.

I stifled a squeal. "He adores you!"

The shade of her cheeks made the scarlet shawl she wore look pink. "You were watching us?"

"Of course. And I have seen enough to know that he adores you. He could very well be in love with you."

She walked past me and slumped down on the sofa. She fanned her hands around her face in a dramatic fashion. "'Love is not real.' 'Love is a weakness.' 'Men do not love, they only desire.' What has happened to you, Charlotte?" She gasped and grinned knowingly. "You have fallen in love."

I raised my eyebrows and put a hand against my chest. "Me? That is an absurd idea, and you know it."

She leaned her face on her hand. "Do not deny it. I observed the way you looked at Mr. James Wortham at the Abbots' two days ago."

I panicked, but refused to admit any feelings I had toward that man. Acknowledging it would only worsen the problem. I frowned, trying to appear nonchalant. "How exactly did I look at him?"

"Like he was happiness personified." She waved her hands in the air and laughed. "Like he was a silken, lace-and pearl-embossed gown. Or a lemon tea cake."

I gasped, sitting beside her and swatting her arm. "I did not!"

She was still laughing, but caught her breath. "And the way he looked at you . . . I daresay he adores you as well."

I shook my head, refusing to believe her. "Nonsense. He despises me."

She gave me a look of disbelief. "That is not true."

"I have given him every reason to despise me, Clara. It makes sense. He is just a very kind man who cannot leave a damsel in distress."

"And what of you? Do you *despise* him too?" Her smile told me she didn't think so.

I sighed. "No. I don't. And I don't love him either, I assure you." "Why?"

I was surprised by her question. "He is—he isn't titled. He isn't wealthy, and Mama would never approve."

"That did not answer my question." She was studying my face, searching for clues. I felt raw and exposed by it.

"I do not love him because I *cannot*. That is why. You aren't required to understand."

She watched me for a short moment longer, then shrugged. "Very well. But if you wish for others to believe that you don't care for him, then I suggest you keep the adoring gazes a bit more discreet." I warned her with a look, but she ignored it, changing the subject. "Mr. Watkins will not be making his usual visit tonight, but tomorrow he will be coming by to remove the stitches."

Drat. I had forgotten about that. I took a deep breath to steady myself. "Perfect."

Mr. Watkins's spectacles were crusted in ice when he walked in our cottage. I poked at the fire in our hearth, trying to coach the orange, flicking light to grow, to make the house warm and to ease my nerves. I brushed bits of ash from my skirts and moved to the sofa where the surgeon was organizing his supplies on the side table.

I swallowed my fear and let him unwrap the bandages. True to tradition, I fixed my eyes on the ceiling. The pain had been minimal over the last week and Mr. Watkins had assured me it was healing well, but I was still afraid to look. The absence of fingers was terrifying. Once I saw it, I would never be able to forget—and I would never be able to remember the way my hand used to look.

"Sit back and relax, miss. I will try to be quick." The surgeon lowered a tool to my hand, and I saw his arm tense out of the corner of my eye. Then he set to work removing the stitches. I bit my lip to keep myself from making any noise, although the pain was intense. And he was not quick.

After what felt like several minutes, he sat back, wiping his tools clean with a towel, then moved on to clean my hand. I let the water soothe my raw, healing skin, and released a shaky breath. My heart pounded in anticipation. I had to look at my hand. It had been several weeks, so surely it couldn't be so very bad. I slid my eyes slowly down my shoulder, across my elbow, over my wrist and . . .

I gaped, a heavy stone of dread settling in my stomach. I squinted. A sudden lightness swam in my head. My hand was an absolute disaster. The skin was misshapen and edged in lines, hanging on by pink scars that were still learning how to be skin. A stub of my fifth finger remained, and the index was gone just below the fingernail. My middle finger was missing above the second knuckle. I swallowed, feeling sick. It was even more ugly than I had imagined.

Whatever unwarranted hope I had held that James might have cared for me was quickly whisked away. He had seen *this*. He could never love me. I told myself not to care, but something sunk inside me all the same.

"Now, I will keep it wrapped for another fortnight, then you may begin to use it again," Mr. Watkins interrupted my thoughts. "The skin will be healed enough at that point in time to bend the joints without tearing. The full recovery should come over the course of two months."

I numbly offered my thanks and showed him to the door. I bit back my tears and leaned against the doorframe once he was gone, the disgrace and shame all catching up to me.

My hand was a true monstrosity. It was hideous. Why had I allowed myself to think of love for even one moment? As much as I hated to admit it, I had wondered what it would have been like if I could love. If someone could love me. But it was clear to me now that it was impossible.

Thankfully, I didn't see James for the rest of the week. I taught my mind to forget the little things I had come to enjoy about him. I even taught myself to only think of him twice a day rather than twice a minute. Instead of sitting around our little cottage, dreaming about all the things I could never have, I set to work cleaning, moving slowly and favoring my left hand. Now that Clara had worked so long as Sophia's governess, we had thought it best that I remain at home and she remain employed. Besides, she never once complained of her time spent with Lord Trowbridge.

When we had first moved here to Craster, Clara had spent a few hours making the home a little less horrid. She had removed the most obvious cobwebs and dusted the tops of shelves and the corners of the room that had been home to insects and inch-thick dust. But there was still much work to be done, and I found that if I was busy, I didn't think so much about all the things that hurt. But also as I worked, I hummed the song Cook used to sing early in the mornings.

I felt guilty for how I had acted toward so many people. I had hurt so much. I had cared only for myself and my own happiness. So shrouded in all my pretty things—a grand house and admired family—I had failed to care about anything else. So flattered by Mama, I had not seen how low I truly was. I was vile, manipulative, and careless. I spit the words out as I tried to squeeze the water from a towel using one hand. Slapping it against the wall, I wiped away dirt.

I remembered the young woman at Kellaway Manor in the summer, the one Dr. Owen Kellaway had chosen over me. The whole ordeal played out in my mind as if it were a painting, covered in a sheet that only now was lifted. Of course he had loved her more. She was kind, selfless, and good-hearted. I was nothing. I had been nothing but a golden shell, pretty and valued without, but hopelessly empty and dull within. The revelation stabbed at me with shame, and I scrubbed harder.

I did not want to be that woman anymore. But still, I missed the old life I had enjoyed. The elegance and refinement and parties. I missed my home, bright sunshine, and Mama's approval. I missed it all so much my heart and soul ached for it. But I did not miss the wicked person I had once been. Looking at the wall I had just washed, I took a deep breath and ran my hand over the surface, smooth and clean. *Smooth and clean.* Kind and selfless. Honest and thoughtful. Trustworthy and caring. Happy.

Day after day, I watched Clara and Lord Trowbridge as he brought her home. Although he lived right down the road, he always walked with her. Surely he would have sent her in a carriage if she had let him. He treated her as if she was nothing short of a princess. I was filled with joy as I saw them together, and Clara and I always chatted for hours about her day when she returned, and how he had looked at her as he bid farewell, and the compliments he had offered. It would be only a short time before he proposed marriage, I was sure of it.

Mrs. Abbot's cook taught me how to bake a set of my favorite cakes, and Mrs. Abbot even sent me home with some of their extra ingredients. I failed the first few batches I attempted, struggling with lighting the fire on my own, and mixing the ingredients in the proper order, but eventually I made a batch I was quite proud of. My injured hand was hardly a nuisance anymore, and I was learning to function quite well without all the fingers.

By the end of the fortnight, as Mr. Watkins had promised, he removed the bandages, instructing me to use my hand carefully, but frequently. I hadn't imagined it possible, but I missed the bandages. Now there was no way to hide the sight of my deformed hand from myself. Or anyone else. I still hadn't seen James.

I wandered into the village one morning despite the cold, eager to do something other than cook and clean. With Clara working as Sophia's governess, we were earning more than enough money to keep us alive with food. So I decided it was acceptable for me to make one small purchase for myself. Wrapping up in my warmest cloak and shawl, I stepped out the door into the chilly air.

It was not snowing today, but the air was crisp, and the sun shone gently over my head, cutting through the cold with an unexpected warmth. Old snow crunched under my boots as I walked along the path to the village. When people came into view, I slipped my hand out of sight under my cloak. I carried with me a small pouch of coins, but held those also concealed, desperately hoping the past would not be repeated with a strange, burly man stealing my money. I shook off the worry, but walked faster between the narrow shop streets.

I scanned the faces I passed, secretly hoping to see James's among them. The last time I had seen him was when we had played music together, and the fortnight that followed had been the longest of my life. I still worried that I had done something to upset him, and I hoped to see him, if only to ask—or even guess—at his behavior. Had he been offended, or was he truly disgusted by me as I thought?

My eyes drifted to the steps of a tiny house, and the image struck my mind with familiarity. A young girl sat on the lap of a man—I assumed he was her father. The girl was shivering, face smudged in dirt, clad in a torn brown dress. My heart ached keenly at the sight, and then her eyes raised to meet mine. They were large and brown and wet with tears.

The first morning Clara and I had been here, I had seen this same girl and her father, sitting on the same steps, wearing the same clothes. James had tried to offer the man money, and he had refused. But he could not refuse anything for his daughter.

I stopped in front of the girl and knelt down, not caring that the dirty snow would soak through my gown and freeze my knees. My eyes flickered to the man, and he watched me through narrowed eyes. I moved my gaze to the face of the little girl. "What is your name?"

"Caroline," she said in a quiet voice.

"Are you very cold, Miss Caroline?"

She nodded, shivering yet again in her thin layer of clothing. I had come equipped with two shawls and a cloak, so I took off the softer, warmer of the two shawls and extended it to her. As I did, the cloak slipped away from my injured hand and she saw it, but she didn't stare. I draped the pale blue shawl over her shoulders and she quickly wrapped it tightly around herself.

I covered my hand again and watched her face. She was so young and shy, lost in the world and a stranger to everything I had known as a child. I had been so very fortunate, and the realization of the life I could have had—the life this girl had—that fate had let me escape brought tears to my eyes. Even my life here in the cold, wet, gray North was tenfold more fortunate than the life of this young girl.

"This is very pretty," Caroline's voice was rasped and quiet. I followed her gaze to the necklace I wore. It was one of the few expensive pieces of jewelry I still owned.

"Do you like it?" I smiled at her as she nodded. "Would you like to have it?"

The man interrupted. "No, no, miss. We can't accept anything else from you."

I quickly reached behind my head and unclasped the necklace. I let it fall gently into her outstretched hand. Her eyes were wide as she watched the light reflect off the tiny gems. "It is nothing." I gave the man a reassuring smile and stood, brushing snow off my skirts.

I felt warm despite the cold, humbled by my heightened under-standing of everything I had. This poor girl had nothing. Little food, little clothing, little shelter. All I lacked was a few fingers. Suddenly it didn't seem so very bad.

The shop I had come to the village for was right down the road from here, so I offered the little girl and her father one more smile before heading in the shop's direction.

When I walked through the door I was greeted by the smell of clean fabric and dye. The shopkeeper greeted me and was able to point out the selection of gloves I would have to choose from. I settled on a pair of smooth black gloves lined in fur. I tried the gloves on, but the right side was still noticeably different, especially where my fifth finger should have been. Looking at the limp, empty areas of the glove, I had an idea. Using strips of fabric from the half-destroyed curtains in our cottage, I could stuff the empty areas of the glove and my hand would appear completely ordinary.

I made the purchase quickly, then wore the gloves as I exited the store. A cold blast of air stole my breath as I opened the door, and my eyes met a pair of handsome, seawater ones.

I jerked back, almost slamming the door on my foot. *Calm your-self,* I whispered instructions to my heart. I ran through my list in my mind. *Never admire the color of his eyes.* I recovered from the shock of seeing James here and stepped out of the shop with my chin held high. My gaze flickered to his face. One, two, three. I looked away. *Never look at his face for more than three seconds.*

I cleared my throat. "James—er—Mr. Wortham. What brings you here?" I brushed my hair from my eyes, trying very hard not to think about the moment he had done the same for me.

He looked confused—and somewhat amused—by my behavior. His expression smoothed over and he smiled. "I came with the sin-gular and determined purpose of seeing you."

My eyes widened and I felt my cheeks tingle with heat against my will. *Do not let him make me blush.* Drat. I had already broken three of my rules in a matter of seconds.

He laughed, but stepped forward and offered me his arm. "But of course you assume that isn't true."

I tentatively took his arm, grateful he had offered me the side of my undamaged hand. I kept my gaze forward and my expression neutral. "Do you not worry that everyone in the village will stare? They may think it odd that *we* are walking together . . . like this."

"Why would I ever object to being seen with a lady on my arm?" I could hear the smile in his voice. "Especially one so lovely." I tried my very hardest not to visibly react. At least I was almost positive he couldn't hear my heart beating.

We walked slowly, in no hurry and bound for no specific direction. I didn't speak for several seconds, and the only noises I heard were the sounds of people as they rushed past—small segments of conversations that didn't make sense, a cool breeze ruffling my hair, costermongers shouting, and in the distance, those blasted fishing traps being hauled out of the water, scraping against the frozen sand.

"Why are you acting so strangely?" James asked. I gave myself three seconds to look at his expression. He was still smiling, but he also looked confused.

"I am not acting any more strangely than you acted before leaving me at the Abbots' a fortnight ago." My voice was clipped and hard. I hadn't meant to sound so hurt, but I was.

I heard him release a slow breath—a sigh. "I had forgotten the time . . ."

"No. You simply wanted to be rid of me." My eyes flicked to his. "Why?"

"That is not true." He stopped walking near the doors of a milliner's shop. "Not in the slightest." I let go of his arm and turned to face him. He crossed his arms in front of him. "I have other responsibilities here I can't abandon. Surely you understand. My men and I are responsible for bringing in a dozen crates of fish each day. I manage our stand in the market every now and again. I need to make a living somehow, Charlotte, and I was not doing anything for myself when I was at the Abbots'. I was there doing a favor for you."

His words stung somewhere deep inside me. "That is all? And you didn't care to see me these past weeks because you have paid me enough favors?"

James shook his head and stepped away but moved back again, this time closer. He looked as if he was about to say something, but stopped the words.

"Mr. Watkins removed the stitches from my hand," I said abruptly. "Would you like to see it? Perhaps the sight will keep you away longer this time." I spit the words out, tugging at my glove through the familiar blur of tears.

"Charlotte. Charlotte, stop—" James reached out just as I pulled the glove away from my hand.

He touched it, softly, with a gentleness comparable to a breath of wind. My heart quickened even though I told it not to. He took my mangled, disgusting hand in both of his, turning it over. He slid his thumb gently over the back of it, over the healing cuts and pink skin. His gaze lifted to mine, but he didn't let go of my hand. Something reflecting torment flashed in his eyes. "It is all my fault," he said in a hushed voice. "I'm sorry. I'm so sorry."

I stopped him. "It is my fault. Not yours. I was stubborn and impulsive and daft to do such a thing."

His eyes flickered downward. I couldn't tell if he believed me, but he shifted my hand in his once again, and my heart picked up speed. "Don't be ashamed of this. Please."

I couldn't find the strength to pull my hand away. "But I have everything to be ashamed of. The place I live, the disgrace of my father, the cruel person I am." I turned my gaze to the ground and tightened my jaw against an onslaught of emotion. "I hate it. My deformed hand is just another thing I cannot escape."

He was quiet for a long moment before speaking in a soft voice, "I saw what you did today for that young child. That was not the deed of a cruel person."

My eyes flew up to his.

He looked down at me, all sincerity and kindness, and it made my heart skip. "If you must be ashamed of the person you once were, then bury her. Start again, here, in this dreaded place of yours, and you can forget shame." He looked at my hand in his, and I followed his gaze, watching for any clues that he was disgusted by it too, but saw nothing. "I am sorry this happened to you, but let it make you stronger. You were determined enough to try to pull in those traps by yourself, and you were determined enough to reclaim music when you nearly abandoned it. Now be determined enough to love your flaws as much as your beauty. And be determined enough to approach the flaws you are capable of changing, and do it. Be a person you can love."

The power of his words settled deep inside me and I clung to them with a tight and desperate grip. I wanted so badly to believe it. "I fear I am not capable of that." I lowered my hand and replaced my glove.

"You have changed so much already—"

"No, I mean I am not capable of *love*." I looked away from the intensity of his eyes and took a step away from him.

"Hate is too heavy a burden to carry, Charlotte. Leave it behind you."

I gave a shaky smile, hoping to lighten the mood by increments. "I suppose I will just settle for something in between, then." My reference to our previous joke brought a smile to his face too, but it was dull and lifeless compared to the way he usually smiled.

"Try to be happy here. Despite everything." He looked at me through sincere eyes that looked oddly gray to match the sky. I had been staring at his face for far too long. I quickly moved my gaze to the ground. What he did next was decidedly unexpected. He reached forward and lifted my face to look at his, nudging his fingers under my chin. I was trapped in his gaze again, and his touch on my face was too much. My cheeks tingled with heat and my heart pounded. His fingertips brushed against my jaw as he dropped his hand, but I still couldn't look away.

He was about to say something more, but I spoke first, without thinking. "I haven't forgotten your kindness to me. Although at times you are terribly confusing. But I wish to repay you somehow."

His eyebrow twitched and he was smiling again. "How so?"

He was so close. I could smell the fresh sea air on him, the masculine scent I couldn't describe, and something that reminded me of home—rolling hills and bright sunshine, although there were none to be found here. His eyes were locked on mine, there was a faint line of stubble on his jaw, his lips were quirked in a smile, and for the first time I noticed the creases in his cheeks that begged to be called dimples. My gaze locked on his smile, and I had to shake myself to look away. I took a deep breath and recited my rules in my head. *Never think about kissing him. Never. Never. Never.*

But it was nearly impossible to obey when he was standing so close to me and smiling in that way and looking at me through those eyes. The only way to focus was to step away, and once I did, I could finally speak again.

"I wish to tell you why I came here. The truth. But in exchange, I want you to tell me about the woman that broke your heart."

"If I must tell you something in exchange, then it isn't much of a favor." He chuckled.

"Fine. We'll call it a trade."

He stared at me for a long moment, surprised by my proposition. I waited, half expecting him to refuse, but finally he nodded. "Very well. But it is awfully cold out here. I know the perfect place for a proper tête-à-tête." A faint smile touched his lips and he pulled off his coat, draping it over my shoulders before I could refuse.

"Where are we going?" I asked, taking his arm hesitantly.

"That is just another secret to add to the books."

Chapter 16

"No legacy is so rich as honesty."

I didn't know why I had offered to tell James the truth, but
the thought of it was filling me with more and more dread
as we walked to the unknown destination James had in mind. I
scolded myself silently for breaking all but one of my rules, then
realized my last rule was about to be broken. *Never spend time alone
with him.* There had been so many people before, sliding past us in
the road, but now it would just be the two of us, in a quiet place with
only dirty snow as a chaperone.

My heart beat frantically, knowing the danger it was in. James
Wortham was quite capable of stealing it, and I feared I lacked the
strength to keep it any longer. I swallowed my worries and walked
with him, reminding myself, in a last effort, to keep every other rule
I had made. If it was necessary that I be alone with him, then so be it.

As we walked, I found myself leaning closer to James as the brisk
wind chilled me to the bone. We were on the same narrow path that
led toward the part of town where I lived. Today it was empty.

My cloak was wrapped tightly around me, so I was unable to
catch myself when I slipped on a thick patch of ice.

I let out a small screech and fell to the ground, arms splayed
meaninglessly at my sides. I stopped my head from hitting the
ground, but my back hit hard, knocking the air from my lungs. I
squeezed my eyes shut, embarrassed. I felt my cheeks burn despite
the cold.

"Charlotte!" James bent over and reached for my arm to pull me up. "Are you hurt?" His eyes were full of concern as he gazed down at me from above. Snow swirled around him in furious gusts. As I imagined the sight of me, sprawled on the ice in a cloak-cocoon, red-faced and scowling, I did something most unexpected. I laughed.

James's hand wrapped around my upper arm and he watched me laughing, a spark of amusement in his expression. "Does that mean you are well? Or are you delirious from pain?"

My stomach ached from laughter and without thinking, I rolled to the side, pulling my arm in one jerky motion. James faltered and I watched his boots fly out from under him. He landed with a thud beside me, sliding backward until his head was just higher up the path than mine.

He grunted and shook his head, eyeing me with disbelief. "You *are* delirious." He brushed snow off his coat and slowly his lips twitched into a smile.

I turned my head up to look at him lying there in the icy snow, and the sight of him brought on a new bout of laughter. He joined me. Despite the cold, something burning and warm grew deep inside me at the sound of his laugh and the sight of his smile. The entire situation was so unexpected and strange that I allowed myself to admire him for just a moment. I allowed my heart to beat fast with that admiration I had been hiding. I studied his features, the way his cheeks creased when he laughed, the glowing blue glint of delight in his eyes, and the line of his jaw and the way his hair was speckled with little flakes of white snow.

I had stopped laughing. So had James. I realized how long and how fervently I had been staring at him, so I looked away quickly, face burning. My heart gave a leap at the thought of how very improper I was, lying here in the snow beside a man. But for an odd reason, I didn't mind at all.

James sat up, a sudden movement. "Well, Charlotte, you have defeated me. May I help you stand without being attacked by your delirium?"

I stared at the sky. "Not yet. The storm has calmed. Look up! The snow is beautiful."

I didn't know why my heart fluttered as James laid back, quiet and slow, and much closer to me than before. The snow wasn't thick here, but it was still comfortable, creating a thin pillow under my head as I stared up at the flurries of snow that spiraled toward me from the sky. It reminded me of tiny white rose petals, and I tried to envision a blue sky and the smell of flowers wafting down in pockets of sunlight. I breathed deeply. It was very strange—the joy I found in that moment, the contentment and freedom. I forgot that I was about to tell James the truth. The strict rules I had set against him were fading into the background of the vision of white and gray and beauty around me. I was relaxed and carefree.

I turned my eyes away from the sky and looked at James. My heart jumped to my throat. He hadn't been watching the sky, but his eyes were fixed on my face. A little smile twitched his lips and his gaze swept over my face like a caress. Warmth filled me to my toes and my heart galloped faster. I looked away quickly and fixed my gaze on the sky again.

James was so close—so close that I felt his breath against my cheek when he said, in a low voice, "How improper we are."

I gave a shaky laugh. "I find I quite like it." My eyes widened and I immediately regretted the words.

James laughed beside me, a deep, rustic sound that made my breath catch. "I thought you learned not to flirt with me. It will never work."

My cheeks flamed. "I didn't intend to . . ."

He propped himself up on his elbow. His face was above mine now, leaning over me with a wry smile that hammered my heart against my ribs. I wondered if he could hear it. "Well, Charlotte, *I* fully intend to."

"It will never work." My voice was choked and shaky. I tried to smile, but all my attention was helplessly captured by James. His eyes looked blue today—the dark color of a roiling sea. He was still smiling as he looked down at me, only inches away. But then his eyes grew serious. His brows tightened subtly in concentration as he raised his hand to my face. His fingers swiped away a snowflake from my cheek, and his gaze slid up to my head and he took a strand of hair between his fingers and melted another snowflake there. I remained perfectly still, watching his face as he went. My heart bounded and my breath quickened.

He looked in my eyes again, and I felt as though he could see it already—every secret and every lie and every dream, playing out theatrically before him. He was drawing out every weakness, every foolish notion of my heart, until I was vulnerable and open. His fingers lifted and he swiped a new snowflake that landed on my eyebrow. My breath shuddered on the way out. I tried to convince myself this was wrong, that I should stand up and go home, and stay away from James forever, but I was too weak. My heart was on fire.

And then I watched his eyes shift, and his fingers traced my cheek and stopped at the edge of my mouth. My pulse raced. There were inches, mere breaths between us. I was glad my hands were wrapped beneath my cloak, otherwise I might have reached up and pulled his face down to mine . . .

I stopped myself. These were ridiculous thoughts, born from the unearthly white all around us and the strangeness of the entire situation. Yet my heart ached with something—some painful, broken thing that told me this was all wrong. James was not mine to laugh with or mine to kiss. I tried to think of all the things he lacked, but could only think of all the things I had come to adore about him. I wanted to stay here, frozen in this moment with James forever. I couldn't deny it.

Perhaps I was delirious after all.

All at once, James's eyes met mine again, a look of regret looming there. I had known he wouldn't kiss me—not like that. He was too much a gentleman.

"Your face is so cold," he half-whispered. "We should be going. I'd hate for you to catch a chill."

I nodded and let him help me up. I was afraid of these things I was feeling. It was all so new and different than anything I had felt before. No man had ever looked at me the way James had just looked at me. I found it unnerving and strengthening at the same time. I wanted to run and hide, rebuild myself stronger apart from James, but I wasn't finished yet. My heart tightened with anxiety again.

Next I would tell James all the things I had been hiding from him. I wondered if I had the strength to do it.

James smiled again, back to his usual expression, and I allowed myself to relax. "If that wasn't enough excitement for you," he winked, "never fear. You will love the place we are going next."

I gave him a quick berating glance but took his arm anyway.

We had been walking for several minutes now, and I surveyed the area. We were approaching the path that led toward my cottage. I was confused, but kept quiet. When we came to Lord Trowbridge's home, James stopped walking and cast me a grin.

"Why are we coming here?" I asked.

He didn't answer, but led me around to the back of the house. It was another long minute before he stopped again. He put a finger to his lips and reached out toward a dead, bare bush and pulled it back by the thickest branch. Behind it was the outline of a short door, half-concealed by dry, once flourishing vines.

"When I was a child, I sneaked around down here all the time," James said. His face lit up at the memory. "Thomas, my brother, was a rascal as a boy, much less stern than he is today. Together we would hide here, in the secret room behind this door when we were making trouble. Here, no one would ever find us." He chuckled. "It wasn't until years later that we learned our mother always knew we were here, but let us keep our secret. She believed that a secret shared between two people was a treasure. It meant trust and friendship. But of course, she always saw good, never bad. She hoped our secret place would keep her sons close all their lives. Now, I don't know if that's the reason, but we have always been friends as well as brothers."

I found myself smiling at his warm story, at the fondness of his mother's memory. I hoped I could be a kind sister for Clara. Somehow I needed to make up for the years we had lost being closer to enemies than friends.

James reached forward again and forced his fingers behind a crack in the wall. He pulled, and the wooden door moved, no longer concealed. The dead vines snapped as he pulled the door all the way open, revealing a narrow, steep staircase going upward. Cobwebs hung from the dark, low ceiling, and dust floated in the air, visible by some hint of light from the clouded sun.

I looked up at James, intrigued by this secret passageway of sorts. "We are going in there?"

He laughed, and I made a conscious effort not to join. "After you, miss."

I scoffed. "There is no possible way. How do I know you are not leading me to my death?"

"What could be in this stairway that is so malicious?" He looked vastly amused.

I searched my mind for a plausible response. "A wicked monster with a sword. Or—or a creature with sharp claws and glowing yellow eyes." I bit my lip, realizing the humor in my reply.

James laughed, then bent down, peering behind the rustic door. "Oh, yes. There he is! One moment."

I watched as he ducked down and walked through the door. He had only taken a few steps before he was swallowed in darkness. I heard several seconds of commotion, dramatic clattering and exaggerated shouting. I had to hold my hand over my mouth to hide my laughter. This was ridiculous. After a moment, James came back into view. He poked his head out of the doorway. I could easily imagine him as a young boy—probably with rosy cheeks and even messier black hair, bright green eyes too big for his face, shining with adventure. The thought was so endearing, I forgot not to grin at him.

"I have killed the beast, Charlotte. Not to worry." He gave me a half smile and reached out and grasped my wrist. I was about to protest, but he pulled me forward and I ducked under the doorway. "We must hurry," he said, whispering now. "I destroyed the creature with the glowing yellow eyes, but the sword-wielding monster still lives."

I slapped him on the arm. What was I doing? As we walked up the endless stairs in the dark, I gripped his arm against my better judgement. He was so warm and strong and safe. I couldn't see him in the darkness, but I could feel him right beside me, and that was almost a greater torture. My heart whispered things I didn't understand here in the black, quietness, but I ignored it. *Hush,* I told my heart. *You are wrong.* I was right. I was always right.

Finally, we paused our climb and James touched a door in front of us. He slid his hand until he found the handle and pushed the door open. Natural daylight flooded in from high above us, and James stepped into the room, then reached down to assist me. My gaze scanned the new surroundings. It was disorienting. Three triangular windows sat just below the peaked ceiling. It was a tiny room, bare except for two chairs, a stone fireplace, a pile of chipped silver, glassware in the corner, and a stack of framed paintings.

I walked over to the artwork to see if it was familiar, but I couldn't place it. The brushstrokes in the top painting were perfect, the colors vibrant. It was a painted landscape of this town—I could tell by the rocky coast and tile rooftops. But the sky was much bluer than I had ever seen, and the grasses much greener. To be sure, I turned to James. "Is this Craster?"

He nodded, a sort of grim look in his eyes. "My mother painted it."

I turned my gaze back to the painting in awe. "It is beautiful. But why did she depict it so differently?"

"It is an identical depiction of Craster in the spring."

I looked at him in surprise. "It is truly this beautiful?"

He smiled. "It is." He walked over to stand beside me, and I watched his eyes sweep over the painting, a sort of longing in his expression. "My mother was ill when she did this. She finished it mere days before her death. This town was such a joy to her, and spring was the only season she had not yet painted it in." He crossed his arms, as if to keep some piece of himself from falling apart. I had never seen him like this, and it shook me in a way I couldn't explain.

"Her hands were always shaking," James continued. "She couldn't even lift a glass to her lips, but when she was painting, they were still. After she died, my father sealed this room from the inside, so the only way to enter was through the hidden outside door, but he didn't know of it. As far as he knew, he had sealed away her paintings forever. It hurt him too much to see them. He passed just a year later, when I was eighteen."

I drew a breath, stricken by the raw grief in his face, the honesty of his words. He turned his eyes away from the painting and back to me. I didn't know what to say, for fear of ruining the understanding growing between us. "I am sorry. That must have been so difficult for you."

He gave a soft smile that melted even my stony heart. He gestured to the chairs in the center of the room and I walked to the far one and sat down. James joined me in the chair to my right and leaned forward. "I understand you have a confession to make?"

Nervousness threatened to stop my breathing. Why had I offered to tell him anything? "You must confess your secret first. Who was the woman you wrote the love letter for?"

He sighed and rubbed the back of his neck, glancing up at me in exasperation. "Only if you tell me one thing." A pause. "Why do you wish to know?"

His question bristled over my skin, a sharp reminder that even I didn't know the answer. Why *did* I care to know? Why didn't I just dispose of the letter and forget that little piece about James? As I thought about what to say, I realized I couldn't tell him the truth about this. The reason I wanted to know was because . . . I envied her. To be loved by a man with as good a heart as James possessed made that lady very fortunate.

I stopped myself. I didn't want to be loved by anyone, especially not someone so far below my ambitions. So why did the thought of that woman choke me with longing for what she had? It didn't matter, because I would never have the same.

James was waiting for my answer, but I still didn't have it. My voice spoke words I hadn't planned for. "You know about so many things that have hurt me. And I realize . . . I don't know about you—about the hard things you have had to bear. I wish to be a comfort, a confidante, a . . . friend, as you have been mine." I looked at him, surprised by the shyness I felt. He was watching me with an expression I didn't recognize.

"Very well," he said finally. "Her name was Mary, of a family well positioned in society, but not wealthy by any means. I was very young, still grieving the deaths of my parents, and she came here during the summer to visit her cousins. She did not like it here, and missed her family in London. Together with our reasons for anger and heartache, we came to know one another, and I thought I loved her." He breathed in slowly and out fast. "I never professed to her my feelings, but she knew. I finally summoned the courage and wrote the note. I planned to deliver it personally, but when I called for her, she was no longer here. She had returned home to marry a man with whom she had a previous engagement. A wealthy viscount with a country house."

His face turned bitter and he looked down at his hands clasped in his lap. "She never loved me at all. She cared for nothing but a title and a fortune, which I lack." He was silent for several seconds, and finally looked at my face again. "Is that all you needed to know?" The smile he usually wore was long faded.

It wasn't. "Why did you carry the letter with you after so much time?"

The question seemed to catch him by surprise, and he hesitated before answering. "I didn't keep it because I still love her, that is for certain. I kept it because I hoped I could find someone else to have it. To put truth behind the words I once wrote from my heart. But I wonder if I am even capable of it anymore. Of love."

Heartbreak cried out in every line of his face and I found myself wishing I could kiss it all away, rules or no rules. Had I ever broken a heart like this woman had broken his? Guilt pooled in my stomach as the realization dawned on me that I was exactly like her. But surely she had made the right decision. What was love compared to a life of comfort and power and happiness? I looked at James's face, at the rawness in his eyes, and saw in him a kindred spirit.

"Perhaps I am the best person to keep your note, then," I said.

His eyebrow twitched upward. "Why is that?"

"Because we are enemies, remember? If love ever threatened you again, you would be in no danger from me." I tried to smile, but it turned out to be a shaky fraction of one. "And at any rate, I am far more likely to hate you than I am to ever love you." The joke seemed far less humorous than it once had been.

James smiled softly, but there was a sort of sadness in his eyes I didn't understand. "Of course."

I tingled all over with an awareness of his closeness, his look, the smile on his lips, the words and agreement that had just passed between us. He was silent for several more seconds, and they were excruciating. The tension in the air broke and he sat back, putting on a much more casual air. "It is your turn. Your confession?"

I took a deep breath and tried to appear calm. I wished I could reverse time and not have agreed to tell him anything. Once he knew the true reason I was here, there would be no hope of him ever respecting me again. But a lingering lie was just as damaging. "I was not entirely honest with you."

"I knew that."

I breathed deeply and rubbed my gloved hands over my skirt. "My sister and I were sent here on an errand." I swallowed. "My father . . . he was familiar with all the gaming halls of London. He gambled away our entire fortune, leaving us in ruin. My mother secured a place for herself to live with one of her cousins, but sent us, her daughters, to a cottage on the tip of England, where no one would know of our disgrace." I tried to keep my voice even, to shun the bitterness. "I had one assignment from her, and it was to secure a match of title and wealth who could save us. Your brother was her primary choice. But I have failed her. And I wish I had told you the truth sooner, but I knew it would only worsen your opinion of me."

I didn't dare look at James in the silence that followed.

"You're fortune hunters," I heard him say. I glanced at James's face. His jaw was set and his eyes flashed. "I suspected it. But not from your sister."

I quickly shook my head. "Clara never supported it! What you see between my sister and your brother is completely genuine. She truly cares for him. I have never been so sure of anything in my life. Please do not worry over your brother. He is ardently loved by Clara, I assure you."

"But *you* would have tried." His voice grew louder. "My brother could have very well lost his heart to you and been betrayed! How does your conscience allow that?"

My pride came to life again, provoked by his anger. My feet jerked beneath me and I stood. "And I would do it again! I will do it again! I do not intend to live in a dirty cottage for the remainder of my life! A woman must be intelligent and understand that a life of ease and comfort is the only happiness that can be afforded. My mother has taught me well." I swallowed hard. "Even if love exists, I want no part of it. It is a destroyer of innocent hearts and hopes that scale too high. It is a hindrance of dreams and goals. It is an imitation of joy and entirely unnecessary.

"Forgive me if I want something more. Love will fade. Freedom and wealth in a marriage will serve me forever and well. Even if Clara manages to save our family from ruin, I will still meet the expectation my mother set for me a long time ago. I am determined to have the future I always wanted." My words choked in my throat, and I shook with emotion. Crossing my arms over my chest, I finished in a softer voice, "One free of love, even if that means leaving behind a broken heart."

I didn't wait for James to speak or move or stand. I turned away and rushed to the door in this hidden room full of secrets I wished I had never shared. The door stood open and I stepped behind it. James didn't follow me.

So I hurried down the dark stairway alone, hastily wiping away tears that dripped off the tip of my nose and streaked down my cheeks. James hated me. Now more than ever. But wasn't this the life I had chosen? Was a life without love just a life of hate after all? It was frightening in the black stairway alone, and I wished for a strong, safe arm I would never have.

When I finally burst through the outside, I gulped the fresh air, calming my sobs and shaking shoulders. What had I done? I pressed one hand against my cheek and walked, stricken with uncertainty and regret. Why had I revealed so much to him? There was pain in honesty and doubt in secrets. Which was worse? James could never respect me. He could never see me again without being truly disgusted. And he could never love me. I knew which of those was the worst, and my chest clenched against fresh sobs. *James could never love me.*

I took a deep breath and scolded myself for caring. It was better that way, because I could never love him either. To love James was contrary to all I had ever dreamed of. No one would be left with a broken heart. I excused the thought—it was nonsense to lie to myself. My heart had already been broken. The only thing that remained for me to do was to fix it. I didn't know how, but I was certain that weeks of distance from a certain set of green eyes would be the best medicine.

Chapter 17

*"Pray you now,
forget and forgive."*

ucy Abbot had an affinity for hats. She did not wear
them often, but kept an expansive collection in her
room, planning to wear them to the first fancy party she was invited
to. Of course, fancy parties were rare in Craster, but that didn't stop
Lucy from visiting the milliner's shop twice weekly.

"Would you like to accompany me today, Charlotte? I would so
enjoy your companionship."

I looked at her over my sketchbook. I had not been drawing, but
practicing each letter of the alphabet with my left hand. I had written my name several dozen times over the page, and each seemed to
become uglier than the last.

The Abbots' home had become a sanctuary. It had been five days
since I had been out of doors besides the walk between our cottage
and the Abbots' house. I worried over seeing James, and couldn't risk
meeting him on the path toward the village.

"To the milliner's?"

Lucy nodded, curls bouncing on her shoulders. "I have a hat
with lace trim and exotic feathers in the process and have scheduled
another fitting."

I glanced out the window at the icy weather and dull skies.
Despite it all, I did long for a break from the monotony I had adopted
these last several days. In the mornings I baked breads and sweets
for Clara and me and scrubbed the cottage until it was pristine. Mr.

Watkins had told me it was acceptable for me to use my hand more freely, and although it hurt, motion was returning and my hand was becoming stronger.

It was strange, feeling the round lumps where my fingers had been severed and knowing they would never return. I still wore the glove when I was in the company of others, but at night when I was alone in my room, I studied the lines and puckers and wilting gashes. After I finished cleaning, I always came to the Abbots'. The memory of James playing with me on the pianoforte haunted this room, but gave it life and joy that I couldn't part from. I was troubled day and night, feeling the keen loss of a dear friend. But I could not let James Wortham scare me away. If he hated me, then that was fine. But I certainly didn't hate him.

"I will come with you," I said to Lucy before I could lose my resolve.

"Wonderful! I will retrieve my things and we will be off." She bounced around the corner, eager and energetic and positively adorable. I thought of the times Lucy had swooned over James, speaking of his bravery and looks. I hoped she hadn't set her heart on him.

I met Lucy at the door and we walked into the cold. I tugged my cloak around my narrowing shoulders. Since we had moved here, I had become thinner from the lack of grand meals and from the increased exercise. At home, I took a daily walk, but never too far, and I never cooked and cleaned. The curves of my figure had lessened significantly, and my dresses fit looser albeit more comfortably. I wondered what else my time here would rob from me.

"I can see my breath in front of my face." Lucy's voice broke my thoughts. "When I was little, my papa told me it was because I spent far too much time with him, breathing in the smoke from his pipe." She giggled. "I believed it."

"When will your father be home?" I asked. I knew he had been away for a business matter, and Mrs. Abbot expected his return soon.

"Just in time for the Christmastide. Can you believe it is only a fortnight away?" She squealed with excitement.

I scowled. My family had never given Christmas much observance. We were often invited to dinners but that was the most of it.

Lucy seemed to notice my confusion, because she looked at me with wide eyes.

"Did my mother not tell you of the festivities? Each year we hold a dinner on Christmas Eve and decorate with all my favorite greenery. Everyone in the town is invited, and we give food and warm garments to all the beggars. Beef and mincemeat, coats, beautiful music and games, and the even bigger celebration comes on twelfth night." She gasped dramatically and squeezed my arm. "Is that all so unfamiliar?"

I smiled weakly and nodded.

"You will enjoy every moment, I assure you. It is without question the most pleasant time of the year. There is little else in this place to ever look forward to," she sighed, rolling her eyes subtly.

I threw her a puzzled look.

"Yes, I am not as enamoured by this town as the others in my family. I hope someday to leave." She shrugged, then lifted her gaze to the dark sky, squinting against the dull glow of the cloud-covered sun. "But I do enjoy the holiday parties."

A welcome feeling of excitement filled me. I had always loved parties. It would give me a reason to dress nicely and feel pretty for the first time in so long. I could keep my hand concealed in my stuffed glove and have a wonderful time. "Must I wait an entire fortnight?"

Lucy laughed just as we reached the milliner's shop. She pulled the door open and a bell rang above us.

The entire time we were at the shop, I couldn't stop thinking about Christmastide. Surely there would be enough people present for me to avoid James, and I could meet so many new people. I made a note in my mind to gather together all the jewelry and extra shawls I had to give the poor townspeople that came for charity during the Christmas Eve festivities. I hardly noticed when Lucy showed me the outrageous hat with the bright feathers. I didn't remember the opinion I gave, but she seemed satisfied by it. When we thanked the shopkeeper and returned to the cold and softly falling snow, I tried to conjure up an image of my small selection of dresses and which one I would wear. I decided upon my berry-red gown with the silver trim before I even arrived home.

Lucy was speaking, I realized too late.

"Pardon me?"

She cleared her throat. "Mr. Wortham is quite taken with you, I believe."

I choked on a breath. "That is absurd." I wished she wouldn't talk about him. "He is much too handsome for my liking. But you don't seem to mind at all, do you?"

She stopped a giggle. "Of course not! But I could never have him, not when his heart is so obviously elsewhere." She threw me a devious look.

I shook my head. "He hates me."

"Do men gaze adoringly at women they hate? I will admit, I used to fancy Mr. Wortham, but the sight of you two is so positively perfect, I cannot possibly steal him from you."

"It is not possible, Lucy. You must have imagined it."

She threw her hand out in front of her. "I did not."

"Well, even if he did not hate me then, he certainly does now. There is no question. And I don't find him particularly agreeable either. He did save me, and for that I am grateful, but nothing stands between us besides an agreement to . . . tolerate one another."

She smirked and flipped one of her dark curls over her shoulder. "Very well. But we shall see if he does not sweep you off your feet at the Christmastide. Many women have fallen ill for his charms during the magic of the holiday."

I was sure I was already ill. It would not be difficult to fall full in love with him, and if Lucy was right, then I needed to stay away from the party. The excitement I had felt before faded away. I decided not to go.

I would stay home and clean and cook and find a safe place I belonged until I could leave this town. My berry-red dress would stay in my closet, and I would keep my heart as a result. I shut out my emotions and made my decision.

There were many things I had enjoyed about my old life, and one of those things had been parties. But at those parties I had been the one claiming hearts and turning heads. It was not wise to attend the Christmastide parties because, for once, I feared that my own heart would be claimed. It was too vulnerable.

"You are wrong, Lucy," I said, forcing a smile.

She tipped her head close to mine, smiling deviously. "We shall see, won't we? Rachel and I have wagered on it."

I gasped, but couldn't help but smile when she burst into laughter. "Oh, and what is Rachel's bet against yours?"

She shrugged. "We both claim that you have already fallen for him."

I scoffed, turning my gaze to the snowflakes falling on my boots as we walked. "What is a proper wager without an opponent? You cannot both claim the same."

"Oh, Charlotte. You provide enough opposition in the matter for both of us."

My eyes flashed to her face, the tip of her nose pink from the cold. She didn't seem to want to continue the conversation, and we were already approaching her house. So I let her words be brushed aside, at least for now.

Hours later, I returned to my cottage in silence, surprised to find a letter from Mama resting unopened on the kitchen table. After sitting down, I tore it open, scanning her words carefully.

My dear daughter,

Charlotte, I am pleased to hear you are indeed progressing toward a match with Lord Trowbridge. I always knew my investments in you would bring reward to our family. Please work to improve your penmanship, as your last letter demonstrated much too stiff curves and loops. It looked very much like the writing of a maid or of Clara. I expect an improvement upon your next letter. I wish very much to see your pretty face and what the lack of sunlight has done for your complexion. My cousin has been recovering from his grief, and his children also. The home has risen from the dull, dreary sadness and the vexing moans and sobbing. We still wear black, but I find the color quite becomes me.

In much happier news, my cousin has struck gold! He has made a business investment with an industrialist and is set to make thousands! Is that not delightful news? Please take comfort in knowing that your mother is happy. I look forward to our next correspondence.

Sincerely yours,

Mama

I set the letter down and put my forehead in my bent arm. Why had I lied to her in my last letter? I should have just told her that Lord Trowbridge was not interested in courting me.

Feeling too weak and unmotivated, I set her letter aside, making a note in my mind to answer later. Once things were settled between Clara and Lord Trowbridge we could write to Mama with the good news. She would be surprised but satisfied with the news and come here for the wedding. Then she would see how terrible it truly was, and take me home with her to Canterbury and I could forget this town and everyone in it. I could reclaim my old life, hiding my deformity and finding a husband even more well set up than Lord Trowbridge. Mama would care about me again. I would be happy.

With determination in my movements, I picked up her letter and walked upstairs to my room, tucking the letter inside a small drawer in my writing desk. I paused, seeing James's love letter lying flat inside. My fingers hovered above it, but I stopped myself. No. I would never read it.

The rest of the day I deviated from my normal schedule, tidying the house for one short hour before settling on the sofa with a book I had found in Clara's room. It was a romantic, adventurous tale, and I believed none of it. But even so, I ended up giddy and short of breath as I closed the final page. How many hours had passed? I could hardly believe it had been all day.

I heard the front door open suddenly, and Clara's head of bronze hair came into view. Without thinking, I tossed the book aside, more forcefully than I intended. The book crashed against the far wall. I jerked my gaze to Clara, hoping she hadn't noticed.

She gasped, eyes wide. "You were reading a novel? A romantic novel?"

"I—" my gaze flickered to the glass of water I had placed on the small tea table. "I—was using it as a . . . coaster." I bit my lip, remembering the time James had teased me about using a book as a coaster when I had accused him of being illiterate.

"Oh, I see." She cast me a knowing smile. "But was the coaster full of damsels in distress and handsome strangers coming to the rescue? Of romantic gestures and happy endings?"

I felt close to bursting and suddenly couldn't contain it. I had thoroughly enjoyed the book. I sighed. "Yes."

She sat down beside me and squealed. "You understand now why I love to read these stories."

I hated to admit it, but I did. "Don't be mistaken, Clara. I will not become some silly romantic because of it."

"Of course not. I would never expect such a thing from you." Another smile.

A subject change was in order. "I trust you had a good day."

Her smile faded slightly and her shoulders slumped. She hesitated. Her lip quivered almost imperceptibly.

I reached forward and put my hand on her arm with concern. "What is wrong?"

"Thomas has been . . . very distant these last several days. I—I don't know what I have done." Her voice was soft and full of hurt.

My heart dropped as I remembered my last conversation with James. I gasped. He must have told his brother about why we came here. James had turned Lord Trowbridge against Clara. It was the only plausible reason he would be avoiding her.

"You have done nothing," I assured her. "It was James. I told him the truth about why we came here and he was very angry. I tried to assure him that you had true feelings for his brother but . . ." My mind spun. Clara could not be hurt again because of me. She deserved every happiness. "It is my fault. I should not have told him. What reason have I given him to believe me? Of course he took his concerns to Lord Trowbridge—Thomas as you call him."

Clara sniffled a little. "I cannot lose him, Charlotte. I—I love him."

"I know. I will speak to James about it as soon as I can, not to worry. We will see this straightened out." Anger bubbled close to the surface of my skin. James was willingly destroying the happiness of his own brother! Didn't he know that what was between Clara and Lord Trowbridge was real? How could he doubt it? Even as the ultimate doubter of love, I believed it.

Nervousness fluttered in my stomach at the thought of approaching James with the very topic we had argued over the last time we had met. But this was not about me. This was about the happiness of my sister.

First thing tomorrow I would find him and do something I never thought I would: I was going to defend love.

*Never look at his face for more than ~~three~~ **two** seconds.*
Never let him see how he affects you.
Never smile at him.
Never stray from a business-like demeanor.
Never let him touch my hand or face or arm.
Never agree with him.
Never forgive him.

I added these few points to my list before leaving for the village. It was important that I had all my rules in order. This meeting was nothing but a brief business exchange. Clara deserved to be happy, and I would not allow anyone to stop that from happening. Especially not James Wortham.

With nervous feet, I walked all the way to the village. The snow had been falling lightly when I left our cottage, but as I continued down the path, the wind blew harder and large flakes of snow hit my face and melted there, leaving me numb and red. I pulled up the hood of my cloak and kept my head down until I reached the market area of the town. Hardly anyone was out. I found myself nearly blinded by this unexpected and uncharacteristically wild storm.

The first person that happened to walk past me, I stopped, touching their shoulder as they passed.

The person turned to face me. It was a woman, middle aged with her hair down, blowing loosely in the wind.

"Is Mr. James Wortham about?" I half shouted over the storm, holding a hand to my head to keep my hood from slipping off.

She scowled, as if annoyed that I had stopped her to ask such a trivial question. Then she was gone, shuffling quickly through the thick layer of new snow. I turned to my right and left, looking for any sight of him, and decided it was useless. He must be home.

So I rotated to the other direction and started toward his house. I cursed fate for making this happen, for making me venture to James's house in the middle of a storm like a traveler seeking shelter. Besides that, I would be forced to be alone with him, which was never a good thing.

I took deep breaths and kept my head down and the snow out of my eyes, recalling the route to his house without looking up to find landmarks. After several minutes, I spotted it, and rushed to the doorstep, cold enough to care much less about the awkwardness of the situation and the confrontation I was about to make.

Knocking three times, I waited. The faint sound of footsteps reached my ears and the door opened abruptly, pushed by a gust of wind.

James was taken off guard, seeing me standing there, but soon recovered and ushered me inside. He forced the door closed behind him, locking the freezing air and snow where it could no longer touch me.

"Charlotte, what are you doing? You will become ill."

I was confused. I thought he would be much more angry than he was.

He reached toward the coat hook beside the door and removed his coat that was hanging there and slung it over my shoulders. Why was he still being kind?

"Come sit by the fire to get warm." He gestured to the sitting room and I walked ahead. He followed and pulled a second chair beside the one near the fire. The silence was awkward as he sat down and crossed his arms. "What the devil were you doing out in a storm like that?" His voice was calm, but he showed genuine concern. I wondered why.

"I needed to see you. To speak with you." My voice was much too quick.

He smiled, but it was halfhearted. "What could you possibly want to speak with me about?"

"I want to know why you have turned your brother against Clara." I gave him the hardest look I could manage.

He didn't deny it, but leaned forward in his chair, so close that I could see the flecks of gray in his eyes. "I care about my brother, and I don't want him to be hurt."

My jaw dropped and I leaned back in my chair quickly, in part to emphasize my words and in part to put distance between us so I could think clearly. "To separate the two of them is the only thing that can hurt him. Do you understand how it is breaking my sister's heart? She is not trying to win his fortune or title. She loves him! You are not protecting your brother by keeping him from her. If he cares for her in return, then let him."

"Perhaps I was protecting him from precisely that. He loved his wife once, and he lost her. It is better to not love at all than to experience the pain that always follows. It isn't worth it." His voice was throaty and full of doubt.

I was even more angry now. "You knew he loved her, and she loved him, and still you turned him against her?"

He shook his head. "It was not my choice. I merely told him the truth about why you ended up here, and he has chosen to spare himself the disappointment of love."

"But they will be happy together! Clara has never wanted anything more. When love is true and good, doesn't it bring happiness?"

His gaze was hard and unrelenting. "I have never seen it."

I paused, letting the silence and power of his words settle. My heart beat loudly and the anger boiling in my veins fell to a simmer. "Nor have I."

My gaze locked on his and my heart threatened to burst. The flames from the fireplace reflected dancing shadows on his face. The air between us was taut with misunderstanding and heartbreak—desperation to understand . . . something. I breathed in slowly, drawing closer to him against my will. No. I leaned back, feigning calm and telling my heart to slow down.

James's eyes flickered over my face one more time and he ran his hand over his hair. "If you are sure, then let your sister prove it to him. Change his mind."

"How does she do that?" I scowled.

"That is for her to decide. There are a number of things she could do to show him she loves him. And if my brother truly loves her, he will stop at nothing to win her back."

Clara would know what to do, but if James had ideas, I wanted to hear them. "What could she do?" I gave a shaky smile.

His gaze focused on my face again, and I felt my heart pound harder. How could he affect me with something so simple as a look? *Never let him see how he affects you.* I lifted my chin and looked him right in the eye, willing myself to look confident, although I didn't feel it.

"Oh, the obvious things. Simple things. If I loved you, for instance . . ." Without warning he reached forward and took my hand in his. Unfortunately I had forgotten my gloves at home, and he had chosen my ugly hand. I cringed through my beating heart and told my hand not to shake. How could he bear to touch it?

". . . I would hold your hand, like this, whenever you needed comfort." He was so gentle, so careful, as he held my hand where it fit so perfectly in his. His thumb traced the scars with the softness of a feather. When I looked at his eyes, the softness there was more intense than before, burning me from somewhere inside. "I would share with you everything I have, every wish, every dream, every secret. Every hour and every kiss." He was still holding my hand, but I refused to look at his face again, so I just stared at his shoulder, where there wasn't a set of green eyes whispering things I didn't understand.

"I would write you notes, saying the things that are hard to say, and tell you how I adore you, and how my heart is yours. I would keep you close, and protect you from everything that is painful. I would whisk away all the sorrow, and all your burdens would be mine. And I would remind you how much I love you if ever you doubt it. I would keep your heart very safe, if I was ever allowed to have it." I heard him draw a breath, slow and heavy. "If I loved you."

I took a brief glance at his face, trying desperately to hide the blush on my own. I was surprised to see the heartache flickering in his eyes, the muscle clenching in his jaw as he released my hand.

He managed to bring up a smile, to excuse every word for something less than they had really been. But there was something alive and real buzzing between us and I wanted it. His words rang in my head like a chant, *If I loved you*. He didn't love me. The things he had said had been mere speculation, nothing meant for my ears or my heart.

"That sounds like an awful amount of effort," I said, trying to smile back. My voice shook. "It is a fortunate thing that you don't love me then."

His expression faltered, and I saw in his eyes one more secret, one I knew he never intended to tell, and I couldn't decipher what it meant. I wanted to know it. I wanted to know everything about him, in fact. I wanted everything he had said he would do if he loved me. My heart ached as I realized it could never be mine. He could never be mine. This was not my place, this was not where I belonged. Mama expected better from me, and so did I. There was no time for ridiculousness and false hopes. Besides, James had deserted love and I had forsaken it.

His jaw clenched again and he looked down at the floor. "Indeed."

Awkward silence fell between us and I stood up, eager to escape the uncertainty in this room and in James's eyes. I had accomplished what I came here to do. Almost. "Will you speak with him at least? Your brother. Help convince him how perfect a match he and Clara are."

James looked up wearily, smiling. "What a romantic you have become. I never would've expected it."

I put a hand on my hip. "It is not for me, but for the sake of others."

"A contradiction, to be sure."

I frowned. "Intelligent."

"Hypocritical."

"Thoughtful!"

He grinned with amusement. "Nothing short of ridiculous"

"I did not come here to be mocked." I lifted my chin and stepped farther away from him. "I came here to help my sister, regardless of how it might make me appear. Now, I thank you for your time, but I must be going. Good day."

I showed myself to the door, and walked out into the snow that had calmed considerably. I had forgotten to remove James's coat I wore in the house, so I left it folded on the steps. Shivering, I pulled my wet shawl back around my shoulders and hurried home. I didn't know if any good had come from that conversation, but I believed Clara could win Lord Trowbridge back.

If there was any good in the world, Clara deserved it. If love could bring happiness, then she deserved all of it. There were still doubts, but I whisked them away to a place I could forget them. A new confidence soared within me, and I made the decision not to run from James any longer. I would go to the Christmastide parties and have a wonderful time, and James would have no effect on me. I would keep myself from falling in love with him or anyone else. I was strong and intelligent and would achieve every single one of my dreams.

Nothing could stop me now. Not a deformed hand, not a cottage in the North, and most certainly not Mr. James Wortham.

Chapter 18

"The course of true love never did run smooth."

When I returned home, I lit the fire in our cottage and warmed myself, waiting for Clara to return home. When she did, I met her at the door, eager to relay my exchange with James. "He did tell Lord Trowbridge why we came here! But there is still hope." I gripped her hand. "You must tell him how much you love him."

Her eyes flew open wide. "No. I cannot do that! A woman should never proclaim her feelings first."

"But he doubts that you love him. The only way to convince him now is to tell him. He has seen it, surely, but there is no proof until you say the words. The hard things."

She pulled her hand away and moved to the chair in the sitting room. She fiddled with a loose strand of hair, deep in thought. "But I cannot." She sat up straight. "No. I couldn't."

"You must." I took her cloak off the hook by the door. "Go back this instant and tell him."

She was clutching her face now, shaking her head. "I can't, I can't, I can't."

I walked over to her and put my hands on both sides of her head, stopping it from shaking. "You can."

"If it is so very easy, then why don't you do it?" She raised her eyebrows in question. "Why do you not tell Mr. Wortham how you care for him?"

My cheeks tingled with heat. "Because I don't."

"I thought you had stopped with the lying. It is quite obvious."

"You said that before," I snapped.

"It has not changed."

I pulled my hands away from her and crossed my arms. "We are not talking about me, we are talking about you. I do not mean to say it will be easy, but it is necessary."

She shook her head. "You just want the family saved from ruin."

"I want you to be happy." I looked her straight in the eyes, to make sure she understood. "If it is too difficult to say, then write a letter."

She seemed to contemplate the idea, pausing. "Fine." She took a deep, unsteady breath. "But you must help me write the letter. You will know the best way to say it."

I threw out my hand. "Nonsense. How could I know? I am not a romantic like you."

She smiled. "That is the worst lie I have ever heard."

We waited until it was dark to deliver the note. Clara and I had spent nearly an hour trying to decide what to write in the letter, discarding and rewriting and screaming. After several attempts, Clara was satisfied with the words she had written, and we sealed the letter.

"There shall be no turning back now." I swiped the note off the table. "I will carry it, but you will put it through the door."

"I will not!" She cringed at the high, nervous tone of her voice.

I laughed, running toward the door. "Very well, but you must accompany me at least. If I were ever caught, then he might assume the letter was from me."

She followed close on my heels, looking close to vomiting all over the back of my dress. "What will I say when I go to work tomorrow? I will see him. There is no way to avoid it. How will I know if he read it? How will I know if his feelings are the same? How will I bear the awkwardness of the entire situation?" She was breathing fast.

"Calm yourself!" I said through a laugh. "He will be overjoyed."

I handed Clara her cloak and put mine around my own shoulders and we stepped outside. A dull breeze carried flecks of snow through the air, invisible in the darkness. The moon offered just enough light, and we walked fast in the quiet, eager to accomplish our mission and get out of the cold and the fright of the darkness.

When we reached Lord Trowbridge's door, I handed Clara the note, and she took it, to my surprise. Her hand shook and her throat bobbed with a labored swallow. In one fast motion, she pushed the letter through the crack between the double doors, turned on her heels, and ran. Laughing, I rapped my knuckles against the door three times, to make sure the letter was received, and ran after Clara.

We were out of sight before the yellow glow of candlelight made a rectangular shape in the distance as the door was opened.

"I cannot believe I just did that!" Clara made a sound, a mixture of a cry, a laugh, and a squeal.

"Nor can I," I said, smiling. "He will love you forever, if only just for your daring spirit."

We slowed to a walk, laughing and breathing heavily. Clara looped her arm through mine. "If this does not work as you planned I will cut your hair in your sleep."

I gasped, rocking against her so she stumbled. She laughed and I scowled teasingly. "If you do that, I will write a new letter to Lord Trowbridge telling him how large his nose is and I will sign it with your name."

"He does not have a large nose!"

It was my turn to laugh as we walked up the steps of our cottage and went inside. I hurried to light new candles in the dark, and warmed my hands carefully above the flame. I turned to face Clara. "I suspect you will be quite incapable of sleep tonight." I laughed. "But you must get your beauty rest because you will see him in the morning."

She put a hand against her stomach and bent over. "I fear I shall be sick."

"Just don't get sick all over Lord Trowbridge's shoes, I beg of you."

She laughed, but it was stiff and abrupt. "How should I . . . behave around him? Should I just enter and wait for him to speak?"

I smiled teasingly. "Oh, he will not say a single thing. Surely he will just step forward and kiss you, right there."

Her face turned scarlet and she sat down on the floor where she stood. I laughed and sat beside her on the planks of wood. She pressed her hands against her face in absolute horror. "That cannot happen."

"Why not?"

"I haven't the slightest idea how to . . . kiss." She spoke the word as if it were poison. "Oh, I sound so very vulgar, do I not?" She sighed. "You must know. Surely you have kissed dozens of men."

"I haven't." My voice was quiet as if I were confessing something embarrassing. "I have never kissed any man, in fact." I had always flirted and coaxed but I had never kissed. Mama had told me to keep from all physical attention until an official engagement was in place. I had no complaints. I had hardly entertained a single thought of kissing before I had seen James's teasing grin and firm jaw and dimpled cheeks. Blast it. "I'm afraid I am just as ignorant as you in the matter."

Clara looked acutely surprised. She examined my face. "You are serious. I suppose I just assumed you would not have told me the story of your first kiss before . . . when we weren't such dear friends as we are now." She smiled fondly and reached for my hand, the ugly one everyone here seemed to prefer. "Thank you for all your help. I will arise early and you must assist me with my hair."

"Of course!" I stood, brushing off my skirts, and yawned. "I will be retiring now as well. Try to sleep."

She stretched her legs on the floor. "I don't think it is possible."

I tipped my head down to look at her and smiled. "Just think— he is probably reading the letter as we speak, pacing the entry hall and running his fingers through his hair—"

"Oh, stop it!" She dove forward and swatted pathetically at my ankles.

I danced away, laughing until my stomach ached. I moved quickly up the stairs. "Good night!" I yelled, only once I was out of sight.

"Good night," she said in a voice close to a whimper. I shut my door behind me and collapsed on my bed and couldn't help but smile. Clara was an absolute mess. I didn't want to know the catastrophic effect love would have on me. But it would not be a pretty sight, that I knew for certain.

We arranged her hair in a simple twist, and as an added accessory, we used tiny shells Clara had collected in the sand our first week here. They were white and tan and small, wedged between thin twists of hair that led to the bulk of her hair in the back. Two long curls hung in the front, framing her face. She looked completely beautiful.

"Is it too much?" she asked, patting her hair tentatively before the mirror.

I stepped back, shaking my head with a smile. "Not at all. You look like a sea princess of some kind."

"I do not," she said, fighting a smile.

"Stop it. You do. Now, are you ready?"

She took a shaky breath, rubbing her palms over the skirts of her simple cream gown. "No. But I mustn't be late." She stood and moved toward the door and steadied herself on the frame.

I put my hand over my mouth to stifle my laugh. "Go on."

She dropped her hand from the door and I watched her walk like a ghost down the stairway. I was afraid she would topple over before she reached the bottom. I stood at the top of the staircase and waved as she walked out the door. I sighed. I couldn't wait until she returned home tonight. Time would crawl by like an ant crossing this room. Patience had never been a virtue of mine.

Clara had already helped me into my gown for the day, but my hair had not been touched. I hurried back to my bedchamber and stepped in front of the mirror. I just stared, taking in every change in my appearance, every newfound flaw. The hand, the diminished curves, the disheveled hair. I expected it to bother me, but something in the sight gave me new confidence, a different kind that I hadn't known before.

It wasn't the confidence that I would catch the attention of every eligible gentleman, but the confidence that I was capable of anything I set my mind to. I had undertaken much over the last months, and still I stood here. I was changing. I was improving on the inside while I was deteriorating on the outside. The realization struck me, and I decided I didn't mind. The people here had taught me that character was far more important than beauty. For now, this was fine. But once I returned to Canterbury, I would find beauty again for just enough time to win my perfect match. But for now, I could find peace in the good changes and uncover a way to forget the bad.

After I had made myself somewhat presentable, I decided to spend the day with the Abbots. When I arrived at their home, Lucy and Rachel were working on embroidery. I sat beside them and watched, knowing I was now incapable of yet another of my previous skills. Soon Mrs. Abbot ordered a tray of food and we all spent several hours visiting in the sitting room, listening to Rachel sing while Lucy played roughly on the pianoforte, and reading our favorite passages from the books we had already spent time discussing.

Mrs. Abbot sat up straight, as if suddenly remembering something very important. "Charlotte, I do not believe I have given you the details of our planned Christmastide parties. It is a tradition."

I smiled. "Lucy told me briefly."

"Oh, the parties are all the rage around here." She fanned her hands in a mock dramatic fashion and laughed. "We would love your assistance with the plans and decoration. The few servants we have are going to be cooking a large variety of food in preparation, and this year, Lord Trowbridge has offered to host! Can you believe it? We will be able to accommodate triple the people from town."

"How exciting!" I truly was excited, but still worried over James being in attendance. I quickly stopped my worries. I could easily avoid him. "I would love to help in any way I can."

"Wonderful. The largest of the parties will be Christmas Eve and twelfth night."

We went on to chat about the parties for another hour, with the three of them telling stories of parties in the past—mistletoe incidents in the servant's wing, spilled bowls of pudding, and the time a man's sleeve caught fire playing snapdragon.

I laughed, becoming even more eager to attend the parties. How delightful it would be to spend night after night with friends and strangers coming together in celebration. The people of this town much anticipated this time of year, especially the poor. How often did they get to enjoy a feast and be given warm clothing?

I left the house late in the afternoon, hurrying home so I didn't miss Clara's return. I realized I had been skipping, and quickly stopped myself, looking around to be sure no one noticed. I pressed down my grin and walked in a dignified manner the rest of the way home.

I hardly had time to open the door before Clara met me there, looking sullen and upset. My gaze froze on her face. Closing the door behind me, I guided her to the sofa.

"What happened?" My voice was hushed.

She put her face in her hands and huffed an audible breath. "He acted as if—as if he hadn't received the letter at all. He went on aloof and distant."

I scowled. "How could it be?"

She was clenching her teeth as she always did when holding back tears.

"Oh, Clara. Tears over a man are wasted. Don't cry."

Her lip quivered and her eyes were wet. She tried to speak but it came out muffled between sobs. "I'm not c-crying. I'm weeping! Th-there is a d-difference!"

I brought her head to my shoulder and cradled it as she *wept*. "There must be an explanation for this. Perhaps he misunderstood the words? Perhaps he didn't read it at all?"

"He must have read it. How could you not read a mysterious letter thrown through your door in the dark?" She swiped the tears from her cheeks and shook her head. "I should have never believed myself capable of marrying a man like him. Living in a home like his, being admired by society. I never wanted any of it before, but

I let myself hope for all the fancy things only because they were attached to him—to Thomas. I loved him first."

"Don't give up," I said, widening my eyes to emphasize my words. "Soon enough he will come to his senses."

She just shook her head, defeated. I couldn't bear to see it.

"He will," I said with more force.

I hoped I was right this time.

Chapter 19

"Love cannot be found where it doesn't exist,
nor can it be hidden where it truly does."

We received another letter from Mama the next morning, as if it had been sent just days after the previous one. Clara and I stood with our shoulders pressed together, heads bent close over the parchment. It shook in her hand.

My daughters,

I have received word that your father had fallen ill while traveling to France and has since died. Although the news came as a shock, I feel unshaken by the information, at ease, if not more free. I hope you will feel the same as I do. I hope you will not find me depraved for saying so, but I quite enjoy being a widow. Please do not bother with mourning; black has never been Charlotte's color.

Yours, etc.
Mama

The silence that followed was strange; the surge of grief I expected to come refused to do anything but rustle over my skin like leaves. I had hardly known the man. Clara was unmoving beside me, reading the words over and over, as if begging herself to feel something more than indifference. I touched her arm, calling her gaze to my face. Her eyes were empty.

"How could Mama say such things?" Clara asked. "He was her husband . . ."

"But nothing more," I said, watching the floor now. Is that what he had been to me? Just a father, nothing more? Not a friend, not a caregiver, not a guardian. He was just a father, filling a necessary space in my life, but leaving behind today the same void that had always been there.

Clara was quiet. "Do you remember when we were little, and Papa carried us on his back? Or when he brought us dolls from the London shops?"

My eyes shifted to her face. The memories were there, but they were faint, overshadowed by the countless memories from when I had grown older and had been ignored, censured, and forgotten. Papa had rarely been home; he had spent most of his days in travel, and, as we now knew, gambling. And when he was home, he seemed to avoid us. Almost as long as I could remember, he had been a stranger. But still, I smiled at the thought of those dolls.

I wrapped my arms around Clara and she drew a deep breath over my shoulder. We stayed that way for several seconds before she said, "May he rest in peace."

My mind traveled back to the last moment I had seen him, that day we had started our journey here from Eshersed Park.

"*Soyez bénis*, Papa." I whispered back. "Be blessed on your journey."

There was only one day left before Christmas Eve, and I had been keeping busy helping the Abbots arrange the greenery for decoration. Lucy and Rachel spent hours cutting up silk and gold paper and I helped pack it into boxes to be taken to Lord Trowbridge. Tomorrow we would help set all the preparations in his ballroom and dining hall. My stomach fluttered with excitement as I worked, eager to be finished and see the result of all our preparation. But I still worried over Clara, going to work each day and returning home more upset and troubled every time. How could Lord Trowbridge have missed the note? I couldn't understand how his prejudice could be so strong against Clara to still snub her after he knew for certain how she felt. Perhaps the letter wasn't enough—perhaps she needed to tell him her feelings aloud.

As I puzzled over this, I sorted the greenery into piles of rosemary, bay, laurel, holly, and mistletoe. The yule log sat in the corner with all the candles that were packed away to be carried to Lord Trowbridge's home. As far as I had been told, the Christmas Eve party would consist of charity toward the poor, possible entertainment from wassailers, games, and plenty of food. The twelfth night party would be something of a masquerade, with dancing and another feast. That was all I knew. I decided I would save my red and silver gown for that night. I smiled widely to myself, forgetting the anxiety of seeing James there. It would be a wonderful evening.

Mr. Abbot returned home that evening. He was a tall man, with pale hair and spectacles. I was sitting at the table when he arrived, and watched silently as Mrs. Abbot rushed to the door to greet him. Her happiness at his arrival was genuine. When he stepped toward her, he dropped his trunk and wrapped his arms around her, proclaiming how much he had missed her. Rachel and Lucy each kissed his cheeks and hugged him as well.

Mrs. Abbot held his hand and he looked at her as if he had been away for years rather than months, and as if she were the only thing he lived and breathed for. It confused me. Papa had never looked at Mama like that. Mama never missed Papa when he was away. She didn't even miss him now that he was truly gone. The ache of his loss hit me a little harder this time.

Mr. Abbot smiled when introduced to me, a wide grin that took me off guard. "Miss Charlotte! A pleasure to meet you. I have heard many wonderful things about you in my letters from my wife and daughters."

Mrs. Abbot hurried to his side, clinging to his arm and gazing adoringly at his face. She smiled at me and reached for my hand. "Charlotte is a very dear friend, indeed."

The following evening, I stood behind Clara in front of the small mirror in my room, trying to reassure her.

"You look lovely! He will come to his senses tonight."

She tipped her head down and took a deep, slow breath. It broke my spirits to see her this way, less excited than I was about the party tonight. A carriage was being sent to convey us to the house, and we were both dressed and ready to leave twenty minutes early.

I put my hand on her shoulder and sighed, trying to sort through my words before I said them. "Clara—I . . . I will speak to James about it again if you wish. Perhaps he can help somehow. He may know something we don't know." That did seem to be a common trend with him.

She shook her head. "Just let it be. I'm tired of trying."

I watched her carefully a moment longer, then nodded. But even though she was done trying, I certainly wasn't. "Are you ready to go?" I glanced out the window and saw the carriage arriving in front of our cottage.

The streets were already filled with people making their way to the party. It was ridiculous really, that we were taking a carriage to a home so close to ours, but I was convinced Lord Trowbridge wanted only the best treatment for Clara.

She forced a smile to her face and nodded. I smiled back and swiped my gloves off my bed, slipping them over my fingers and stubs of fingers to make my hands look as natural as possible. The pieces of curtain I had torn and stuffed inside looked strange upon close inspection, but it would have to suffice.

Together we hurried down the stairs and through the front door, wrapping our shawls quickly over our shoulders. The footman helped us into the carriage and soon we were moving forward, rumbling over the narrow, uneven road. As we approached the house, I could already hear music and boisterous laughter. The house was lit brightly, and through the windows I could see smiling faces and long tables of food. I stared in awe—I had never seen a party so lively and full. The parties in London were certainly crowded, but never so exciting and genuine as this.

When the carriage stopped, we were let down from the step and Clara and I walked arm in arm to the entrance. I had spent the early part of the day decorating, but could never have imagined how beautiful the house would look at night, lit by candles and the yule log in the fire.

As we came through the door, Mrs. Abbot rushed toward us in greeting. She wore a deep green gown with white satin trim. Her eyes shone with excitement and joy. She looked absolutely radiant. "Come in! Oh, you both look so beautiful."

She took our shawls and guided us around the corner where tables were lined with all kinds of food. Crowded around them were dozens of people I had never seen before, talking, laughing, and eating. Many of them were dressed in old, ragged dresses, mended together with neat seams and scrubbed clean of dirt. It warmed my heart to see them here, so happy and having such a wonderful time.

Mrs. Abbot was watching my face, waiting to see my reaction to it all. My smile grew and I turned to her. "This is perfect. Perfect!"

She sighed contentedly. "The preparation is always taxing, but the result is worth every moment." She watched the crowd a moment longer, then turned her attention back to me. "After the feast, we will see a performance from the wassailers and any other volunteers."

I scanned the crowd again and saw Lord Trowbridge standing with Sophia against one wall of the ballroom. I followed his eyes where they were set on Clara.

I looked at her face—she hadn't noticed him yet. I nudged her arm and nodded my head discreetly in his direction. She glanced at him, then turned her head away in one swift motion. "Charlotte!"

I gave her an innocent look. "What is the matter? He deserved to be caught if he was going to stare so unabashedly at you." I winked.

A crease set between her brows as she scanned the room. Her gaze focused on something across the room and her forehead softened and her mouth quirked upward. "Oh? Then we must put a stop to *that* immediately."

I followed her eyes to where James stood, watching us—watching me. I looked away quicker than Clara had, and tried to decipher what I had seen—briefly—in his eyes. Was it resentment?

Frustration? Admiration? I couldn't tell, so I allowed myself to look at him again.

He was wearing a formal jacket, white cravat, and his hair was neat, black as the sky, the contrast of his eyes as stark as the candles shining from the windows. His jaw was set, his eyes fixed on me, and I tried to draw a breath. Slowly, a smile formed on his face, and my heart skipped. Despite my every effort, I smiled back—careful, tentative, and uncertain—and then he was walking toward me.

I didn't know what to say to him, but then I looked at Clara, the sorrow on her face as she watched Lord Trowbridge across the ballroom, and I knew what I needed to say. James stopped just in front of me, that look I couldn't name still in his eyes, hidden and careful.

"I need your help." It came out quick and not at all the tone I intended.

"Your servant awaits." He smiled, and I had to look away. "For what do you require my help?"

"I know you don't truly wish to rob your brother of happiness. Just look at him," I nodded my head toward where Lord Trowbridge stood, "and look at her." Clara was standing, shoulders slack, engaged in a quiet conversation with Rachel. Her eyes darted across the room every few seconds without fail. "What can we do?"

James rubbed his jaw and slowly a grin lit his face. "This is a dangerous game, Charlotte. You wish to play matchmaker with me as your assistant? A dreadful team we will make I daresay—especially with business of the heart."

"We must try, at least. We are both partially to blame for their separation. You told your brother things that you knew would distance him from Clara, and I should never have told you the truth in the first place." I cringed at the bitterness in my voice. "You will never forgive me for it."

His eyes searched mine and I found myself trapped in them; I couldn't look away if I wanted to. And I wasn't sure if I did. James took a deep breath. "I wish I could stay angry with you. But I can't." He crossed his arms, smiling with a gentleness that melted my icy charade. "I'm glad you told me what you did." He stepped forward and smiled in a teasing way. "Otherwise I may have fallen madly in love with you."

His words hit me hard, and my heart quickened. I searched his face despite the dangers of doing so, hoping to find clues of some kind. His eyes were so difficult to read—teasing one moment and serious the next—hiding a misunderstanding behind blue and green and unspoken words. I clutched my skirts and adjusted my gloves. "How fortunate then . . . that I told you the truth."

James's jaw tightened and he looked down, but quickly replaced the expression with another smile.

I tugged at my gloves another moment longer, trying to dispel the discomfort between us, then cleared my throat. "What shall we call this operation?"

He raised an eyebrow in confusion.

"If we are to play matchmaker, we must be discreet." I gave a sideways smile. "Shall we call it . . . Lady Trowbridge?"

He rolled his eyes dramatically. "That is not discreet at all."

I put a hand on my hip. "Your ideas?"

"There is plenty of greenery to draw inspiration from . . . holly, bay, laurel . . ."

"Mistletoe?" I suggested, "That's romantic."

He smiled with mischief. "Only if you plan to use it. If we could somehow drive them both toward the servant's wing, there is plenty of mistletoe there."

I laughed, and he joined me. "I don't wish to ruin my sister's reputation! We shall call the plan 'Rosemary.' It is completely unrelated to love and there is no significance to it."

He leaned his head down, lowering his voice to a whisper. "But rosemary is one of the most significant scents in my opinion."

I scoffed. "How so?"

"It never fails to remind me of you." He winked and my cheeks burned.

"I smell of rosemary?" I tried to smile.

"The very best kind."

I rolled my eyes at him and stepped away, trying not to enjoy the sound of his laugh that followed. I recovered my thoughts and cooled my cheeks. "Before we begin, you must know the rest of the story. Several nights ago, Clara wrote a letter to Thomas, telling him how she felt. We slipped it through his door, and he has not acknowledged it at all. I worry he didn't receive it, but I don't see how that can be possible."

James listened carefully, then paused before speaking. "It may not have been enough." He scowled. "He has been hurt before; it may be difficult for him to believe someone could love him. His wife never did."

I frowned. "What do you mean?"

"His late wife married him for the sole purpose of obtaining a title and a large sum of pin money." His voice was bitter. "She never loved him, but he loved her more than anything. I fear he has never recovered."

A thread of guilt stitched through me, and I crossed my arms to contain it. "How awful," I mumbled.

His gaze focused on me, but I refused to look at him because I knew the guilt would be too much. That woman was just like me, carving yet another broken heart in her path. Was I capable of doing such a thing?

"What else can Clara do?" I asked in a quiet voice.

"The only thing left for her to do—she must tell him her feelings aloud," James said.

I glanced over at Clara and knew it was impossible. "She's too timid," I said. "Just delivering the letter nearly made her ill. We cannot ask such a thing of her."

James seemed to consider this, darting his gaze between the two of them, thinking. Before he could speak again, I saw Mrs. Abbot rushing toward us, face still shining with excitement. "Charlotte! I am sorry to interrupt, but will you assist me for a moment? We need to gather the guests around the music room to hear the performances."

James started to step away, but Mrs. Abbot caught him by the arm. "Mr. Wortham, will you please treat us to a piece on the pianoforte?"

I had only seen it once or twice before, but his confidence faltered. Then his eyes met mine and he smiled. "Only if Miss Lyons will accompany me."

My breath caught and I tried to protest, but Mrs. Abbot gasped too loud to compete with. "Yes! Please, if you will. Do you sing?" She turned to me with wide eyes.

James answered for me. "Your guests will not be disappointed, believe me. But the method of our performance must remain a surprise."

She pressed a hand to her chest. "Now I am very anxious to begin." She smiled and kissed my cheek. "I am taking this quarter of the room, and my daughters will help with the west and south sides. Will you usher the north guests to the music rooms?"

I smiled despite how nervous I felt. "Gladly."

With another smile and squeeze of my arm, she left, leaving me alone with James again. I gave him a hard look. "Why did you say that? Now everyone will know of my injury."

His look was a gentle reprimand. "I told you not to be ashamed."

"I would still prefer that the entire town not suspect there is something amiss. If they discover the truth . . . they will despise me for it." I took a deep, shaking breath, and a tear slipped from my eye. James reached for my hand with a reassuring smile.

"They will not."

I scowled. "How do you know?"

He chuckled and swiped away my stray tear with his thumb. My heart pounded, and I tried to ignore it, but I was too aware of James's closeness and comfort and safety. "Because it is fairly impossible to despise you. Most of the time."

I couldn't stop my smile, feeling thoroughly ridiculous for being so afraid. Did it even matter? In that moment it seemed that the only opinion of me that mattered was his. If he was the only person in the world that didn't despise me, it would be enough. My heart beat fast with the lies I had been telling it, the secrets I had been keeping.

I pulled away from James, wiping away my own tears and taking a deep breath. "I will meet you in the music room then. But first I must see to the guests."

When all the seats were full, people still stood around the outskirts of the room and in the hall surrounding it. Even Lord Trowbridge's home couldn't entirely accommodate such a large group of people. I wiped the sweat off the palm of my hand—the hand that would play the keys beside James. Mrs. Abbot had added us to the program, the last performance of the night. I wished I could sit back and enjoy the music, but my stomach fluttered too violently.

My eyes met James's across the room, and he smiled, trying to reassure me. But he looked nervous too. That made me feel better. I sat back, trying to breath normally. After an eternity, the song preceding ours ended. A young boy had played the fiddle while his sister sang, and I waited to compliment them before standing. I left one of my gloves on the seat of my chair when I stood, knowing how strange it must have looked to still wear a glove on one hand.

I sat down on the bench first, and thankfully it was longer than the one in the Abbots' home. James sat beside me, and I watched as he positioned the same music we had played before in front of us. I put my hand over the keys, but it shook. I focused my gaze on the music, and glanced at James once before I began. He nodded, I breathed, and I played the first note.

James joined in at the perfect moment, and I lost myself in the music, the beautiful stillness of it, the precise and flawless way it fit inside my heart. I forgot the spectators and any judgments they may have against me.

When the song ended and the room burst into applause, I stayed sitting at the bench a moment longer before turning around. James gave me a smile, a lopsided tip of his mouth and a warmness of his eyes that cheered and unsettled me at the same time. How could I go a day without seeing *that*? I didn't want to know the damage it would do to my already mangled heart.

I found my seat again, troubled and suddenly anxious to leave. I hadn't forgotten my rules, I had disregarded them. Staying away from James was the only way to reverse this change within me, to keep my feelings hidden and to remember my goals. It needed to stop. I considered not coming back, staying home alone for the twelfth night party, but then I remembered Clara. I could not abandon her.

Project 'Rosemary' was still necessary, and I hated to admit it, but I needed James's help.

For the rest of the Christmas Eve party, I avoided him, accepting the compliments of other guests and promising to send the same to James, although I knew I couldn't speak to him again tonight—not when I was so confused and emotional. I rubbed my eyes, eager to return home.

It was long after midnight when Clara and I finally climbed in the carriage and drove back to our cottage.

"Thomas didn't speak a word to me tonight," she said as she sat down on my bed, running a comb through her hair.

I yawned, pulling my blankets around me. Hope was waning, and I struggled to hold on to it. "James is going to help. If nothing changes by twelfth night, we will fix everything at the party. Not to worry." She just stared at me, not saying a word. Sorrow was heavy in her eyes and I hated to see it. I wondered if she could see the same in mine.

"How you have changed, Charlotte." Clara smiled, a subtle, reassuring lifting of her lips that buoyed my spirits. "It is wonderful to know that, for the first time in my life, someone cares for me."

I frowned. "Mama cared for you. She still does."

She shook her head. "I have been forced to believe that all Mama cares for is herself. I wish it wasn't true, but anything else is a lie."

"I *know* she cares for me. She wants only the best for me. She always has." My voice was growing shrill with a hint of uncertainty.

Clara sighed, tugging on the last knot in her hair. "If you choose to believe that, fine. But I cannot."

I was tense, and relaxed after her words. "It is only because the two of you do not always agree." I said. "Mama and I have the same beliefs, the same goals and opinions, so I suppose that is just why we get along better than the two of you."

"But do you still? You have changed and I'm not certain Mama's beliefs are truly yours any longer. You can be happy without all the things you had before, without all the pride and advantage of a calculated match." Clara's eyes showed true concern, but I tried to ignore it, choosing also not to listen to her.

"I—I cannot. It is all I have hoped for and dreamed of my entire life." My own voice seemed to be coming from a place that was much weaker than before—much more uncertain.

"That was before you came here . . . before you learned all you have, met the people you did. Before you met Mr. Wortham." She gave me a knowing glance.

I froze, feeling suddenly defensive and angry. "Don't suggest that he will keep me here, Clara. The very moment I have an opportunity to leave this place, I will. I'll forget everything about this town. I will not miss it. I won't." Even as I spoke the words I wasn't sure I believed them.

Clara sighed, long and slow. "The day you admit you love something, anything, anyone . . . I will probably faint out of disbelief." She gave a brief smile, then moved toward the door.

I stopped her, and sat down on my bed, head spinning with the memory of spinning lights from the party. "I wish I understood how you love so easily," I said in a quick voice.

She turned, halfway out of the doorway. "It is only difficult if you make it so." She smiled again and faded into the dark hallway.

I waited until I heard her door shut and saw the flicker of candlelight on the walls swallowed by the darkness. Exhausted and utterly confused, I fell back on my pillow. I did not want to think about anything right now, not Clara's words of advice, not Mama's expectations, not my own, and certainly not James's smile.

So I just fell asleep with an overflowing mind and a dry heart, trying to decide what was right and what was wrong—what was truth and what were lies.

Chapter 20

*"I know no ways to mince it in love,
but directly to say 'I love you.'"*

Twelfth night came on a Wednesday, and snow was falling. The days had been filled with an abundance of silk ribbons and golden papers, fresh greenery, and the decorating of masks—and my determined avoidance of James. I found that my head was clearer in his absence, but there was a deep well in my chest when I thought of him—which was more often than I liked.

To make tonight's twelfth night party entertaining, Mrs. Abbot, Rachel, Lucy, and I had created dozens of masks for the masquerade dance. They were also used for performances, so I finished painting the upturned lips and exaggerated eyes of one of our eccentric masks. I was proud that it turned out especially unique due to my limited use of my right hand. I held it up in front of my face and sneaked behind Lucy.

"Charlotte!" She gasped, clutching her chest. "That is truly dreadful." She laughed, holding up her own mask, a neat painting of pursed lips and triangular eyes.

"Horrifying," I said through a laugh.

I sat back and started on another, leaning my elbow on the windowpane beside me. We were almost finished, and soon I would return home to prepare myself for the party. I had spent little time thinking about how to help Clara and Lord Trowbridge. I felt terrible for being so selfish, but most of my worry had been directed at seeing James again, and how I could manage to avoid him. As far as I knew though, nothing had changed for my sister—Lord Trowbridge still seemed indifferent toward her, although I knew it wasn't true. There must have been a way to bring them together. I just needed to find it. But the letter was still a mystery to me. How could he have missed it? I bit my lip, struggling to understand so many things that seemed impossible.

"How is your hand healing?"

The question came from Rachel, breaking me from my thoughts. I cleared my throat. "Very well."

She eyed my glove. "You don't need to keep it covered around us. I assure you, we will not judge you for the sight of it."

I smiled. "That is very kind of you, but I am . . . more comfortable this way." I shifted in my chair.

"Quite well, I was just curious, that is all." She gave a soft smile and set to work again on her mask. "Who do you hope to choose as your partner tonight?" Her voice turned giddy.

My brow furrowed. "What?"

Mrs. Abbot looked up from her work, surprise crossing her face. "You have not heard of the tradition?"

I shook my head no.

"It is the very best part of the evening. Just before the dance, each lady draws a slip of paper from a hat with the name of a gentleman written on it. In the ballroom, she may look at the paper and find the gentleman there who will be her partner for the rest of the party."

Lucy grinned wickedly. "Last year I picked the name of the most handsome man . . ."

Her words quickly faded into the background of my thoughts. I could *not* pick James. Avoiding him had seemed possible, but if that happened it would be much more difficult. I quickly calmed my worries, reminding myself of how unlikely it would be for me to draw his name from so many. I relaxed, taking a breath to steady my nerves.

"So . . . who do you hope to pick then?" Rachel was looking at me again.

I shrugged, trying to appear more calm than I felt. "It doesn't matter to me."

"Of course it does!" She gave a sly grin to rival her sister's. "You hope to be partnered with Mr. Wortham."

My heart jumped. "I do not."

"You do! Oh, would that not be perfect?" She turned toward Mrs. Abbot. "We have spoken about how perfectly matched the two of you would be." She smiled at me. "And I can tell he is absolutely smitten by you."

Why did everyone keep saying that? "I can assure you he is not." I stood from my chair, eager to leave all these searching gazes that knew far too much about me. "I will leave now, but I'll be sure to return early for the rest of the preparations." I gave a shaky smile before turning toward the door and walking as fast as I could outside.

My heart quickened with every step, growing more and more nervous about this evening and what it could entail. I had too many questions—my heart was concealing too much from me, and I wasn't sure if I wanted to discover the truth it had to tell. Lies often served as a convenient barrier, a shield from the pain and complications truth always brought with it.

It was growing late, and I only had a few hours before the party would begin. When I stepped through the door of our cottage, I stopped. Clara was sitting on the sofa, wiping hasty tears from her cheeks. I hurried over and wrapped my arm around her, pulling her head to my shoulder. "What is the matter?"

She sniffled, and I felt something wet fall to my arm. "I—I can't do this anymore. I don't want to go to the party. I don't w-want to see Thomas ever again."

I patted her back, releasing a long breath. "I don't want to go either." My voice was nearly a whisper. Silence fell in the air, broken only by her irregular sniffling and the whimpers she tried to conceal. "But we must go," I said finally. "Try your very hardest to dry your tears, and we *will* go to the party."

She didn't seem to listen, but closed her eyes. "Perhaps you were right to want to leave this place. It would be much easier to live without Thomas if I wasn't forced to see him every day and if the reason he didn't love me was because I moved far away and he forgot about me."

I sighed. "Don't give up just yet, Clara. Something is bound to change tonight, I just know it."

She looked up at me, a puffy-eyed mess of tears. "But why don't you want to go to the party?"

I searched my mind for something to say, a way to skirt around the truth, but found nothing. "Because . . . *I* don't want to see James ever again."

She snorted, a strange noise that I couldn't tell if it was a result of crying or laughter. "I knew you loved him."

I sat back against the cushions, defeated and too exhausted to argue. I rubbed my head, trying to somehow push away all the thoughts that battled for my attention. Clara sat up straight and huffed a heavy breath. "But you are right. We must go to the party, and we will have a wonderful time."

"Yes." I sat up and looked her straight in the eyes. "We will both look more beautiful than ever, and we will not allow two silly men to destroy the happiness of our first twelfth night party."

She laughed. "Are you sure they are the silly ones? Look at us."

I smiled, pulling her into a quick embrace. "If Lord Trowbridge doesn't see what is right in front of him, then he is the silliest one for certain."

She took a deep breath and smiled. The sight warmed my heart and calmed my nerves. We hurried up the stairs to get ready for the party. It was beginning to feel like an obligation, but despite my misgivings, it would probably be an enjoyable evening. I had plenty to keep my mind occupied while I was there, but I would choose to just relax and have a wonderful time. Everything would be all right.

I stood in front of the mirror in my room and smiled. Before Clara came in to help me with my hair, I found my old list in the drawer of my writing desk. I unfolded the list and reviewed all my rules, running them through my mind like a tedious thread. *Never let him see how he affects you. Never admire the color of his eyes. Never look at his face for more than two seconds. Never let him make you blush. Never think about kissing him. Never spend time alone with him.*

Never fall in love with him.

The silver trim of my gown matched the pins in my hair perfectly. I wore a different pair of gloves, long white satin ones that reached my elbows. The fabric was thin and didn't conceal my hand as well as my thick, black ones, but at the moment I didn't care. My hair was pulled up with several curls pinned at the back of my head, with long strands framing my face. I stared into my own eyes in the mirror and saw a stranger dressed in these fine clothes and looking beautiful. It was odd, seeing my face looking back at me, and hardly recognizing it at all. My hands shook as I smoothed back a stray hair and straightened the scarlet skirt of my gown. Taking a deep breath, I turned away from the mirror.

Clara stood beside me. She wore an ivory dress with lace capped sleeves. Neither of us wore jewelry. We had sold or given away nearly all of it. I found I didn't miss it. I gave Clara a reassuring smile and moved behind her to straighten the bow at her waist. "You look beautiful, as always. Do not worry over Thomas. Let him go if you must and accept that you are well enough without him."

"But I cannot let him go. That is the problem." Her eyelids drooped and she released a heavy, burdened breath. "The very worst part about going to this party is knowing that I will see him and know that he *can* let me go. He already has."

"I don't believe that." I put my hand on her shoulder and tipped my head down to look at her, making up the few inches we differed in height. "Can you not be happy without him?"

She looked down at the floor. "I can . . . but I don't want to."

I stepped away, feeling the weight of her broken heart weighing heavily on my own. Determination found a home in me then, and I knew what I needed to do. Tonight I was going to do all I could to fix a broken heart, but not mine. Clara's heart was altogether kinder, happier, and more precious, and for the sake of the world, it needed to be whole again. There was no other option. Feeling a strange sense of new strength, I walked toward the door and held it open, smiling widely in an effort to lift Clara's spirits and ignore my own fears.

"Let us go now. Take a deep breath and walk through that door. We are going to the party and we will have—"

"A wonderful time," she finished, half of a smile on her lips.

When we stepped outside, the same carriage that took us to the Christmas Eve party was awaiting us, and we climbed inside. I watched the sky outside as we drove. The sky was dotted with stars that appeared to be much closer than they really were, and my muddled mind decided they were intentionally put out of reach, made to look like pretty dots of innocent light, but if ever one came close enough to touch, it would only burn and destroy. So the stars remained magnificent from a distance. Only from a distance.

My eyes caught similar dots of light in the windows of Lord Trowbridge's home, and my stomach fluttered against my will. I rubbed a layer of frost from the window for a better view, but my quick breaths quickly replaced it.

After the carriage had rolled to a stop and we had stepped inside the house, the smell of cinnamon and all kinds of herbs filled my nose. The house was warm with fire and friendly faces, and I spotted several guests who had brought masks of their own to wear. My smile widened.

As I surveyed the crowd, I noticed a familiar child standing beside her father, licking the pastel icing off the top of a tiny cake. She wore a familiar and oversized necklace, adorning a ragged brown dress and a sullen face that had been wiped clean with soap and a smile.

I walked over to her, and she noticed just as I came a few feet away. Her face lit up with recognition and her fingers flitted to the necklace at her collar.

"How lovely you look tonight, Caroline," I said as I stopped beside her, stooping to her height. "And what a beautiful necklace." I winked at her.

Her eyes grew brighter. "Papa let me wear it one last time for the party. Tomorrow he will sell it for food."

I considered her wide expression, full of joy and amazement. Where did she find the strength? "I'm afraid that was not a very wise decision by your papa. Just look at all these young boys he will have to keep away from you tonight."

Caroline giggled, casting her eyes up to her father, who glanced at us casually. He raised a single eyebrow and half his mouth lifted in a smile.

"Are you enjoying the sweets?" I asked her.

She nodded, offering a shy smile.

"May I teach you a trick?" I dropped my voice to a whisper. "If you tuck the top layer of your skirts into the ribbon at your waist, you may carry dozens of cakes out the door to eat tomorrow."

She giggled, a quiet bubble of a laugh. "Is that what you do?"

"Always." I winked. "We will be the same. But please keep it a secret."

"I will." She gave a resolute nod that made me smile. I glanced at her hair, lighter now than it had been before, washed free of the dirt. It was styled in a single braid down her back. I reached up to my head and removed one of my silver pins, making a strand of hair fall out of place. I took the end of her braid and twirled it around itself into a small knot at the base of her neck, and secured it with the silver pin.

"There. Now we look the same too. Although . . ." I tapped my lip, "I daresay you are the most beautiful girl in the entire house tonight." I smiled as she felt the pin on the back of her head in awe. "Have a marvelous time at the party." I stood up straight and stepped away before she tapped her father's shoulder to show him the new style of her hair.

My smile seemed irreversible now, and as I walked away, I steadied myself and refocused on the task I had come here to accomplish. A voice from behind me made my heart jump.

"I didn't think you could become more beautiful."

I turned slowly, steeling myself. James was smiling, just a soft lift of his lips that fluttered my heart and reminded me of every single smile and word and laugh that had belonged to him. Every piece of me he had stolen was reflected in his eyes, and I had no power to reclaim them. My cheeks tingled with heat at his compliment.

"I didn't think you could become more presumptuous."

He laughed, looking down at his boots, then back at my face. "Forgive me."

I smiled, hating myself for how much I enjoyed being beside him, talking with him, teasing him, laughing with him. It was all so unfair. "I assume you came to me because you have a plan to accomplish the deed we call 'Rosemary'?" I said.

"That is one reason." He smiled but it lasted one brief moment before it was gone, replaced by the same uncertainty from before, a secret and an unspoken question.

"How can we bring them together?" I asked quickly, keeping my gaze moving around the room, not settling for too long on his face.

"Do you know for certain that she loves him?" I heard the suspicion in his voice.

I dared a glance at his face. "Yes, I have no doubt. She has loved him for a very long time."

James's eyes were careful, withdrawn, and looking far too deeply into mine. I was afraid he could read my thoughts. My heart beat fast, begging me to believe that the words I spoke belonged to James, that I had loved *him* for a very long time. I wondered if it were true.

"And your brother? Do you know that he loves her?"

James took a deep breath and his eyes did not leave my face. "It was difficult to believe at first, but now there is no question. He loves her more than anything."

"Is there anything we can do? Or should we trust fate to the task?"

He smiled, one side of his mouth lifting more than the other. "If there is anything I don't trust, it's fate. Come now, Charlotte, we're clever. We'll find a way."

I searched the room, looking for clues and looking for a distraction. The awareness I felt of James standing beside me, every breath, every movement, was too much to bear at the moment. "We must separate. You speak to your brother, I to my sister, and we will meet again later to . . . conspire with our new information."

He nodded, trying to hide his amused smile. "Where will this conspiracy take place?"

"In this very spot. In one hour."

He chuckled. "Very well. I will see you in an hour, then."

I nodded and turned, eager to escape his gaze. My mind raced as I walked through groups of people, searching for Clara. I couldn't find her, so I just tried to find the farthest corner of the ballroom that I could hide where James wouldn't find me. Not now, not in one hour. I leaned against the wall and breathed, squeezing my eyes shut. I did not love him. I did not love him. *I did not love him.*

I opened my eyes and saw Mrs. Abbot and Lucy standing nearby. Relief flooded through me and I hurried toward them, knowing their conversation would serve as the perfect distraction. Mrs. Abbot looked up as I approached. "Charlotte, welcome! Did you try one of the cakes yet? We have them prepared every year but this year they reminded me of you." Her eyes crinkled at the corners and she whispered, "I must warn you . . . they are quite addicting."

The thought of eating cake right now made me sick. "I will have to try one." My smile was forced.

Mrs. Abbot glanced at the large clock hanging on the north wall then turned to Lucy. "Will you go fetch the guest book from the front room? The ladies will need to pick names soon and we ought to begin making the papers."

My stomach flipped over as Lucy left and I remembered that particular tradition. "How many gentlemen are here?"

"Oh, at least fifty unmarried. They are the ones who participate. Some are from out of town and considered quite eligible." Mrs. Abbot winked at me.

I allowed myself to relax a little, knowing my chances of being partnered with James were very slim. I spotted Sophia standing with the housekeeper just outside the ballroom in the hallway. She wore a pale green dress to match her eyes, with a ribbon in her hair and that familiar brown twine tiara partially concealed beneath ginger curls. I excused myself and walked over to Sophia, putting a smile on my face for her sake more than my own.

"Darling girl, I have missed you!" She heard my voice and looked up, grinning instantly.

She pulled her hand away from the woman's and walked over on the tips of her toes, holding the skirt of her dress.

"You look quite lovely this evening," I said, earning a giggle. "Would you like to help me with something? It is a very secret task, and I think we will make a perfect team."

She nodded, her face showing she intended to take the duty seriously.

I smiled. "First, tell me, are you fond of Clara?"

"Oh, yes! She is very kind and very smart. She is teaching me how to read, and how to count, and how to sing. I like her very much."

"I am glad to hear it. And does your father care for Clara?"

Sophia's forehead crinkled. "I don't know . . . he doesn't talk to her like he did before."

I leaned down and whispered, "That is what we need to fix. Because Clara loves your papa, very much."

Her eyes rounded. "She does?"

"Yes."

She gasped and rubbed her hands together in excitement. "Will she marry him?"

"I hope so. But first we must be sure your papa knows that Clara wants to."

"Will she tell him?" Sophia's voice was quiet now.

"She is afraid."

A crease settled between her eyebrows. "I tell Papa I love him every day."

The look on her face was so endearing I had to smile. "Then I suppose you are much braver than most. Clara did try to tell him, but she wrote him a letter instead. But that is the mystery, because we do not know where the letter went, or if your papa ever found it."

Her face lit up. "Miss Clara wrote a letter for me too! I can't read it yet, but when I'm big, I'll know how to read the fancy writing." She clasped her hands together and rocked back and forth. "I was in my night dress and sneaking a cake from the kitchen after bedtime, and then the letter came through the door, just for me! I peeked outside, but no one was there!"

My breath caught in my throat. "What?"

"I opened it up and it said Miss Clara's name at the bottom, so I put it in my bedchamber and I will read it when I'm big."

She was beaming now, and I was still trying to process her words. Sophia had the letter all this time! Lord Trowbridge never received it. I bent down and grabbed Sophia's arm. "You must find that letter. It was for your papa!" My mind spun.

"It wasn't for me?" Her face fell.

"Clara will write a new one, just for you. She will even teach you to read it if you wish. But first, please find the letter, and bring it back."

She gave a quick nod of her head and hurried across the ballroom and out the opposite door, holding her skirts up with one hand, showing several inches of her stockings.

I watched her until she was out of sight, then scanned the crowd for Clara, anxious to tell her of my new discovery. I found her standing alone on the outer edge of the ballroom, watching the crowd with the look of someone who wished to be anywhere else in the world but here.

"Clara!"

She looked up, surprised.

"Sophia has the letter! She had it all this time!" I lowered my voice. "Thomas never read it. He still doesn't know how you feel."

The color had begun to drain from her face, and I started to worry she would faint.

"Sophia is bringing the letter back to me, and we can dispose of it if you wish. The only thing left for you to do is tell him. Tonight! Tell him that you love him tonight."

She exhaled, slow and shaky. "But—there are so many people. Rejection with an audience is far worse."

"He won't reject you!"

I followed her eyes across the room to where Lord Trowbridge stood beside James. My breath hitched and I tore my gaze away. I looked at Clara again just in time to see her eyes fly open wide. "No," she breathed. Her hand clutched my arm. "No. No. No. No."

"What is it?" My gaze shot across the room again, and I gasped. Sophia was standing beside her father, holding up a folded sheet of parchment. I moved a step forward but knew it was too late. Lord Trowbridge looked down at her with confusion, taking the letter tentatively. Her lips moved, and she raised a tiny finger and pointed it in our direction.

My eyes flickered to James. He was watching me, one eyebrow raised in question. I was frozen where I stood, and my arm was turning numb from Clara's grip when Lord Trowbridge unfolded the letter and his eyes scanned the written words. The moment he looked up, Clara released my arm and rushed out the door behind us. I considered following her, but realized Lord Trowbridge already intended to, pushing past groups of guests, carried by long strides toward the same door she had exited through.

I pushed back a squeal of triumph, and found my gaze returning across the room to James. Instinctively, I looked away, but checked the clock. It had been one hour. There was no way to avoid him now.

When I looked at him again, he was already walking toward me, a baffled expression on his face. I met him in the middle of the room, near the same place we had met earlier. I cursed my heart for beating so loudly.

"As co-conspirators, I feel as though I should've been informed of that tactic," James said, smiling, a look of awe on his face. "Care to enlighten me?"

I explained everything from the night the letter was delivered to my conversation with Sophia.

"A stroke of genius on Sophia's part." He chuckled. "Perhaps you should've always consulted her before me."

I shrugged. "A girl not six years of age has bested us. She understood what we did not, I suppose."

"Love must be much simpler than either of us suspect." He was smiling, but there was something hidden in his eyes.

"I wish it was." The words came without my permission.

James looked at me, locked in my eyes like a door without a key, and the air between us grew taut and painful with too many questions and too much heartache. I wished it was easier, I wished a future in the South living in a grand home and making my mother proud wasn't such a contradiction to this man, his contagious laugh and endearing smile, his words of comfort and that overwhelming feeling of acceptance and safety. It stung, deep inside, and I begged my mind to forget him. I wished that was easier too.

It was only a few seconds later when Lucy appeared beside me. I tore my eyes away from James with effort, and tried my hardest to smile.

"All the ladies are to meet in the drawing room immediately. We are picking names," Lucy said.

I nodded, allowing her to pull me with her by the arm. I glanced at James one more time, but he was looking down, scuffing his boot across the marble floor, arms crossed.

Once we reached the drawing room, the giggling I had heard from a distance before was now a full roar, echoing in high trills as a top hat filled with miniscule slips of paper was passed from lady to lady. I searched the room for Clara and found her, standing beside Rachel, eyes scanning the room. They landed on me, and her face broke into a smile and she rushed to my side. Relief flooded through me at the look on her face—a mixture of joy and surprise with a hint of embarrassment.

She pulled me away from the crowd of ladies and whispered, "He loves me, Charlotte! You were right. You were right! And—and he said he was wrong to be so aloof, and that he was sorry. And . . ." Her cheeks turned pink. "He kissed me."

I couldn't stop my grin. "I am not surprised."

She took my hand, and I noticed in her eyes a brightness that had been missing for a long time. "Thank you. If you had not intervened I would still be grim and Thomas would still be blind. You are the world's most amazing sister."

"Stop with the flattery." I rolled my eyes half-heartedly. "You owe your gratitude to little Sophia. Your future stepdaughter?" I raised an eyebrow in question.

"He didn't propose marriage yet, but we were interrupted." Her cheeks were still flushed and her smile could not have been wider. "Do you think he will?"

"Of course." I shared her smile, trying to absorb happiness from her, to somehow replace the confusion and emptiness I felt within myself.

I turned at a tap on my shoulder from behind where a young woman with black hair stood, extending the top hat to me. "Have you chosen a name yet?"

I shook my head as she held the hat closer to me. My hand was shaking and I hoped no one noticed. There were still several names inside the hat, but each was well concealed, folded in quarters and tucked in at the corners. I peered at the papers, trying to guess which paper would have James's name written on it, so I could be sure not to choose him. It was impossible though, so I just reached in and grabbed the first one I saw.

I crumpled it in my fist, too afraid to read it, and looked at Clara.

She plucked a paper from the top of the pile inside the hat and raised an eyebrow, keeping hers concealed as well. "What name did you choose?"

"I don't know yet."

"Shall we read them together?" Her cheeks were still flushed with joy and I felt a small pang of jealousy. I pushed it away. Clara's worries were over with for the time. She was happy, free. I tried my best to feel the same.

My breath quickened as I fought with myself over wanting James's name, desperately, to be written on that paper, and hoping I could somehow depart from this party—from this town—without ever seeing him again. I didn't know which option would cause me more pain, but it was all so complicated it made my head spin.

All around me ladies were already reading their names, each face either squealing in delight or marred with a frown. "Very well, Clara. But no cheating."

"I wouldn't dream of it." She smiled. "On the count of three. One."

"Two."

"Three!"

I opened my hand and rubbed the paper between my fingers to flatten the creases before focusing on the name written on it. The ink had smudged on the first letter, but the rest was easy to read.

The Earl of Trowbridge

My eyes flew to Clara in shock. Her eyes lifted from her paper and she scowled at my expression.

"I have Lord Trowbridge," I said, my voice hushed.

It was difficult to tell, but a wisp of a smile touched her lips. "You must switch names with me then. It is only fair. Please."

I nodded, and after checking to be sure no rule-abiding woman would come snatch the papers from our grasp, I slipped my paper into Clara's hand and she did the same with hers. A brief look of triumph settled on her face but it was peculiar, something hinting at mischief behind her eyes.

"I will meet you in the ballroom." She slid out the door with the other young ladies. I frowned and my gaze drooped downward, toward the new paper I now held. It was folded twice, and I opened it in one swipe. *No.* My heart skittered and I covered the words again, holding the paper against me. I sneaked one more peek, hoping I had imagined it. But no, written in the softest, graceful hand of Rachel Abbot were fourteen letters, arranged to create the name I had most feared to see.

Mr. James Wortham

Chapter 21

"My drops of tears I'll turn to sparks of fire."

I cursed my sister under my breath. How could she knowingly put me in this situation? Even after all I had done to help her with Thomas? My gaze darted to the door, but she was long gone, and the trail of ladies I could see in the hallway through the open door were all laughing and smiling. My chest constricted with a sudden fear. I was afraid of the things James made me feel and how they were such a parallel to the things I had been taught were to be frowned upon.

Without thinking, I was moving toward the door and the hall of giggling young ladies. We had been told to meet our partners in the ballroom, where we would be given further instruction. I tried to stop myself, but I followed the line into the ballroom, and my eyes had to adjust to the dim light. It was warmer in here. My hands grew slick with sweat inside my gloves.

And then there he was, across the room, smiling that devilish smile, eyebrow cocked as he watched Clara find Lord Trowbridge and show him his name on the paper that used to be mine. Then James's smile softened to one of relief as he watched them together and my breath caught. Oh, he was loved.

I feared I couldn't do it. The slip of paper that bore his name was now an embarrassing ball in my hand. My fist was clenched so tight I felt the sting of my fingernails against my palm. All around me, the room was full of excitement and hearty laughter, faces drawn in shock over the good fortune—or misfortune—of their assigned partners. James was standing alone, and I made my decision, or rather, my feet made the decision for me. I was walking forward, more shy than I had ever been in my life. More afraid. More raw and vulnerable and confused. I watched the floor until I was a short distance away.

I stared at James's boots until the blasted man lifted my face to look at his, nudging my chin up with a bent finger, half a smile on his lips and a question in his eyes. "How many pounds did you have to pay out to secure my name?" He was looking at the crumpled paper in my hand.

"Only a thousand."

"I'd wager you planted a few facers too, as you fought madly over me, just to be sure you met success."

"One of the women is nursing a nosebleed as we speak." It was a wonder how these conversations came so easily, even when I really didn't want to make him smile.

"As I suspected."

"I did it for Clara," I blurted. "I chose your brother's name first, and she offered a trade, but that was before I knew it was your name she had picked."

I expected him to grin, make another joke, but instead something in his expression seemed to fall. He smiled anyway. "Ah. Clever move on your part, of course, partnering your sister with my brother against all odds. Sacrificing your chance with a wealthy Lord in exchange for an evening with me that is to be *endured*."

I peeked at his face and realized all traces of humor were gone. He looked hurt, and it tugged at my heartstrings. "James—I won't apologize for having ambitions. But rest assured I have given up on pursuing your brother." My voice was defensive, and I realized how terrible I sounded—how heartless.

He bristled, but after a moment, his face washed over with calmness and he rubbed his forehead. "I wish I could stay angry with you, Charlotte" he repeated. "It would make everything much less . . . complicated."

I didn't have a chance to ask what he meant before Mrs. Abbot was calling for our attention, her husband at her side. "I welcome you all once again to our annual town twelfth night celebration. I see you have all found your partners." A mumble of approval rolled through the room. "As the most anticipated event of the evening, we will begin, as always, with a waltz."

My stomach was very near depositing its contents all over the slick marble floors. Mrs. Abbot signaled the musicians and I knew the song would begin soon. Blood rushed past my ears and heat tingled my face. I didn't move, scowling in Mrs. Abbot's direction, begging her to change tradition.

"Come now, Charlotte. The other guests will worry."

I turned my scowl back to James. His face was careful, tentative, as he reached slow and unwavering for my hand. "I am the only one who knows what that frown of yours really means." His other hand wrapped around my waist, gentle at first, then more pressing, pulling me closer to him as the music began.

My breath was lodged in my throat, and I found my gaze trapped on the creases his smile marked beside his eyes, the dimples in his cheeks, and the points of his lashes when his eyes were narrowed down at me so closely.

"And what does it mean?" I found it difficult to frown when his smile told me how much he enjoyed the sight.

"It means you adore me, remember?"

"No, I'm afraid I don't."

"You don't remember, or you don't adore me?"

"Both."

Although he was smiling, he looked far from laughter, and I knew why. This topic of conversation was much less humorous than it once had been. We turned to the song, and I found that I didn't think once of the steps, the poise I had practiced for hours with my instructor, or the ridicule from Mama as she watched me and told me my back was not straight enough.

I could think only of James, the warm strength of his hand, the way he didn't care that my deformed hand lay in his, and how his eyes bore into mine, searching for answers that I didn't have or dare to discover.

"Perhaps if I inquire of your feelings for me often enough, one day you'll give me the answer I want to hear." His voice was quiet. I might have imagined it, but his hand at my waist pressed me closer.

This wasn't fair. How could I remain so close to him, knowing nothing for certain, a prisoner of a heart that didn't even belong to me anymore. The longer I looked at his face, the more I wondered how long my heart had been his, and how he had managed to manipulate it without my permission.

"I can't."

His smile was gone, a broken look replacing it, one that made me ache to see. "You can't, or you won't?"

I thought of my hopes and dreams. Of Mama's approval and society's praise, and my jaw set firm against the tears behind my eyes and I said, "Both."

He was silent then, and it was James that looked away from me, with him keeping his secrets and me keeping mine. The dance wasn't over, so still we turned to the haunting music, and it was all I could do not to beg his forgiveness and tell him the truth.

So we danced, a handsome young man scarred by love, and a pathetic young lady who didn't want anything to do with it.

"Was that really necessary?"

Clara had her hand planted on her hip when she walked through our door a little after midnight. I was still slumped on the sofa, unblinking and quiet.

"You would pretend to be ill just to be driven home early. Just to escape Mr. Wortham?" Her gaze didn't waver.

"Yes," I croaked.

She walked over and pushed my legs off the sofa so she could sit beside me. "You are such a hypocrite."

Her bluntness surprised me.

"How do you put forth so much effort to ensure my happiness but do nothing for the sake of your own? You have been an advocate of love these last weeks, Charlotte, yet you deny yourself any part of it. Why?"

I didn't feel like speaking. I hardly felt like doing anything but squeezing my eyes shut and falling asleep, if only to stop the tears. But as soon as I shut my eyes against Clara, my throat tightened in a knot and tears fell from the corners of my eyes anyway. I breathed a shaky breath and stayed silent.

I sensed Clara's disposition change, and her voice fell to a gentle apology. "You could have such a joyful life here. It really is beautiful if you look hard enough. The people are so lovely and kind, and the Abbots have treated us so well. I will be here, I hope. I don't mean to be presumptuous, but I will likely be living just down the road. There is no place else for you to go. So choose to be happy here because that is the only option. And you and James . . . Charlotte, you must know that you are loved. I love you, the Abbots love you, he loves you."

My eyes snapped open. "He doesn't love me." I stood, swaying on my feet at the sudden movement.

"Charlotte—"

"No." I put my hand up to stop her words and walked toward the stairs. She didn't follow me.

Still wearing my red gown and satin gloves, I almost tripped up the narrow stairs and my hand slipped on the railing. When I reached the top I turned toward my room. All I was aware of was my breathing, the hitched sound as I fought against the onslaught of emotion that roiled through me. I pushed through the door and to my desk. After pulling my gloves off, I pressed my palms against it and leaned forward, trying to calm myself and discover why I was feeling the way I was.

What if Clara was right? What if I could be happy? I looked up at my reflection in the mirror above the desk. My eyes were rimmed in red and my lips were pressed tight. What if I was forced to stay here forever? The thought struck me with fear. How could I be comfortable knowing all the things I was missing, and all the things I could never have again? I refused to settle, to not achieve what eighteen years of instructing had intended me to achieve. I replaced the bars around my heart stronger, more unwavering than before.

But then I looked at the round knob of the drawer of my writing desk, and my heart softened all over again. I was too curious now.

I pulled the drawer open and withdrew James's love letter with a shaking hand. I held it like it was a fragile, infinitely precious thing as I unfolded it. I realized as my eyes first met the parchment, that I had never really seen James's writing before, and every line, curve, and shape seemed to suit him flawlessly.

I made one more attempt to stop myself from reading it, but I was too weak, and every piece of me longed for something that belonged to him, for some piece of his heart to hold. I swallowed hard and let my eyes lap over the page, reading the words that weren't mine.

My love,

I wish I had the courage to speak these things aloud to you, but I don't. You have stolen my heart, and your friendship has been a balm for my aching heart these last months, and I wish to dearly thank you. You will forever be in my heart, and although you find me lacking, I can't bear the thought of being without you. Even if you cannot find it within you to return my love, then please return to me. Let me see your face again. I will be waiting, always, for you.

James

I ached everywhere, and pain burned through me for James's sake, for his broken heart. I clutched my throat, where a tight ball had formed, and tears streamed down my cheeks. It wasn't fair. None of it. It wasn't fair that this woman had been so cruel and it wasn't fair that James had been so hurt. Guilt clouded my eyes. I read the words again and again, until it was too much to bear.

And then I tore it in half. Squinting through angry tears, as well as my poorly functioning hand would allow, I tore it in half again and again, until it was a pile of disjointed words on the desk. When I was finished I stared at the shreds with wide eyes, dazed and shocked, and then I put my arm down on the table and lay my head in the bend of my elbow. I was shaking.

I tried to puzzle out why it had affected me so much. It could have been because I cared about James, and I didn't want him to be hurt, or it could have been because it was so hard to believe that James had loved like that, and how real he had made it seem. And maybe because somewhere deep inside, I wished every word had been for me.

I stood from the chair, legs shaking, and plodded in a daze to my bed. My brain was tired of thinking and my heart was tired of feeling. As I faded off to sleep, I imagined a life where I stayed in the North forever, and where I smiled on the worst of days, all because James held my hand. It was ridiculous, and I tried to stop imagining it, but again, I was too tired.

Chapter 22

*"Let me be that I am
and seek not to alter me."*

When Clara returned home the following day, her smile was so wide I worried her face would become frozen that way. Lord Trowbridge had offered for her, and she had accepted, of course.

I was happy for her, and it took all my energy to cling to her excitement and joy when I found it impossible to find my own. Clara's cheeks were touched pink, and she looked simply radiant. I smiled as she relayed to me every detail.

"We are to be married in two months' time," she said. "That will allow plenty of time for his aunts to travel here to help with the preparations. Did you know he has six aunts? I hear they are all delightful . . ."

She carried on with the details of her day while we sat together on the sofa. It was strange, the joy I felt at seeing her now. The way her dreams had all come true, and I couldn't help but compare them to my own. A sinking feeling mingled with the happiness I felt for her as I realized how hopeless the possibility was of me ever accomplishing my goals and returning to the life I had before. My head ached from the events of the previous day, and I found myself easily distracted.

I shook myself and cleared my throat to speak. "Mama will be pleased to hear it."

Clara froze. "I'm not telling Mama."

"Why? You must! Don't be ridiculous."

She looked down at her lap, wringing her hands together. "Well . . . I—I just don't want to tell her. Please don't say a word."

I scowled. "There must be a reason."

Clara was suddenly defensive. "She will claim responsibility for the match. She will reap the benefits of our living and . . . after how she has treated me, treated us, our entire lives . . . I don't believe she deserves it." Her voice carried a hint of bitterness that surprised me. She recognized the harshness of her words and tried to recover, eyes wide. "I would just prefer that her opinion of me not be based upon the advantage of my marriage. Does that make sense?"

I thought about what she said, a warning that I didn't recognize flashing in my head. "But she will still expect that I marry him, and I can't continue lying to her."

"Then don't." Clara's eyes bore into mine. "Tell her you do not wish to marry for advantage."

"But I do!" My voice was rising now.

"Whose advantage, Charlotte?"

Her words rang in my ears. "What?"

"Whose advantage would you marry for? Because not allowing yourself to love, clinging to these ridiculous ideas of a happy life . . . it's ruining you. Tell Mama the truth and don't let her stop you. Make new dreams for yourself, set new goals, let go of the things you left behind because they have certainly let you go. Please, I beg of you, don't become the person you once were."

I felt defeated, and a thousand questions rolled through my head at once. "Do I have a choice?" My voice sounded hollow.

She smiled, a soft shift of her lips and a gentleness in her eyes. "Make the most of your life here. Find James and tell him how you feel. You helped me and now it is my turn. If I must be a meddlesome scoundrel, I will."

For the first time, I truly considered it. Living here in that tiny house of his, smiling and laughing, shopping in the village under a gray sky, eating fish and spending evenings playing whist with Clara and Lord Trowbridge, while Sophia ran about in her pretty dresses and twine tiaras. A fierce longing for that life came over me in waves.

But all the while I saw the edges of my imagination barred in steel. There was more than this. How could I ever settle?

My eyes fell downward, and I noticed Clara shift in her seat. It was a subtle movement, but I saw a corner of a torn piece of parchment fall hidden beneath her skirts.

"What is that?" I pointed.

Her eyes flew open. "What?" She shifted again.

I reached across her and pulled what appeared to be an opened letter out from beneath her. "This." I frowned when I saw the wax seal—our seal. "This is from Mama? Why did you try to conceal it?"

Her face fell. "Please stay, Charlotte! I know you won't want to, but please."

Hardly listening to her, I unfolded the letter and read, heart pounding with anticipation.

My daughters,

It has been four long months, and I presume that if you haven't been engaged by now to Lord Trowbridge, you never will. Therefore, I took matters into my own hands. Mr. Bentford, my dear cousin, has finally opened his eyes and my schemes have met success. We are to be married! He offered for me not two days ago. He is growing richer by the day with his miraculous business investment and is gaining respect among society. I expect they should all overlook our past disgrace and accept us anew. Our good fortune does not end there. Two young men have moved into town, Mr. Webb and Mr. Morely. They both have inherited large estates in the country and Mr. Webb will soon obtain his father's title. We invited them to dine with us and both were quite smitten by your portrait, Charlotte.

So, in light of these recent events, remaining in Craster will no longer be necessary. I have sent a coach to convey you home which should arrive promptly on the eighth, should the weather hold. I look forward to your arrival and our reunion.

Mama

The air seemed to have been drawn out of the room, and silence hung heavy. I stared at the letter until my eyes went out of focus. Mama was inviting me home. I read it again, just to be sure it was real. There the words were, right in front of me, plain and certain. My gaze shot to Clara. "Why would you keep this from me?" My heart thumped. "The eighth . . . that's tomorrow."

"Don't go, Charlotte!" she cried. I hadn't noticed the tear on her cheek.

I was quiet as my mind spun, trying to piece together the news I had just received. I had been so close to excusing the possibility of ever returning home, but now here it was, an invitation and a second chance. I would be a fool not to take it.

"I'm going."

Her eyebrows tipped down and new tears wet her eyes. "Don't make such a mistake! You are not thinking clearly. Please. Please stay!" She held my arm in an unrelenting grip, as if that alone could keep me here.

"No." I was still in a daze, hardly believing what had just happened. A stroke of good fortune was as rare as a living flower in this dreary town.

"Charlotte, please! Don't be so rash. Think of James!"

That made me stop, and made my heart quake a little. But I set my jaw and made my decision. How could four short months be enough to reverse the beliefs I had upheld for years? I shook my head clear and tucked my heart away where I couldn't find it. I pulled my arm away from Clara's grasp.

"Please help me pack my trunk."

She slapped a hand over her mouth, biting back muffled sobs. "No, Charlotte! Don't do this. Don't do this."

I looked away, standing up and walking to the staircase, numb and determined. This was what I wanted. This was what I wanted. My feet stomped on the wood, creating a rhythm for the chant in my head. *This was what I wanted.* Wasn't it?

I could still hear Clara on the main floor—the soft whimpers and sniffling. I stood in my doorway for a moment, wondering why she cared so much. The thought of leaving had been so impossible, and the news that I could leave had been so sudden that I hadn't stopped to consider how it would affect everyone here, including myself. Clara could still be happy. She was marrying the man she loved. She would live in a beautiful home and never work another day of her life. She would have Thomas, Sophia, Mrs. Abbot, Rachel, and Lucy. And I would have Mama and perhaps this Mr. Webb, and a beautiful home of my own.

As I considered this, I was struck with the realization of all the things I wouldn't have. Clara, the Abbots, James. *James.* My heart pinched at the thought.

Trying to distract myself, I hurried to my trunk and began packing my things. And as if to remind me of an important thing I had forgotten, my hand stood out pale against the crimson gown I packed away. Mama didn't know about the injury. I had chosen not to tell her, but I had nearly forgotten about it myself. Everyone here didn't seem to notice it. But what would Mama think? I tried to reassure myself, packing with renewed energy. All would be well. She had always cared about me. Nothing could change that. And even if she did despise it, I could conceal it in my glove and find a suitable match, and then all would be well. I tried my hardest to smile as I worked, but every time James crept into my thoughts, I found my smile wiped away.

Would I ever come back to this place after I left? How could I, if I knew James would be here? I cursed fate for making him so poor, yet so easy to love. My chest constricted with the ache of knowing the last time I would see him was the previous night. He couldn't know. I would leave without bidding farewell to him. It would be easier that way for both of us.

I didn't know for certain if he cared for me at all, or if everything he had done and said was just a result of his much too kind heart, but I couldn't help but wonder what me leaving this place would do to him. Was anything worth breaking such a heart? I thought of the woman he loved before and guilt jolted through me as I realized that if he did care for me, I was just like her.

When my trunk was full, I placed my thickest gloves on top of it. The sky outside was dark, and my eyelids were growing heavy. The things I felt now would pass. I would forget everything about the past four months and remember the way life was before I met James Wortham. And if I was capable of forgetting him, then surely he could forget me. His heart would heal and so would mine. Tomorrow I would leave Craster at last.

Clara was gone most of the following day, and she had hardly spoken to me that morning. I had positioned my small trunk by our front door. I waited, trying not to think or feel, watching out the window as fat snowflakes spiraled in slow motion from the sky. As always, I counted them as they fell.

Hours passed, and still no carriage arrived. I was afraid to step outside, knowing the possibility of seeing the Abbots, or James, was very real. While I hoped the carriage would arrive soon, I also wanted to bid Clara a proper farewell before I left. She usually returned home at this time, but there seemed to be a delay.

I grew impatient, trapped within the walls of stone and wood and distorted glass. I shivered, and tightened my cloak around my shoulders. Where was Clara? Although she didn't approve of my decision to leave, I needed her here, if only for the company. I didn't know how much longer I could bear to be alone with my variable and indecisive thoughts. Taking a deep, quaking breath, I pushed the door open and stepped outside, dragging my trunk behind me. I breathed the fresh, chilling air, and walked down the steps to where I could see the sky.

Flakes of snow landed in my hair, in the strands that hung in drab chunks on my shoulders. I stared at the sky. I never thought I'd miss the color. I wondered if I would ever see the same shade again. The thought made me sad.

I don't know how long I stood there, breathing the cold air that smelled faintly of fish and salty seawater, but when I closed my eyes I was hoping, against my will, that I would never forget that smell.

Feeling a sense of release, I turned, prepared to retreat back to my perch in the doorway, but something caught my eye and set my heart racing.

There, passing the nearest snow-blanketed tree—walking straight toward me, was James.

In an instant I turned away and turned back again, caught between being weak and being strong, staying or hiding. What was he doing here? I had strengthened my barriers, reminded myself of my goals and dreams, and how close I was to finally achieving them. But all that resolve had already begun to fall apart at the sight of him. James was moving fast, and soon he would be here beside me, too close and too safe, and I would fall apart.

I begged myself to relax. My legs were already shaking, and my heart was pounding so hard it hurt. My rules were disassembled in my head. But they were no use to me now, so I just crossed my arms over my chest to keep myself from bending and breaking any more for him.

James was only a few paces away now. He stopped, an abrupt change, and I tried not to look too closely at his eyes—at all the things I knew would unravel me. I raised my eyes to his face, trying to appear as if nothing were wrong. But the sight of him then, the raw emotion in his expression, told me he already knew. There would be no more pretending. No more lies.

We both just stood there, not speaking, as snow fell all around us—softly, slowly, a barrier between us that I wished were stronger. He knew I was leaving. He would try to stop me, but I couldn't let him. I tightened my grip on my heart.

"How did you know?" I asked. My voice shook and I looked away.

He drew closer, careful and slow. "Your sister told me."

Of course. Didn't she know I had already made my decision? That seeing James would only bring unnecessary pain to both of us?

"Don't assume you can make me stay," I blurted. "The carriage will be here soon."

"I never assumed that. I have learned that no one can make you do something you don't want to do." He took a deep breath, and his eyes searched my face. "But the reason I'm here, is because I'm not sure you want to leave."

I bit my lip against the sudden tears that stung my eyes. "Yes, I do." My voice was quiet and uncertain, and I hated the sound.

"Are you certain?" he asked.

My eyes snapped up to his face, and I regretted looking the moment I did. A broken heart was reflected there, in every line, every inch, and it tore me apart to see it. Then he came closer. His head tipped down to look at mine, and I wasn't capable of looking away this time. His eyes bore into mine, begging, soft and fragile. James had never been fragile. That had always been me.

"Please, Charlotte," he whispered. Nothing could have been a sweeter, crueler sound than his voice speaking my name, *Charlotte*.

Everything that had been holding me together, every defense, every bar and tightly knotted thread was coming undone. James had some power over me. He always seemed to pull out the weak and broken things from inside me and make me feel things I didn't want to feel and hope for things I shouldn't. Every thought, every reason I was leaving came pouring out in anger and wrenching heartache.

"I have to leave!" I cried. "Nothing can keep me here! Do you know how long I have waited for this? My mother wants me to come home! She didn't banish me here forever! I will go home and finally accomplish everything I have worked for my entire life!" My voice sounded unfamiliar to my own ears, broken by emotion and stifled sobs. "I w-won't fall short again, and I won't disappoint her! This is my l-last chance to please her and secure the future I have always wanted!" I breathed and swiped my cheeks. "It is my last chance to show her I can be the d-daughter she wants and then maybe she'll love me."

James reached out and cupped one side of my face with his hand. My body shuddered with another sob, and I was too weak to push him away. My tears fell hot down my cheeks and his hand.

His eyes looked into mine, firm and gentle at once. "Charlotte, that isn't love! Approval of meeting expectations isn't love. You deserve more. You have undertaken too much and *you* have become too much. You are kind and generous and thoughtful, utterly maddening at times, and selfless. Don't let her change that. You deserve to be loved for those things, nothing less."

I stepped back, away from the warmth of him and I shivered. "You know nothing of love." I shook my head. "It is pain and suffering. A weakness. What has it done to you? It has done nothing but break and destroy and hurt. Why should I aspire to that?"

He was quiet for several moments, watching me without an answer. Finally he said, "You're wrong. Love only does those things when you push it away." He looked down at me, and a thousand things I didn't understand were written on his face. "So don't."

I stared back at him, at the snowflakes on his shoulders and his hair, and the raw heartache in his eyes. How easy it would be to say yes, to be wrapped in his arms and never leave. I didn't know it would be this hard. My heart beat fast, like wings learning to fly, trying desperately to escape my chest and land safely in his hands.

"No. No!" I stepped even farther away and wrapped my arms around myself. "I need more than that."

"You think you need wealth and prestige to be happy? Don't make such a mistake. Those things won't last."

"And love will? How can you say that, James? *How* after all Mary did to you?"

That silenced him. He stepped back, rubbing his face and then he drew a ragged breath. "Because she never loved me. Not really. If she did, she would never have made the choice she did."

"That cannot be true." My voice was hard and cold. "Perhaps she was just stronger than her heart. She needed more."

"More than me?" James's eyes were framed in betrayal and sorrow. When he spoke I wished I hadn't been forced to hear the sound—all shattered fragments of the voice I knew. "And is that what you need too? Is that what you want?"

I didn't know how to answer. It wasn't a fair question. He didn't know the truth and I could never let him know it. If he knew I loved him, then he would never let me leave. He was still standing several steps away, and I shivered in the cold. I kept my lips pressed tight as quiet tears ran down my cheeks and fell from my chin, not willing to answer him. I didn't know my answer. And I had lied to him too much already.

"Charlotte," he ran his hand over his hair. "Please stay. You will learn how to be happy. You will learn how to love."

"I can't." I shook my head. "I can't."

I looked up at him and immediately wished I hadn't. His cheeks were streaked with tears of his own. His voice trembled. "Don't do this to me again." He didn't have to explain what he meant for me to know. I was Mary. "I thought I loved her, Charlotte. But I know now that can't be true. Because I no longer care. I have moved on, I have recovered. But if you leave . . . I shall never recover. My heart will never forget you. I'll never stop loving you. I didn't say these things to her, but I'm saying them now, to you. I'm begging you to stay."

My heart pounded fast. It was too much—everything he was offering me. I ached with longing everywhere, but there was danger in the unknown. It would haunt me forever. Not knowing what I was abandoning by staying here. Not knowing the life I could have had. I closed my eyes and I could see it. My dreams, my pursuits and ambitions, approval and happiness. Never had I been so conflicted.

I searched my mind for any reason that his declaration could be false. "How can that be true? If you loved me, then why did you leave me so abruptly at the Abbots'? Why did you act as if I—as if I *disgusted* you? You told me. You said you couldn't love. Not again." I was shaking my head.

James gave an exasperated sigh. "I was afraid. I have seen so much heartache, so much pain and suffering at the hands of love. I was afraid of what you were doing to my heart, Charlotte." His eyes met mine, careful. "You were stealing more and more of my heart, day after day, but I knew how much you hated me. I knew that I was not worthy in your eyes. I knew, too well, how acutely you would come to hate me for what I caused to happen to your hand."

"James! Please don't. It is not your fault." I pleaded with my eyes. "I don't hate you. I never will." A fresh tear slid down my cheek and my chin trembled.

"But you don't love me." His voice was final, a statement begging to be contradicted. His eyes pulled at mine, as if he were waiting for an answer.

There was nothing I could say. He couldn't know the truth. Not this time. I did love him. I knew it with a deeply embedded certainty that scratched all the way through my heart. The thought crossed my mind again—the question of staying or leaving. No. *No.* My decision had been made. I couldn't let James reverse that decision! I couldn't let something as fickle as love change that decision.

The pain stung me anew, and a fresh wave of sobbing choked me and I turned away from him. "I-I'm leaving! You can't change my mind! I'll just f-forget everything! I'll forget the village and the gray skies and the s-sea and this house. I'll forget the Abbots and their kindness and their pianoforte. I'll forget my lost fingers and lost music. I'll forget everything I've lost and everything I'll never have again." I was choking now. "I'll forget the p-pain and suffering and sorrow! And eventually I believe I can even forget you."

There was a brief lapse of time, a moment of indecision, before James moved. One step and one breath before he was there, my face in his hands, and he was kissing me.

There was nothing I could do to stop it. My left hand clutched his jacket, pulling him close, and my other hand rested at his neck, his hair, a broken hand that he didn't mind at all. His kiss was all desperation and heart, a warmth that reached to my bones, begging me for something I couldn't give. I tasted the salt of tears on his lips, mine or his, I couldn't tell. My legs were shaking beneath me and I trembled in his arms.

I knew this needed to stop. Now. It was wrong, it wasn't fair. And then his lips slowed, his kisses so gentle my heart broke all over again, and he pulled away, just far enough that I could see his eyes and the tears that shone there.

"But you won't forget that. I promise you won't," he said in a hoarse whisper.

I sighed, a shaky sound, and allowed myself a moment to feel, to love and be loved. I pressed my face into his shoulder, breathing the smell of him, trying to memorize it before it was too late. I knew what I was doing. I was making the right choice. It was the only choice I was capable of.

"Good-bye, James." My voice cracked the moment my heart did.

I waited three seconds, then pushed myself away, crossing my arms over my chest again. I didn't dare look at his face because of how close—how very close—I was to letting him win. Letting him change my mind.

The rattling of wheels called my attention, and I saw the carriage, the one meant to take me home, rolling down the road toward us. Before I could be weakened again, I turned and took hold of the handle of my trunk. My arms shook as I dragged it behind me, leaving a trail in the new snow as the coach parked in front of my little cottage. I bit back the tears that came and tried not to think about James standing there alone in the snow. But then my trunk lifted behind me.

I turned, surprised to see James carrying it. My hand fell away and something broke inside me.

He always was too kind.

His jaw was set, and his eyes flickered to me one more time as he helped the coachman strap it to the back of the carriage. He knew I had made my choice.

I stepped inside the carriage, where my maid sat, sent to accompany me. The door was still open, and I wanted to thank James, to apologize, to say *anything*, but nothing seemed to be enough. I just looked at him as he walked away, memorizing every detail, and altering the stooped shoulders to be strong, and the tears I had seen in his eyes to be ones of laughter. I didn't want to remember him this way. I wished I hadn't broken his heart.

I tore my gaze away from James and the carriage rolled forward. Don't look back, I ordered myself. *Don't look back.* But I panicked, disobedient, and sneaked one more glance at him. He just stood there, watching me leave until I couldn't see him anymore and he couldn't see me. He was gone. I had been holding my breath, and I let it out, slowly, a hitched sound that resembled a sob.

And as we barreled down the road toward home, I looked out the carriage window and watched the flakes of snow fall. And then I counted them.

Chapter 23

"Absence from those we love is self from self— a deadly banishment."

I slept for most of the first day of the journey. The carriage hadn't picked me up until the afternoon, and when I opened my eyes, the sky out the window was black. Moonlight danced off the shadows in the carriage, darkening one half of Anna's face. She was sleeping. As I watched her, guilt flooded through me. I had treated her so terribly. She had done so much to assist me as my maid and all I had done was belittle her. Had I ever thanked her? Had I ever treated her with any measurement of kindness?

She stirred, and a shiver rolled over her. I looked down at my lap where two blankets lay. Anna had already traveled at least nine days to accompany me, and now she would endure the same trip again. Poor girl. Her forehead was creased as she slept, and her breath exhaled in mist from the cold. I lifted one of the blankets off my lap, shook it out, and stood, steadying myself with a hand on the roof of the carriage, and draped the warm fabric over her, tucking the corners under her chin. Then I sat down again and tucked my legs beneath me to stay warm without the weight of both blankets.

My head ached from the events of the day, and I could still feel where my tears had dried on my cheeks. I leaned my head against the window and the cold glass soothed the pain throbbing in my skull. I breathed out and closed my eyes. I hadn't seen Clara again before I left. She had underestimated my ability to keep my wits with James begging me to stay. She had assumed he could stop me. She was wrong. Perhaps I could convince her to come visit Mama and me after she was married. The thought provided enough peace of mind for me to relax. But still my conscience whispered fears and questions to my mind, battling against the decision I had etched in stone.

I hadn't noticed Anna open her eyes, and I wondered how long she had been watching me. My stomach dropped when I saw the look on her face. The only way I could describe it was cowering. Her eyes were wide as if she were afraid to blink, as if I would accuse her at any moment of stealing the blankets. It wrenched at my heart.

"I thought you looked cold," I said, my voice raspy from hours of silence.

Her brow flinched in confusion as she watched me, still on guard. "How is Mama?"

She took a moment to recover from the shock of being spoken to, and cleared her throat. "She's well." Her eyes dropped away from mine.

"And how are you? Surely this journey has worn on you." I tried to make my voice gentle.

Anna shifted and when she spoke it was a small, quaking sound. "I'm as well as I'm able, miss."

I watched her, the sad slump of her shoulders in the dark, the weight of a thousand things I didn't know about, and I hadn't cared to know before. How had I treated such an innocent, weak girl with so much spite? It seemed incomprehensible to me at this moment. I needed to fix it. I couldn't sit here any longer before I did.

"Will you please forgive me?" I asked. "Please, Anna, forgive me for my unkindness to you these last years, growing up, I was so terrible, I—" My head was shaking. "How could you forgive me? I cannot expect you to. But please know how awful I feel and that I am sincerely sorry." I waited, feeling a switch of roles as I begged for her acceptance and sheepishly awaited her reply.

Anna's face was difficult to read, but I saw no bitterness there. A long moment passed before she said, "Yes. I forgive you." It had a stronger sound than her voice usually held.

I breathed a sigh of relief and felt lighter than I had all day. "Thank you," I choked.

She was still looking at me as if I were a foreign creature, but then she nodded. One of her ghostly white hands peeked out from beneath the blankets and she pulled them off of herself. "Please take it back, miss."

I stopped her. "No. You need it far more than me. See? I have a cloak and gloves. I am warm enough, I assure you."

She hesitated, but finally wrapped herself up again. I couldn't see her well in the dark, but after a short few minutes I heard the high whistle of a snore. And then I promised myself, there in the dark, that I would never speak an unkind word to her again. Never hurt her, never make her shrink. Returning to Canterbury would change nothing but my place of residence. I wouldn't be the cruel person I was before. Never again.

We stopped at an inn called the Rose and Crown that night, and although it was dirty and surely haunted, I had never slept so soundly in my life. I had never been so tired.

The days passed in a blur of colors. Night was black, morning was gray, and afternoon was white. The snow fell lighter the farther we traveled south, and occasionally I'd spot a patch of green out the carriage window. Anna spoke more too. I learned that she hadn't seen her family in five years. Her father had fallen ill when she was very young, and she was forced to move wherever necessary to find work as a lady's maid. That was how she had been employed by my family. It was remarkable to me that I had never noticed the sheen of grief that covered her eyes and the way she carried a broken heart with such poise. I hoped one day I could be like her.

On the last day of the drive I began to sweat. My stomach fluttered. Would I even belong here anymore? I recognized the tall trees and the frosted hills and the larger houses. We were only a few short miles away now. My legs were stiff from the cold and the lack of use, so I stretched them, breathing out a jagged breath.

"Anna," I whispered. "Anna."

Her eyelids fluttered open.

"I am sorry to wake you, but we are almost home." The word *home* tasted like a lie. We were set to arrive at the house of Mama's fiancé, Mr. Bentford. My gaze drifted out the window. "It has been so long."

Her yawn turned into a smile. "It's only been four months, miss."

"But what will Mama think of . . . my hand?" I had spent one afternoon of the drive telling her the story of the entire incident.

Another wry grin. "It is but a keepsake—from your time away from her. A piece of artwork, that is."

I smiled. I had learned that Anna was not nearly as timid as she appeared. "I worry she will hate it."

Anna's face grew solemn but she didn't answer. Perhaps she thought it to be beyond her bounds to speak her mind in this instance. At any rate, I wasn't sure I wanted to hear what she had to say.

The rest of the drive passed in silence, and I had almost drifted to sleep again when I noticed the carriage start to slow. My head bounced against my seat as we rumbled over the uneven drive of Bentford Manor. It was a stately looking house, with crisp corners and pristine windows. I sat up straight.

The carriage came to a halt and I was too full of nerves and excitement to remain still any longer. Without waiting for the footmen, I jumped out of the carriage. My feet stung as I hit the ground. Anna stifled a giggle of disbelief from behind me as the footman intending to assist me stopped, showing an uncharacteristic display of surprise. I smiled and breathed in the southern air and used it to tuck away all my worries and wayward emotions. When I reached the front door, I saw the flash of an emerald gown and a narrow frame through the window. Mama.

Before I could reach out for the handle, the door swung open. Mama stood in the entry hall, a faltering smile on her lips. A great need for comfort overcame me and I didn't hesitate, but rushed forward and threw my arms around her. My face buried in her bony shoulder. Her arms hung at her sides and she grew stiff with alarm.

"Charlotte! What *are* you doing?" Her voice was more shrill than I remembered.

My face burned with embarrassment and I stepped back, nearly tripping over my skirts. Mama wasn't looking at me. She was running her hand gingerly over her sleeves. "I just had this gown made three days ago. You will soil it."

"I—I'm sorry . . ."

Her eyes shot up to mine, piercing green and wide with shock. "What has happened to you?" Her gaze slid over my face, my hair, and she stepped around me like a cat circling an inadequate kill. "You have grown so thin! And your hair so dirty. Your cheeks have no color . . ." She gasped. "My poor girl. We shall change that straight away. Mr. Webb intends to meet you in one week! This is your grand opportunity, Charlotte."

Self conscious under her gaze, I smoothed my hair away from my forehead. Her eyes sharpened in on my gloves.

"What are those shabby things?"

My heart pounded. "I use them to cover—to cover my hand." I swallowed. "I did not want you to worry while I was away. I had a—well . . . I had an accident."

She didn't flinch. "An accident?"

"I will keep it covered. I assure you, no one will know." Panic was creeping into my voice.

Mama watched me out of narrowed eyes as she stepped forward and pinched the tip of one gloved finger. She pulled, and the glove slid slowly off my hand. First she saw the scars, then the missing fingers. Clumps of torn curtains fell to the ground.

She jumped back, throwing the glove to the floor as if it were a deadly thing. Her face contorted in disbelief and revulsion. She covered her mouth and turned away, as if she expected to be nauseous, and squeezed her eyes shut. "How did this happen?" Her voice was a scratchy whisper.

"I was attempting to handle fishing equipment, and it . . . was a disaster." I struggled to hold her gaze.

She was rubbing her head, facing the back wall, and peered at me from over her shoulder. "Why were you doing such a thing? I did not raise you to behave with such foolishness!"

"Yes, I was foolish. A man challenged me to it, and I accepted. He never thought I would, and he felt dreadful about it. But it is over, Mama. Nothing can be done to change the past."

"A man? Surely he was an uneducated, dirty, impoverished scoundrel to do such a thing." She turned around and her eyes flicked to my hand again. She grimaced.

"No," I said in a firm voice, "it was my fault entirely. He did nothing wrong. He was a gentleman." Speaking about James made a shard of grief stab me.

Mama shook her head forcefully, making the large pendant at her neck swing. "I should not have brought you here. No one will have you now."

Her words hit me hard and panic began to flood through me. "No, Mama! I will keep my hand hidden!"

"For how long?" she snapped. "I will be ruined all over again if society should learn I am the mother of a—a *deformed* child."

It was a blow to my chest, a deep, throbbing pain in my heart. How had I ever imagined she would understand and accept me this way? How had I been so naive and foolish? The silence hanging in the air burned me to my bones. Blinking back tears, I stooped to the floor and picked up my glove. "I will keep it hidden forever," I said in a quick voice. "It will become the latest fashion to wear gloves at every social event. Watch and it will happen." I slipped the glove over my hand again and Mama's shoulders seemed to relax a little.

"But how will you write? How will you stitch and draw? And you cannot even play the pianoforte!" Her voice rang shrill in the air and when she looked at me, it was as if doing so was an arduous task.

"I will prove it to you, Mama. You'll see. I will court Mr. Webb and hide my hand. We will not mention that I ever knew the pianoforte!" I felt like I was grasping at smoke in the air. Nothing I said to reason with her seemed to work.

"Have you considered how you will excuse yourself from performing at parties with people who knew you before? They will expect you to play for them." She was fanning her face.

I froze. I hadn't thought of that before. "We will—we will think of something. Perhaps I am resting my hands for a performance for the Prince Regent?"

She scoffed. "Who would believe such a thing?"

I bit my lip, mind racing.

As if searching for something she had forgotten, Mama's eyes darted around the room. "Where is Clara?" she demanded.

My eyes rounded and the words came spilling out. "She stayed. She is marrying Lord Trowbridge."

For a moment I thought Mama would faint. Her eyes flew open in surprise and she clutched her chest. Then a slow smile formed on her face, starting at her lips and creating a sly glint in her piercing green eyes. "I never would have thought it possible," she whispered. "Clara. Clara a countess? Hah!" She paced the black and white tiles and I felt like I was shrinking before her. She turned to face me, a wild excitement in her eyes. "When society hears of this I shall be praised to no end. I managed to secure my plainest daughter a match with an earl!"

I opened my mouth to speak, but stopped myself. *You did nothing. He loved her.*

"Why was I not informed of this sooner?"

I swallowed. "It was recent news, the letter would not have reached you before I did."

Mama seemed satisfied with my reply and continued her pacing. "How did she do it?"

"Pardon me?"

"How did she win him over you? Surely your hand deterred him from you, but Clara? How did she win him?"

I wasn't sure I was hearing her correctly. Did I really speak that way before? I frowned. "It was not a contest, Mama. She didn't wish to marry him. At least not before falling in love with him."

She laughed, a high, grating sound. "She fell in love with him? Nonsense. She must have ensnared him."

"She didn't."

"You truly believe she loves him? You have lost your head, Charlotte. What has happened to you?"

I scowled, head spinning. "I don't—I don't know. I am tired from the journey."

She reached out and touched my cheek, her fingers cold as ice. "Despite recent events," her gaze flashed to my hand, "I believe you may still make a fine match for me. Can you imagine? All three of us so well married." She chuckled. "I always knew Clara had potential. Learn from her and you will not disappoint me. In the coming week we will plump up these sunken cheeks of yours and have your gowns taken in." She pinched a strand of my hair between two fingers and dropped it again on my shoulder. She cringed. "And we must do something with this hair."

I nodded fast, willing to do anything to win her favor.

"And no one shall know of your deformity. Do you understand me?"

I nodded again.

Chapter 24

*"One may smile, and smile,
and be a villain."*

Mr. Bentford was a quiet sort of man, prim and meek in Mama's presence. He was like a strand of ribbon in her hands, effortlessly bent and twisted however she liked.

"Mr. Bentford, Charlotte and I have had three new gowns made. I do hope the bills will not be too much for you." She fluttered her lashes from across the dining table.

His cheeks splotched a pink color. "Nothing is too much if it shall please you."

Mama sat back and sipped from her goblet. Only I could recognize the sheen of victory in her eyes. My gaze traveled around the table to where his two daughters sat. They were younger than me by several years. Louisa was twelve and Eleanor was fourteen. Both girls had tightly curled pale hair and brown eyes, much like their father. They didn't seem to notice the manipulation my mother was practicing, nor did they care. In the six days I had been here, I had only spoken to them once or twice, and they had acted as if it were the last thing in the world they wished to be doing. They were rather oblivious to their surroundings, but I had learned better.

My eyes traveled between Mama and Mr. Bentford, and I recognized a puppet pulled by invisible strings, entwined in her hands and her coy smile. While I had once aspired to such behavior, watching it now made me sick deep within my stomach.

I pushed away from the table, making my fork clatter against my plate. "Please excuse me. I wish to retire early."

The surprise in Mama's eyes faded and she gave me a knowing glance. "Very well. You must receive adequate rest this evening, for tomorrow you will meet Mr. Webb."

I smiled but when I turned away my face fell. Why was I not anxious to see him? Before I would have been filled with excitement and anticipation over the prospect of winning the attention of a wealthy gentleman, of flirting to my heart's content. But now, all I felt was a glaring emptiness, devoid of emotion. I walked like a ghost to my room. Anna was there to help me prepare for bed. It was strange that the most comfort I found here was in her friendship and company.

We each spoke about the events of our day as Anna brushed my hair and I was overcome with longing for Clara. Oh, how I missed her. She must feel so betrayed, so angry and upset with me. I couldn't blame her.

Anna seemed to sense something was wrong, just as she had when I had stepped into the carriage when I was leaving Craster. But much like then, she didn't pry.

"Sleep well, Miss Charlotte. Tomorrow will be an eventful day, I trust."

I took a deep breath. "Indeed. Thank you for your help."

Anna watched me, an inquisitive look on her face, but left without another word. I blew out the candles and climbed in bed, thinking in the dark. Why was I feeling this way? I had never imagined I would feel like such a stranger here, after only four months of being away. Mama looked at me differently now. She was more critical and disdainful, the way of treatment she had always saved for Clara. I thought of the way she had looked at my hand that first day, how disgusted she had been.

My chin quivered and I bit my lip to keep from crying. I had longed to return here for so long, but now that I was back, I was vastly disappointed. I hadn't known that freedom meant missing what I had before. My thoughts wandered to James. It was a practice I had shunned since that first mile on the road home, but I allowed myself to think of him at times like this when I was the most weak.

I wondered how he had spent the past fifteen days we had been apart. I wondered how long it had taken him to forget me. I wondered if he had really ever loved me, and if he did, how long it had taken him to hate me instead. Because I knew, without a doubt, that he hated me now. How could he not hate me after all I had done to his heart? I shivered and tightened my blankets around me and for the first time I wondered which fate was worse—living here in the South and knowing James hated me for leaving him, or returning to the North and knowing I disgraced Mama.

Burying my face in my pillow, I took a deep breath. No. Even if I wanted to return, I couldn't. James would never forgive me. I couldn't bear to be around him and know that he wouldn't smile and tease me and laugh with me. He would never play the pianoforte with me, or comfort me, or assure me that my decision to come back had been the right one. Perhaps he had even found another girl in town to love. Someone much kinder and more deserving of him than I was.

I scolded myself for even thinking of him and closed my eyes. This was my home now. I wrapped up my emotions and put them where they couldn't be found. Tears pooled beneath my eyelids but I didn't let them fall. This was what I wanted. I would court Mr. Webb and perhaps my luck would turn. A voice inside me whispered that I had made a mistake, that I was a fool, but I shushed it. Mr. Webb could offer me a beautiful home, dozens of dresses, and months every year in London. What more could I ever need?

Eventually my breathing relaxed and my eyes dried. Yes. When I met Mr. Webb, I would do all I could to secure a match with him. It was just within my reach now. My heart would have nothing to do with it.

It will be easy, I told myself, because my heart is in a place very, very far away from here.

The following day was eventful indeed. I spent the morning hours trying on my new gowns while Mama circled me, eyebrow raised.

Anna made several attempts at my hair; Mama swiftly made vocal her disapproval at all of them. By the fifth attempt, Anna's hands shook, but she managed to create a style Mama found acceptable. I watched Anna's eyes in the large mirror. She was terrified. I made a note in my mind to apologize for Mama later.

"Wear the blue gown," Mama said. "It matches your eyes." She turned and walked toward the door. "And it looks least absurd with the gloves." The door slammed shut behind her. I flinched.

When I finally came down the stairs that afternoon, Mama, Louisa, and Eleanor waited at the bottom. I was nervous for Mama's reaction, but was relieved to see her smile. Louisa and Eleanor looked as if they would enjoy nothing more than to strangle me.

"I daresay Mr. Webb will be smitten out of his wits tonight." Mama's voice was full of mischief. "You look absolutely beautiful."

I tried to believe her, but I didn't feel beautiful. Not at all.

Mama threaded her arm around my elbow and guided me to the drawing room. She closed the door. "Do you remember what I need you to do?"

"Lean in close. Let him speak about himself. Laugh at every humorous comment he makes. Touch his arm." My voice was stiff.

"And the smile . . . ?"

I demonstrated my best flirtatious smile.

Mama gave a huffed breath. "I suppose it will have to suffice."

My smile fell.

"Now. You will avoid sitting on his left side. Keep your hand far away from him. He must not suspect anything."

"I will try my best, Mama."

She watched me from the corner of her eye as she walked toward the pianoforte on the left side of the room. She ran her fingers over the keys, shaking her head. "What a shame that you will never play again." Her voice was cold.

My words came out without permission. "No, I am still quite capable of playing."

Her head snapped in my direction. "How?"

"In Craster . . . there was a man who taught me. Well, we played music together, really. He played the right hand and I played the left—"

"Who was this man?" Mama demanded.

"His name is James." I realized my mistake as Mama's eyes widened in shock. "I mean—er—Mr. Wortham."

"James?" Mama's face was pulled tight with indignation. "How improper, Charlotte. I have taught you to be better than that low-class talk. How well did you know this man?"

My heart pounded. "Too well. But he was very kind to me. A wonderful friend."

"And his station?"

I paused. "Below mine. But he is very kind and agreeable and—"

"That will be quite enough!" Mama rushed forward and clutched my arm, her face firm and unyielding. "Thank heavens I was wise enough to call you home from that wretched place. I was right. You *will not* play the pianoforte again, because you will never see this 'James' again."

My voice was a mutter. "I do not plan to."

She smoothed her hair. "Good. Very good."

I gave a quick nod. Awkwardness hung in the air around us and I knew that I couldn't stay in this room a moment longer. Too many things were racing through my mind and heart, and I needed to be alone to sort through them.

"I am going to my room to rest before Mr. Webb arrives."

Mama glanced her approval at me and I hurried to the door. When I was out of the drawing room, I paused in the hall, breathing the air that I had thought was my escape but now felt like a prison. Our family portraits hung just ahead of me, joined now with the Bentfords'. Mine had been painted just two years before. I stepped closer, examining Mama's portrait. Her eyes were sharp as always, and there was an overall air of disdain in her countenance. Her head was upturned slightly, and her face seeped confidence and condescension. Her lips were pressed tight, implying that the only thing that could make her smile would be money and power and entitlement.

My gaze slid carefully to my own portrait, and my stomach sunk far to the ground. There, on my face, was the same look as Mama. The same selfish, cruel, unrelenting face. Beautiful to the outside eye, but I knew better.

I thought of the miniature portrait Mama wore in the pendant at her neck. Never had I considered Mama's depth of devotion to her own mother. Picturing the straight spine, the heavy eyes, the calculated smile of her own mother, the resemblance was more striking than ever before. I had never known my grandmother. But it seemed she had taught Mama the same things I had been taught; she had schooled a heart into rigid discipline. And Mama thrived off of it. Would I be the same?

My heart pounded with dread as I thought of tonight, how I would meet Mr. Webb, and how I was expected to be that girl in the portrait. I feared I couldn't do it.

I stepped back against the wall to steady myself and wondered for the first time if I really wanted this—if I really wanted to be like Mama. Because to be like her was the only way to please her. And I knew deep within my soul, that if Mama was still the same woman in that portrait, then she wasn't capable of love. Not now, not like this. So what was I trying to do? Mama could accept me, and she could approve of me, but I would always fall short. Was that enough to make me happy? Did I even deserve to be happy?

I turned away from the portraits in disgust and ran. My feet slapped against the marble floors in loud echoes as I made my way to the staircase and up to my room. I couldn't afford to think this way. I had made my choice. There was nothing left for me anywhere else. Everyone I had dared to love now hated me, and surely they would not allow me to return to them. I simply needed to be strong and move forward.

Two hours later, I walked down the stairs again, and Mr. Webb and Mama waited with uninviting smiles at the bottom.

Chapter 25

"I love you more than words can yield the matter."

The water running over my hand was cold. Chill bumps erupted over my arm and I sighed, enjoying the soothing coolness of the stream on my skin. It was finally warm enough to venture outside. I had never been much of an adventurer before, but any form of escape was worth every precious moment.

I stood and brushed the dirt off my skirts and wiped the hair away that had fallen in my eyes. The woods were thick behind Bentford Manor, and I had discovered this little stream only a week before. Since then it had become a fortress of relief and distance from a certain much-too-watchful man. I had spent hours alone here, practicing my writing with my left hand, sketching the trees, and hoping Mr. Webb wouldn't find me here.

Taking a deep breath, I filled my lungs with the fresh spring air and looked up at the sky through the trees. It was gray with heavy clouds. I watched them move through the sky, a slow roiling that captivated me. It would rain soon, and I knew I should go inside, but I couldn't look away. The color reminded me of the sky in Craster, and I took a moment to wonder whether or not James was standing under the same colored sky, and I wondered if it were possible he thought of me as much as I thought of him.

241

Kicking the grass ahead, I slipped my gloves back over my hands as I walked out of the woods. Almost immediately, I heard a familiar shout.

"Miss Lyons! Where have you been? I have been so lonely without you." His voice cracked with exertion as he ran toward me. Mr. Webb stopped, breathing heavily. He doffed his hat and extended his arm to me. A sheen of sweat covered his forehead. "Are you unwell?"

"I could ask the same of you," I said.

He laughed and wiped his forehead with his sleeve. His wavy auburn hair was sticking to the sides of his head. His eyes settled on me, a brown color that I had come to associate with the mud on the bottom of the stream. "I could run miles and miles, dear Charlotte, if it meant I could see your beauty once again. Your eyes remind me very much of the blue satin bow my cat wore when she was just a kitten."

"Oh?" My voice was flat. He had offered the same comment on at least two other occasions.

"Yet I fail to make any comparison that would adequately describe the lovely color your eyes possess. I have never seen anything like it."

"Thank you, Mr. Webb. You are too kind."

He shrugged and flashed a winning smile. Then he went on to tell me every detail of his meeting with his man of business, and how he had acquired another small inheritance from a distant cousin. "Would you like to take a ride into town? I know how much you like to see the new fabrics in the mantua maker's shop. You like that, do you not?"

"I do . . . but we did go yesterday." I didn't know if I could manage to undertake another ride with him.

He stopped walking. "Well, what else do you like?"

"I like lilacs, summer breezes, ribbons, lace, dancing." It was not entirely a lie, but I wasn't allowed to say the things I really liked. Playing the pianoforte, sketching alone in the woods, eating lemon tea cakes, rocky coasts, the sea, and beautiful memories that I had taken for granted.

"You forgot one thing!" he said emphatically. He turned to face me, pulling me close. Sunlight filtered through his pale lashes and glinted off his sweat. "Me!" He laughed and spun me around. "You like me most of all, I think."

I dislodged myself from his arms as quickly as possible and faked a smile. "Of course."

He brushed my hair from my eyes and I cringed. "You are so very beautiful," he said again.

I didn't have the energy or the desire to reply. I stepped back, feeling sick and empty and more lonely than I had ever felt in my life. "I must go. I need to prepare for dinner."

He nodded with understanding. "Oh! Please wear your lavender gown tonight. It is my favorite."

I didn't look back. But I made a promise to myself that I would never wear my lavender gown again.

Mr. Webb was a good man. He was friendly and agreeable, but dull and disconcerting at the same time. Mama had been married just a month before, and shortly after she returned home from her wedding trip, she had assured me that I was well on my way to securing a marriage with him. She had smiled, and although I had expected her words of approval and her smile to comfort me, they just left me dry and cracked inside. I lived day by day, hour by hour, always dreading the next. I was miserable. I hated hiding the truth, wearing that stuffed glove day after day, not because I hated the sight of my hand but because Mama did. Every time she looked at me, her eyes flickered to that glove, and glinted with disapproval that etched embarrassment and inferiority in my soul with every glance. I felt choked and trapped by it and I didn't know how to escape. I doubted I ever would.

Dinner came at its usual time, and I wore my brown dress with the ivory ribbons. Mr. Webb's smile faltered when he saw me, and when he cleared his throat he sounded frustrated. We hardly spoke at all throughout the meal, and I could feel Mama's eyes on me the entire time, digging a hole into the side of my face.

When the dishes were cleared away and the women were preparing to move to the drawing room, Mr. Webb stood. His throat bobbed with a swallow. "I would like to request a . . . private conversation with Miss Lyons."

Mama's eyes rounded and returned to normal within a second. "Oh, yes. Of course." She looked as if it took all her concentration not to leap from her chair and drag Louisa and Eleanor from the room by their ears. "Stepdaughters. Mr. Bentford." She stood and they followed her from the room, a quiet clattering of chairs and muffled footsteps.

I stood too fast, panic throbbing through my veins. I knew what he was going to say. "Mr. Webb, I—"

"Miss Charlotte Lyons, I cannot express to you the extent of my feelings." He stepped close to me. "I find you enchanting, mesmerizing, and I expect that I never should grow tired of gazing upon you."

My stomach lurched.

"And there is much I am ready and capable of giving you, if you would accept my proposal. Therefore, it is much to your advantage and mine, if you agree to be my wife." His face broke into a smile, as if his explanation and proposal had been horribly romantic rather than an equation. "Marry me, Charlotte. I daresay we shall make a lovely couple."

My mind spun. This was not right. Was this really what I had always dreamed of? Mr. Webb was growing wealthier by the day. I had seen his estate and it was beautiful beyond words. The few months his uncle remained alive marked the time before Mr. Webb would become an earl. It was as if all my dreams were in front of me, gazing through a pair of muddy eyes, but they appeared in this moment as nothing more than a trap, a ruse, a thorn disguised as a rose. I didn't want this. I was shaking my head now, and the smile on Mr. Webb's face was fading.

"Do you really know me at all?" I asked, my voice hard and fast.

His brow wrinkled. "Of course! I *have* been courting you these last three months."

I shook my head again and stepped away from him.

"But—but that does not matter. We shall come to know one another better. We have years to be together!"

The thought of spending years with Mr. Webb, seeing his face every day, and always wondering what it would have been like if I had stayed in Craster, if I had chosen love instead . . . I couldn't bear it. The walls of the room seemed to be closing in, and I could hardly breathe. "You are a good man, Mr. Webb. And I believe you could make someone very happy, but that woman is not me."

"Please, Charlotte! Why do you refuse me?"

"Why do you want to marry me?"

He was silent. "Because I have never seen a woman more beautiful, more lovely, more magnificent—"

I stopped him. "That is the problem. One day I will be old and ugly, and you will wish you had never met me."

"That is not true," he said in a low voice. "You are perfection."

Releasing a sigh of frustration, I tore my glove away from my right hand and threw it to the ground. I lifted my hand up to where he could see it. His eyes flew open and he stumbled back.

"Does this change your mind?" I didn't look away from his face, even as much as it hurt me to see the distaste in his eyes.

"What—how?" he stammered. It was all he could manage to say.

"I didn't show you before because I knew what you would think. These pretenses were not acceptable and I apologize. But even so, my answer remains the same. I will not marry you. And if my suspicions prove correct, you won't wish to marry me now either." I watched as his gaze slid over my hand and back to my face. His expression was contorted in quiet shock and a bit of guilt. He didn't speak.

"Be careful, Mr. Webb. One day there might be a woman who steals your heart. Make certain she loves you or surely she will break it. You will be hunted for your fortune and there are many women like me who might have said yes just now." I walked backward toward the door and paused in the open doorway. "Be careful."

He nodded and I saw him slump down in his seat the moment I closed the door behind me. I took a moment to calm myself. I hadn't noticed how my legs were quaking and how fast my heart was beating. It was over. There was no way to recover now. I stared at the puckered scars on my hand pressed against the wall. What had I done?

"Charlotte!"

I turned at the sound of Mama's voice and told myself to be strong.

"Charlotte!" Her gaze settled on my uncovered hand. An eerie stillness settled on her face. "You have made a dreadful mistake."

My eyes stung with tears, but I stood tall, feeling more free and brave than I had in months. "No. I made a mistake when I decided to return here to court these men. I cannot—I will not deceive any longer. I will not be the woman you taught me to be. One of your daughters managed to make an acceptable match for you, but I will not."

Mama spoke through clenched teeth. "I made it clear that you were to keep your hand a secret until after you were married. He will never have you now!"

"And I am glad! Because I don't want him!"

"How dare you—"

"You do not need an advantageous match from me! Not anymore. I thought that was what I needed too, but I was wrong. I will not marry a man of your choosing, of your—of your requirements." My voice echoed in the hall and Mama cringed.

"I did not invest all these years, all these hours in a daughter that would become a spinster!" she screeched. "Mr. Morely has not met you." She walked forward and gripped my shoulder. "I will invite him to dine with us next week and you will not ruin such an opportunity again."

"No!" I pulled away and she gasped. "I mean what I say! I never should have returned to Canterbury. I miss Clara!" My throat tightened in a knot. "I miss James." Tears dripped from my eyes and Mama threw her hands in the air with exasperation.

"Go back then! Leave!" she shouted. Her voice and demeanor calmed and she turned away from me. "Go. Marry this James. I have no use for you now."

Something burned and ached inside me and I fought the urge to reach out and cry into her shoulder and beg for her forgiveness. But I knew she would only push me away. She could have thousands of creases in her sleeve, but each one would always mean more to her than her two daughters. I had learned that—I had finally seen it. It seared a hole in my heart nonetheless.

So I turned and walked away, leaving her in the corner of that empty hall. I sniffed and wiped the tears from my cheeks. How had I been so foolish? I had doubted Clara's wisdom before and now every inch of me cried out in the agony of regret. I had doubted the strength of love, and now I was left with nothing but longing for it. I still loved James after all these weeks, and if it were possible, then maybe he could love me too. Maybe there was still hope.

I rushed to my room with renewed energy, clinging to my little drop of hope with eager hands. I threw the door open and headed straight for the bell pull. Anna arrived a long five minutes later, and I stood from my bed, heart pounding. "I need your help."

She noticed my disarray and handed me a handkerchief. "What is it, miss?"

"I need your help to write a letter."

I had known Anna was educated before coming to work as a maid, but was amazed by the perfection of her writing. Two hours later, we still sat in the dim light of my room, and Anna penned the final curve of the 'e' at the end of *Charlotte*.

"Would you like to read it over? To make certain I wrote everything as you wished?" Anna asked. She blowed the ink dry and extended the letter to me.

I took it, my hand shaking, and read.

Dear James,

By the time you read this, four months will have passed since I left you, and eight months will have passed since I met you. I thought too much of myself then and I thought I had changed, but I was wrong. Because I thought myself capable of forgetting you, and I know now that is impossible. Since I left not a day has passed that I haven't thought of you. I have little experience with love, but I have no doubt that I have felt it. You captured my heart when I didn't know I had one, and for that I am forever in your debt. A wise man once told me to write the things that are difficult to say, so here it is: I love you.

I don't expect you to forgive me, but please accept this apology, and know that my heart is written on this page, and that I wish for you to keep it always. I lived without a heart once, and if I must, I will do it again.

Charlotte

I folded the letter as soon as I finished reading. My courage was wavering, and I didn't know how much longer it would last. I handed the letter back to Anna.

"Please post this first thing tomorrow." My voice shook.

She gave a gentle smile. "Of course."

I rubbed my head and laughed, a crazed sound in my throat. "I'm mad."

"Love does such things to a person."

Gratitude surged through me. "Thank you for helping me."

"'Twas my pleasure. I should be heading downstairs now. Mrs. Jennings will likely murder me for being away so long."

I smiled, a tired twitch of my lips. "You are a wonderful friend. If ever I find a way to repay you, I will do it."

She smiled before turning and leaving the room with my letter clutched in her hand. My stomach turned over and over at the thought of James reading those words. My cheeks burned. There was nothing I could do now. Nothing but wait.

I avoided Mama the following day, spending the morning hours by my stream in the woods. I brought a novel with me today, one I knew Clara would have liked, but found it impossible to focus on the story. There were too many other matters on my mind.

I watched the birds in the trees jumping from branch to branch, chirping in a language I didn't understand. I lay back in the damp grass and propped the book under my head. I closed my eyes.

"Charlotte!"

The voice came from Anna. I sat up. She was running toward me, and I squinted. There was a square of parchment in her hand.

"This came for you," she panted as she stopped beside me. "I said I would deliver it to you."

"What is it?"

She didn't speak but held the letter out in her hand. It came to my eye level where I sat on the grass. My heart lodged in my throat. It was from James.

I was afraid to touch it. How could I bring myself to open it? I was filled with so much anticipation and worry and excitement that I thought I might burst. For a moment my spinning mind thought that he had sent this as a reply to my letter, but Anna had just posted it this morning. He had written this—whatever it was—several days, if not weeks, before now for it to be arriving today. My hands were sweating and shaking as I took the letter from Anna. It was so unexpected, so nerve-racking, that I worried I would faint.

"Go on," Anna said, smiling encouragingly. "Read it. Read it!"

I held the letter at the corners, and tore the seal with a delicate hand. James had held this letter not too long ago—he had written the words I was about to read with his own hand. With one final leap of my heart I unfolded the letter and let my gaze touch the parchment.

Dearest Charlotte,

I thought I knew what it was to love before. I thought I knew what it meant to be hurt by love. I thought I would see an end to this suffering, this longing for you, but I know I never will. You told me love wasn't real, and that it wouldn't last, but it seems that I have proven you wrong yet again. If what I'm feeling isn't real, then please tell me why I can't sleep at night, why I see you every time I close my eyes, and why I want nothing more than to hold you in my arms and never let you leave me again. Because I know more surely than I have known anything before, my lovely friend, that my heart has chosen to love you forever. My words might not have kept you here, and they might not bring you back, but at least you will know you are loved. Because, dear Charlotte, you deserve to be loved.

It isn't my intention to keep you from your dreams, no matter how strongly I disagree with them. If they will make you happy, and you are certain I cannot, then please disregard this letter. But if by some miracle you've changed your mind, and will dare to give your heart to a rugged fisherman, then please return to me.

I can't offer you a life of grandeur. No endless wealth and entitlement, but I offer you my heart. I hope that will be enough.

James

I could hardly breathe. I sat there in the wet grass, reading the letter over and over again, until my eyes stung with tears and my heart threatened to burst. James loved me. He hadn't forgotten me. I read the last line again, *I offer you my heart. I hope that will be enough.* It was more than enough. It was everything I ever needed. How had I been so blind?

I blinked my eyes dry and stood on my shaking legs. Anna was still standing there, and when she saw my smile she smiled back. "Oh, Charlotte! Is it good news?"

I laughed, a choked sound, and her grin grew wider.

"He doesn't hate me!" I wiped my nose with my sleeve and grabbed Anna's hand. I was practically jumping. "He wrote me this beautiful thing . . . a love letter. For me." I shook my head and more tears, joyful, relieving tears splashed from my eyes. "He doesn't hate me."

She squeezed my hand. "Upon my word, it would be nearly impossible to hate you."

"I must go back!" My heart pounded. "I need to leave today."

Anna nodded and her curls bounced. "I will have your trunk and carriage prepared immediately." She started to walk away, but I stopped her.

"Come with me."

Her brow wrinkled. "Of course. Your mother would never have you travel unaccompanied."

I shook my head. "That is not what I meant. Leave your work for this household and come to live in Craster! Clara and Lord Trowbridge will surely employ you. You will be treated with kindness and I am certain your wages will improve. You have become such an invaluable friend these months, Anna, and you deserve every happiness."

Her eyes were round with shock. "Are you certain?"

"Yes!"

She hesitated for a moment longer before her face broke into a smile of such gratitude and joy that my heart melted. "Thank you."

"Shall we leave in the morning?" I asked.

Anna nodded. Everything I had been missing these last months came flooding back to me, and all the hopelessness and uncertainty fled. I knew, without a doubt, that I would travel anywhere in the world if it meant I could see James again. I also knew, without a doubt, that the next ten days would feel like a lifetime.

Chapter 26

"And ruin'd love when it is built anew,
grows fairer than at first,
more strong, far greater."

My feet touched the rocky path in front of the home of Lord and Lady Trowbridge in the late afternoon. Everywhere I looked I saw green. From bright, lush green to deep and dark emerald green—all breathtakingly beautiful and like nothing I could have imagined. The sky was still gray, but with patches of blue that peeked through the thin clouds. I heard trills of birdsong, and I could smell flowers and sweet, salty sea air. The breeze was cool against my skin. My eyes swept over the surrounding landscape, and my heart beat fast with joy and nervousness and a strong sense of belonging all at once.

My mind traveled back to when I had seen the painting James's mother had done in the secret room. The colors were even more vivid now, seeing Craster in the spring through my own eyes. Everything seemed so different than before, and as I walked away from the carriage, it felt like I was breathing for the first time in four months.

I inhaled slowly in an effort to calm my racing heart and scattered thoughts, and savored every detail of this place I had missed so dearly. I was home.

Anna followed at a distance behind me as I made my way toward the front door. I glanced heavenward and prayed that Clara would be home . . . and that she would forgive me. James could be anywhere, and I needed her and Thomas's help to find him. My stomach fluttered violently at the thought of seeing James again. What would he do? What would he say?

I thought of when he had kissed me, and my face tingled with heat. A small part of me still wondered if these last ten days had changed his mind all over again. Love was a fragile thing in my mind, and I feared every second that passed could still break it. I needed to see him to be certain his words were honest, that he did love me, and that he would forever. And I needed to be sure that he knew the same was true for me. I loved him. I couldn't bear to be without him. Not a moment longer.

I walked faster, and soon I was at the door, waiting to be let inside. The butler opened the door with an inquisitive eyebrow, but then Clara appeared behind him. My face broke into a smile and my eyes welled with tears. "Clara," I choked.

She gasped and ran forward, throwing her arms around me. "Charlotte! You are here! When did you arrive?" her voice was quick. She pulled away to look at my face. She looked shocked to see me, happy, but also frantic.

"Just now," I said. "I'm very sorry, Clara. I should have listened to you, I should have stayed. You were right." My head was shaking. "I wish I had been here for your wedding. I'm sorry I didn't reply to your letters. I was just—" I sighed, at a loss for words to explain my stupidity. "I cannot wait to speak with you in length, but right now I must find James."

Her eyes were round and she put a hand over her mouth.

"What? What is wrong?" Dread pounded through me. I looked up and saw Lord Trowbridge walk into the entryway. Clara stepped back and whispered something to him. His gaze fell on me and his brow creased with concern. Clara turned to face me again and she gripped my shoulder. "Charlotte . . . James left this afternoon. He informed us of his departure, but he didn't say where he was going or how long he would be away."

My heart fell. What could have made him leave? "He didn't give any reason? Nothing at all?"

Lord Trowbridge stepped forward. "He said nothing, but he had a letter. I suppose it was something important. Perhaps a business matter that required immediate attention."

I whirled around to where Anna stood just beyond the open door. She must have heard it too, because her eyes were wide with shock and disbelief. *Your letter*, she mouthed.

Of course! James would have received the letter I wrote to him by today. He must have read it and chosen to come to me instead. It was a dreadful misunderstanding. I needed to stop him! Panic took flight inside me. He was several hours ahead of me. How could I reach him before nightfall at least?

"I must catch him!" I faced Clara and Thomas. "Will you help me?"

A small grin lifted Clara's lips and Lord Trowbridge just looked confused. Neither of them moved.

"Please, I must stop him." My voice came so fast I could hardly understand it. "He sent me a letter, you see, but I sent one to him first, and now he has received mine before I returned here to him, so I conclude that he is on his way to Canterbury as we speak, where he thinks I'm waiting for him. But I am *here*." I took a deep breath.

Clara gasped. Then she laughed, a high pitched, girlish sound. "How romantic! Is that not awfully romantic, Thomas?" She turned her nose up to her husband and he smiled with such adoration that her cheeks turned pink. "How shall we help them?"

Lord Trowbridge planted a quick kiss on her forehead and turned to me. "He cannot be more than an hour ahead. I will have my lightest phaeton equipped immediately."

"Thank you!"

Clara rushed forward and squeezed my hand. Anna had inched through the doorway and stood several feet away, but I pulled her toward us. "I informed Anna that you had need of another maid. Surely little Sophia and her spoilings could use another set of hands."

Clara smiled. "Of course!" she said, reaching for Anna's hand too. The sight warmed me to the core and banished my nerves. Why had I ever priced anything above friendship? It seemed absurd to me now.

A short few minutes later, Lord Trowbridge had returned and guided me outside with Clara. Both of them would accompany me. My heart jumped about in my chest like a wild thing as I climbed in the phaeton and we set off to catch James. I couldn't wait, I couldn't think, I could hardly breathe. We sped down the winding paths and my heart leapt every time we skidded past a rocky ledge, and the open air whipped my hair into tangled knots. I didn't count the minutes or the hours, but remained silent, for it was all I was capable of. Each second that passed meant I was closer to James. But what if he hadn't received my letter after all? What if he had left in a completely different direction and I had only fantasized the entire thing? I pushed these thoughts away and told myself to relax.

It wasn't until the sky was streaked with the peach of sunset that we spotted him. Lord Trowbridge saw the carriage first, a dot in the distance, and our horses trotted faster. My uncovered hands shook, and I watched with unblinking eyes, stretched wide with sudden panic. I couldn't do this. *What was I thinking?*

I considered telling Lord Trowbridge to turn around, but I knew Clara would never let him. My heart pounded so hard it hurt. As we drew closer, Lord Trowbridge half-shouted over the rickety wheels. "That is certainly my carriage!"

I slumped in my seat, clinging to the side. "I cannot do this," I whispered to Clara.

"Well, I fully intend to force you, so you have no choice in the matter." She winked.

"What an awful sister you are." I growled, sick with nervousness.

"I'm only as awful as you." She grinned. "Take it as an act of vengeance."

Our phaeton followed closely behind the carriage until it began to slow down. We came to a halt at nearly the same moment. I stood in one swift motion, knowing that if I didn't move now then I would never do it—I would never stand or speak or see James's face.

"Did he travel alone?" I asked in a quiet, shaking voice.

Lord Trowbridge nodded but I hardly noticed. He stood and let me down from the phaeton. My hands shook. Clara squeezed my shoulder before I touched the ground.

I took two steps forward, squinting under the dim evening light. The outline of James's carriage loomed just ahead of me, and I moved toward it, relying for the first time on something uncertain. It scared me.

Rows of prickly green plants grew off the path, and the setting sun made them glow purple. My feet crunched over the road, but it was just a muffled sound, blocked out by the sound of my own heart. I was so close now. I stepped around the front of the carriage at the precise moment James jumped down from the coach box. My heart leapt.

His eyes glinted blue in the waning light. "Charlotte," he breathed.

I was too shocked to move a muscle, too afraid that this wasn't real—that he wasn't really here standing in front of me. I hadn't known it was possible to miss something so much, a face that had comforted me countless times, a set of kind eyes, and ever-untidy black hair . . .

"James. I am so sorry." My voice was hoarse with emotion. "I was a fool. I didn't mean to break your heart. I accused myself of being selfish, when I didn't know that truly, I had broken my own heart as well. I wrote my letter to you before I received yours." I took a deep breath. "And I meant every word." I stepped toward him and spoke the words I never imagined I'd say. A great crevice in my heart filled and I smiled, shaky and unsteady, but more certain than I had ever been in my life. "I love you. I love you, and I am so, so sorry."

His face broke into a smile—a smile that assured me, all at once, that I had made the right decision. James filled the space between us in five steps. His arms wrapped around me, so perfect and strong and safe, and he kissed me. He kissed my lips, my cheeks, and my lips again, holding my face in his hands as tears of overwhelming joy fell down both our faces. He whispered my name, over and over, and countless other beautiful things as we stood there, free and happy and oh, so loved. Everything was suddenly right, every piece I had been missing for so long fell back together perfectly.

I didn't know if I belonged in the North, but I knew without a hint of uncertainty that I belonged with James, wherever he may be. This was home. This was my new dream, and I would cling to it always.

At last he pulled back just enough to look in my eyes. "What changed your mind?"

"I didn't know if you would ever forgive me, but I realized that to be alone would be better than to live such a lie. I took a chance writing that letter, and I never thought you would do the same. I thought you hated me." I laughed, a breathless sound.

He leaned his head down with a smile. "I could never hate you, Charlotte," he half-whispered. Then his hands slid down my arms and grasped mine. With a gentleness that made my heart melt all over again, he lifted my hand—the one Mr. Webb and Mama had so despised—and pressed his lips to my fingers. His smiling eyes met mine again and fresh tears streaked down my cheeks. "And after all," he said, "I thought it was you who hated me."

A teasing grin lit his face and I smiled. "Of course, I do."

He laughed. "That is the worst lie I have ever heard."

Epilogue

Our song was a flowing melody, quick and steady, intertwined with speeding trills and imperfect measures. My eyes streaked over the music in front of me and down to the strong hand that played deftly beside my own. A laugh of thrill and energy bubbled in my chest.

"Turn the page!" I exclaimed.

From the corner of my eye I saw James's other hand flick to the music and move the sheet we had finished out of my way. "Play faster," he said. I heard the smile in his voice.

My fingers bounded over the keys and every muscle in my body tightened in concentration. My heart soared, and James chuckled beside me as he struggled to keep up. The song was almost over, and we finished in a dramatic slowing of the notes. The resonating sound echoed off the walls until it had faded into silence. And then the room burst into applause.

I looked up at James, sitting beside me on the bench. He smiled, and the sight fluttered my heart as it always did. "Well done," he whispered. Then he leaned forward and kissed my cheek. I laughed and ducked my head as my face bloomed with heat.

"We have an audience," I berated.

He raised an eyebrow and looked behind him. "Well, then . . ."

Before I could object he pulled me against him and kissed me, deeply and slowly, making me melt and momentarily forget our spectators. "See what they think of that," he whispered against my lips. I pulled away, laughing and blushing even worse than Clara. I swatted his arm, shaking my head at the wink he threw my way.

The pianoforte had been a wedding gift from the Abbots. It was the very instrument that had been in their sitting room for all those hours I had played it. Mrs. Abbot had insisted that we have it, even as I had tried to refuse such a generous gift. But it had been moved to our little home the day of our wedding six months before. And it hadn't moved since. The pianoforte fit so perfectly here with its chipped keys and fading colors. Our house was small, but it was more comfortable and safe and much more of a home than anything I had ever had before. I wouldn't trade it for anything.

I turned my head over my shoulder, smiling without reservation. Mr. and Mrs. Abbot sat on the end of our uneven sofa, and Lucy and Rachel crowded on the other end. Clara and Thomas sat on the chairs closest to the pianoforte. Anna smiled up at me as she poured their tea.

Clara wasn't clapping—her hands were occupied with her squirming baby, Henry. She planted a quick kiss on his sagging, round cheek and his tiny fingers wrapped around a strand of her hair. He pulled and Clara gasped, laughing as she held him at a distance.

"Naughty boy, Henry!" Sophia rushed to Clara's side and tapped the baby's nose with one finger. He giggled. "You will hurt Mama!"

I smiled and rotated on the bench so I faced them. I leaned against James. Sophia adored her little brother. I watched as she smoothed the fuzzy tuft of hair on top of his head. He reached for her hair but she skipped away, shaking a finger at him. James's laugh rumbled against me.

Sophia hurried over to where we sat at the pianoforte. "Auntie Charlotte and Uncle Jamesy! Your song was very pretty." She stepped closer and plinked out a few notes on the keys beside me. "It's my birthday tomorrow," she announced for the tenth time that day at least. "I will be seven."

"How very old! You are growing up far too fast," I said. James and I had already crafted a crown from the twigs in our garden that I planned to have her wear on the special day. I had picked several different colored ribbons to intertwine with the crown, and James had helped me assemble them. It had turned out beautifully. I hoped she would like it. The longer I had been here, the more I realized that the simple gifts that came without cost were always the sweetest.

Clara piped in from across the room. "You will love what Auntie Charlotte and Uncle Jamesy have for your birthday gift."

Sophia squealed and clasped her hands together in excitement. "Is it cousins? I would like to have cousins. Very much."

The room erupted in laughter and Sophia eyed my belly carefully. James smiled. "No cousins yet, my dear, but perhaps for your eighth birthday we might have such a gift for you."

She jumped into a twirl, clapping. James laughed and tugged me closer, planting a kiss on top of my head. Sophia climbed into her father's lap and leaned over to tickle Henry's face with the lace cuff of her sleeve. My breath released as a sigh.

Everything in this room was beautiful, a dream made possible by hope and friendship and love. There was nothing more I wanted. Even with winter thick in the air once again, I knew there would be much joy to be found—much warmth despite the cold and the dreary sky. Spring would always come again to Craster, and love would always last.

James's hand slid around mine and I held onto it tight.

Discussion Questions

1. When considering the relationship between Charlotte and Clara, what did the two sisters learn from each other? How did they change throughout the story? What similarities do you see in your own relationships with your sisters?

2. How does Charlotte's view of the environment of Craster in the beginning of the story change by the end? How does this apply to her own personal change and perspective?

3. Charlotte uses the pianoforte as a sanctuary and a distraction from the things that trouble her. What is your sanctuary in hard times? When Charlotte loses the ability to access that relief, she is devastated. How would losing your own sanctuary affect you? How can you relate to Charlotte?

4. Compare and contrast Charlotte's relationship with her mother and Mrs. Abbot. In what way does Mrs. Abbot uplift Charlotte? What attributes do you find in common between these two women as mothers? What differences do you find in the treatment of Lucy and Rachel by Mrs. Abbot and Charlotte and Clara by their own mother?

5. When James is first introduced, he tries to retrieve Charlotte's money from a thief. What does this initial act show us about his character? How do we see these attributes shown in the rest of the story? What do we learn through James about forgiveness, kindness, and love?

6. Why do you think the author chose to have Charlotte return home to her mother? What did Charlotte need to realize through that event? Although James could have chased Charlotte home for a storybook ending, why did Charlotte need to make that decision to return to Craster on her own?

7. Both James and Charlotte make sacrifices for one another in the story. How does this strengthen their relationship? What role does sacrifice play in love? Why is it necessary, and how does it build Charlotte's character?

8. The love story between Clara and Lord Trowbridge is built off-stage. How would you envision their love story? How might their personalities have complemented each other? What unwritten events might have led to them falling in love? Discuss and imagine your own scene ideas of what might have happened.

9. Considering Charlotte's upbringing and the pressures of her society, do you find any justification for her views and actions? How do her selfish roots ultimately transform to a change of heart?

10. Why do you think James kept his love letter after so long? What did it mean to him? Have you ever found it difficult to let go of something?

About the Author

Ashtyn Newbold was introduced to the Regency period early on, and the writing soon followed. Fascinated by the society, scenery, and chivalry, she wrote her first novel, *Mischief and Manors,* receiving a publishing offer before high school graduation. Ashtyn is currently attending college with plans to obtain a degree that will help her improve in writing and creativity. In her spare time she enjoys baking, singing, spoiling her dog, spending time with friends and family, and dreaming of the day she'll travel to England.

Scan to visit

www.ashtynnewbold.com

Acknowledgments

I was the first person to love this story, and I was worried I would be the only one. Special thanks to my mom for being the second, Anna for being the third, and Aunt Megan for being the fourth. Your words of encouragement and feedback were exactly what I needed.

Thank you to my creative writing class for reading this book in its beginning pages and forcing me to write through our Nanowrimo competition. Thank you to my family, for showing me the meaning of unconditional love long before I wrote these characters. Thank you for letting me learn from my mistakes like Charlotte, letting me dream like Clara, and for showing me kindness like James.

Much appreciation to everyone at Cedar Fort, especially to my editors Hali Bird and Jessica Romrell for your wonderful insight, uplifting words, and hard work; and Priscilla Chaves for the gorgeous cover design. It's perfect!

I also must acknowledge England for being so beautiful, the Regency period for being so fun, and William Shakespeare for providing such wise and powerful quotes.

And finally, I express my gratitude to my Heavenly Father for giving me stories to tell and blessing me with an ability and love for writing them. May there be many more to come.